DAMAGED!

A Walker Brothers Novel

J.S. SCOTT

Damaged!
A Walker Brothers Novel

Copyright 2017 by J.S. Scott

Cover Design by Ashley Michel/AM Creations

ISBN: 978-1-946660-41-1 (E-Book)
ISBN: 978-1-946660-42-8 (Paperback)

CONTENTS

PROLOGUE	*Dane*	1
CHAPTER 1	*Kenzie*	6
CHAPTER 2	*Kenzie*	14
CHAPTER 3	*Dane*	19
CHAPTER 4	*Dane*	22
CHAPTER 5	*Trace*	30
CHAPTER 6	*Dane*	36
CHAPTER 7	*Kenzie*	39
CHAPTER 8	*Dane*	48
CHAPTER 9	*Kenzie*	51
CHAPTER 10	*Dane*	59
CHAPTER 11	*Dane*	61
CHAPTER 12	*Dane*	67
CHAPTER 13	*Kenzie*	69
CHAPTER 14	*Dane*	77
CHAPTER 15	*Kenzie*	80
CHAPTER 16	*Dane*	88
CHAPTER 17	*Kenzie*	96
CHAPTER 18	*Dane*	105
CHAPTER 19	*Kenzie*	109

CHAPTER 20	*Dane*	115
CHAPTER 21	*Kenzie*	120
CHAPTER 22	*Kenzie*	127
CHAPTER 23	*Kenzie*	138
CHAPTER 24	*Kenzie*	144
CHAPTER 25	*Kenzie*	148
CHAPTER 26	*Kenzie*	151
CHAPTER 27	*Kenzie*	158
CHAPTER 28	*Kenzie*	160
CHAPTER 29	*Kenzie*	166
CHAPTER 30	*Kenzie*	169
CHAPTER 31	*Kenzie*	176
CHAPTER 32	*Dane*	178
CHAPTER 33	*Kenzie*	184
CHAPTER 34	*Dane*	187
CHAPTER 35	*Kenzie*	189
CHAPTER 36	*Kenzie*	196
CHAPTER 37	*Kenzie*	201
CHAPTER 38	*Kenzie*	207
CHAPTER 39	*Dane*	213
CHAPTER 40	*Kenzie*	221
CHAPTER 41	*Kenzie*	226
CHAPTER 42	*Kenzie*	234
CHAPTER 43	*Kenzie*	239
CHAPTER 44	*Dane*	244
CHAPTER 45	*Kenzie*	249
EPILOGUE	*Kenzie*	256

PROLOGUE

Dane

EIGHT YEARS AGO...

*T*here was nothing I wanted more than to just be left alone.

I listened to the rain hitting the roof of the small shack that was the only existing structure on my new private island. As soon as I'd been discharged from the hospital, and saw the reactions to my altered appearance, all I needed was just to get away from the horrified glances I'd gotten every time I stepped out my door.

I looked like a monster.

I felt like a monster.

So, I *was* a monster, at least to myself.

My two brothers even had a hard time handling my appearance now. Neither of them said what they were thinking, but I could feel the awkwardness between the three of us. It didn't take a rocket scientist to figure out why.

Hell, I was only eighteen years old, and my entire life had just gone up in smoke.

Literally.

I couldn't remember much of the plane crash that had killed my dad and his new wife, but I was feeling the effects of it now. My whole damn body ached from the newly healed burns and other injuries I'd sustained from the accident.

My brothers, Trace and Sebastian, kept telling me I was lucky to be alive. I didn't *feel* like I'd been somehow blessed to survive the horrific plane crash. There had been times in the last several months when I wished I'd just died with my father. Recovery had been touch and go, and the pain had been so bad that I wasn't sure I'd live through it, even with medications.

"I can live alone," I mumbled to myself. I sat up in the small bed, and was met with nothing but darkness.

It seemed strange to be completely solo. I'd spent my life surrounded by family and friends. To be suddenly stuck on a private island with not another soul around was both a relief and painful at the same time.

I flopped back onto my pillow, trying to tell myself that I'd fix up the island, make it my own. It wouldn't be so bad after I was able to get a real residence here.

The first thing I was going to do was build a decent house so I could sleep in a comfortable damn bed.

My brothers knew very little about what I was up to, and I didn't feel the need to inform them that the island...well...it needed some work.

A house.

Indoor plumbing.

An airport.

Roads.

Some kind of studio so I could continue to work on my art.

I was disappointed that I'd never be able to attend a university or college. I looked so damn bad that I couldn't inflict my appearance on anyone right now. Before the accident, I'd been accepted to one of the best art programs in the world. I couldn't do it now. There was no way I could handle the piteous expressions of the other students on campus every time I tried to walk from class to class.

Maybe someday, my face wouldn't look so mangled, and my body would regain its strength. But right now, I was broken, and I knew it.

Mind.

Body.

And soul.

At this point, I wasn't quite sure which was suffering the most. All of the pain seemed rolled in together until I was just one big mass of agony.

I'd purchased the expensive island in the Bahamas as a place to recuperate and try to get my head back together. There would be more surgeries to try to fix some of the cosmetic issues, but in the meantime, I'd have a place to escape from other people.

Yeah, I'm running away.

Maybe I was also trying to outrun myself. I wasn't sure. My head was all fucked up.

I'll be okay. I just need some time.

Unfortunately, I'd found out just how many *real* friends I had after the accident. The only ones who had genuinely been there for me were my brothers. When the expensive parties stopped, and I needed my buddies, there was nobody who was interested in babysitting an invalid who barely had enough strength to walk across a room.

"I'm pathetic," I grumbled, wishing that I hadn't needed to leave Sebastian and Trace. I missed them, but they were both involved in their own lives, and I could tell they just wanted to put all this behind them. Unfortunately, the accident wasn't over for me. In fact, I felt like my hell was just beginning.

Yeah, I'd told my brothers that I'd be fine.

Problem was, I actually *wasn't* fine.

I absolutely *wasn't* doing well *at all.*

However, I *was* healed, even though the end result of the accident wasn't pretty.

I'd wanted my brothers to go on with their lives. They'd spent months worrying about me, dealing with grief over my dad's death, and it was time for them to concentrate on rebuilding their lives without our father. Trace was busy trying to run our father's multi-billion-dollar corporation, and Sebastian was going back to his engineering studies.

And me? I was going to hide out on my new island for a while to figure out how to handle my life now that it wasn't as charmed as it used to be. I was still licking my wounds. Well, not literally, but figuratively. I was behind my brothers on mourning my dad since I'd had a month or two when I hadn't known the whole truth. And then, I'd been so sick that I couldn't deal with it.

I guess I'd never really known how good I had it until everything fell apart.

"Suck it up, Walker," I said morosely into the dark room.

I turned onto my side, cursing at the lumpy mattress I was resting on.

Tomorrow, my first priority would be to get a comfortable bed delivered to the island so I could get a decent night's sleep.

The wind started to howl, and I hoped to hell I wasn't in for a nasty tropical storm. I hadn't checked the weather, and I was in a hurricane zone.

It was only my second day on the island, and I was already tired of the quiet and the isolation.

Be careful what you wish for, dumbass!

Earlier in the day, I'd *wanted* noise.

Unfortunately, I was getting exactly what I'd asked for, but not at all in the way I'd hoped it would happen.

I felt so damn lonely. The sudden isolation on the island was pretty extreme.

I wasn't used to being completely without somebody to talk to about my problems. My mom had died years ago, but my dad had always been there for me when I was growing up. I'd never missed having a mother because he'd been such a great father. If I had problems, he'd immediately want to discuss them and help me solve them.

Jesus! I wanted him back so damn bad that it physically hurt, my chest aching so badly that I almost couldn't stand it. Maybe I couldn't remember the crash, but I still mourned the loss of my father, the only parent I'd ever known.

How in the hell was I supposed to live without him?

I guessed that I'd work through it, just like my brothers. Right now, I wasn't ready to accept the fact that I'd never see my dad again, but I knew I'd have to eventually come to terms with the fact that he was gone.

My heart clenched, and I put a hand over the left side of my chest, trying to somehow fill the profound emptiness, and the painful ache that was suddenly trying to take me over.

"I miss you, Dad," I said in a hopeless tone.

Unfortunately, nobody answered.

Reality was beginning to sink in. The numbness of denial was starting to go away.

Dammit! I *wanted* my denial back because it hurt too damn bad to think about being without my dad.

I was on my own to handle my shit all by myself.

I'll be fine alone. I'll get used to it.

I closed my eyes, but it was a long time before I finally fell into a troubled, restless sleep.

CHAPTER 1

Kenzie

THE PRESENT...

I'd only flown in an airplane twice in my entire life. Once to Los Angeles from Boston when I was eighteen years old. The second time I was on my way back home to the East Coast after all of my dreams had been shattered a couple of weeks later.

I could still remember the long coast-to-coast flight, being crammed into the cheapest economy seat I could find. Both directions had been uncomfortable, and I was happy that I'd never needed to fly again.

Until today.

Having been dirt poor all my life, nothing could have prepared me for my current flight to the Bahamas in Trace Walker's private jet. I'd set out late this morning for my new job opportunity. Now, it was almost dinnertime, and I knew we had to be getting close to Dane Walker's private island in the Bahamas.

I almost hated to see the flight end, even though I'd been in the air for over five hours. There was any number of things to occupy myself on the luxurious plane. I could even go take a nap in the bedroom of the jet, but I was too nervous to even consider that option. I'd eaten a gourmet lunch, and then watched a movie, so the time on board the jet had flown by.

Now that we were getting close to the Bahamas, I was getting nervous.

"Can you fasten your seatbelt, Ms. Jordan?" The friendly flight attendant's request snapped me out of my thoughts.

"Of course," I replied as I fumbled with my seatbelt. "Are we landing?"

The pretty, thin brunette smiled at me. "We're descending. We'll be on the island shortly."

I sat up straight in the comfortable leather seat and snapped my seatbelt on. "Thank you for being so nice to me," I mumbled, not sure quite what to say to the woman who'd made sure I had every available comfort on my flight.

"It's my job," she answered. "But it's been a pleasure to serve you on this flight."

"I appreciate it," I told her. "I've never been on a private jet."

I was pretty sure she already knew that. I'd been gawking at the interior of the aircraft like it was some kind of mirage in the desert from the moment I'd boarded.

"I hope you enjoyed the experience," she commented politely.

"It was amazing," I replied honestly. "I just hope Mr. Walker likes me."

My new job as billionaire Dane Walker's assistant on a private island in the Bahamas was a dream job. Not only was I being paid a small fortune in comparison to my previous jobs, but I was going to be working with an amazingly talented artist. During my short employment as a receptionist at a New York art gallery, I'd gotten to view one of his pieces in person. Not that it had stayed on display for long. It had sold for an outrageous price, and I'd mourned the loss of the beautiful work of art the moment it had been removed from the wall. I'd admired Dane

Walker's work for a long time, and I'd really hated to see the canvas go off exhibit so soon.

"You'll be fine," she assured me. "I haven't met Dane Walker personally, but his brothers are both very good men."

Maybe she *had* to say that because Trace Walker was her boss, but I had a feeling she meant what she said. "I haven't met him either. I haven't met any of the Walker brothers in person," I confessed.

It had been a long flight, and I'd had plenty of time to chat with Mary, my accommodating flight attendant, during the flight. I'd told her that I was going to be a new employee to Dane Walker, and that I was nervous about whether or not we'd get along.

"Relax," she said in a soothing voice. "I'm sure he'll be as nice as his brothers."

I hoped she was right. "It just seems strange that he lives on an island all alone. He *has* to get lonely. And why would he want to be away from his brothers? From what I can gather, they're the only family he has."

I'd been reading about the effects of prolonged isolation, and they weren't good. If Dane Walker had been mostly alone for eight years, he could be completely nuts.

Mary shrugged. "I'm not certain, but he's an artist. Maybe he's just a little... eccentric."

That was probably a tactful way of saying he was a little—or a lot—crazy.

I glanced out the window, noticing that we had gone down in altitude fairly quickly.

"Maybe," I agreed in a noncommittal tone. I wasn't certain exactly what I'd find on the island, but I was hoping for the best.

"You could travel to the populated islands on your time off," she suggested. "It's beautiful here."

I nodded politely, knowing I wasn't doing much of *anything* until I got paid. I had exactly five bucks in my purse. I'd been *just that close* to going broke in New York City after I'd lost my receptionist job because my boss had been a total dick. I'd still worked in a convenience store part-time, but living in New York was pricey, and there had been no way I could afford my part of the rent on the apartment I'd shared with several other women.

Trace Walker's job offer to work for his brother had come completely out-of-the-blue, and it couldn't have been offered at a better time. It had saved my ass from homelessness.

My best friend, Paige, had gotten engaged to Sebastian Walker, the middle billionaire Walker brother. After graduating from Harvard Law, she'd moved to Denver to work for Walker Enterprises. I hadn't seen her since I'd left our apartment in Cambridge to move to New York City. I'd never even had the chance to tell her that I'd lost my job in the gallery, so she'd never known quite how bad things had gotten for me.

Honestly, I hadn't *wanted* to tell Paige that I'd lost my job. She was so happy, and she deserved every moment of joy she could get. The last thing I'd wanted was to bring back any gloom and doom to her life.

Unfortunately, everything in my life sucked, and I was a total downer.

I figured I'd get by somehow. I always had. I'd been alone most of my life, and I had always managed to survive.

However, I *was* lucky that Trace and Sebastian had called me to offer employment. If they hadn't, things had been about to get really bad. Like, *homeless bad.*

Finally, I answered the brunette beside my seat, "I want to see everything. I haven't really been able to travel."

I didn't count running as fast as I could to another town as *traveling*, but I'd done some pretty quick relocations in my life. I'd had no choice.

"You'll love traveling," Mary said enthusiastically. "I love my job because it takes me to so many different places in the world."

"I'm sure it will be okay," I said, without much enthusiasm. I was too concerned about meeting Dane to think about anything else.

This job has to go well. I don't have a plan B.

Mary patted me on the shoulder. "I have to get into my seat. We'll be landing soon."

I shot her a weak smile as she went to sit in one of the cream leather seats behind me and fastened her seatbelt.

Really, I had no idea how all this was going to work out, but I *had* to get along with Dane Walker. My survival depended on it.

I didn't know what exactly I was required to do as Dane's assistant, but I was willing to do most anything to keep a high-paying job that would lift me out of the world of poverty I'd been stuck in my entire life.

I worked hard, but I never got anywhere. I didn't have a college degree, so there was very little hope of bettering myself. The only thing I'd known was how to stay alive.

Everything will be fine. Paige wouldn't have let Trace and Sebastian send me here if it wasn't a good opportunity.

I missed Paige so damn much. She'd not only been my best friend for years, but my *only* true friend. I was desperately hoping I could get to her wedding. Trace had told me that he wanted me to help Dane get organized so he could attend Sebastian and Paige's big event, so obviously Dane would be going to the nuptials. Since the wedding was in the serious planning stages, I knew the date would be set soon. Would my new boss be willing to give me time off so I could attend the wedding? Since he'd be going to the ceremony, maybe he wouldn't need me for a while.

I flinched as the tires of the jet hit the runway. The sound was still unfamiliar to me.

As I took a deep breath, I tried to convince myself that everything would work out okay. I just needed to make myself agreeable to Dane Walker, and deal with the fact that I was going to be doing things very much alone on the private island.

The difficulty was that I *hated* being completely alone. Maybe I didn't have many real friends, but I'd always lived in the city where there were distractions. If I had too much time to think, I'd end up conjuring up memories I wanted desperately to forget.

I waited as the jet continued to taxi and it finally came to a complete stop. Mary was already getting my suitcase out of the closet and handing it to the pilot when I rose from my comfortable leather seat. I gathered my purse and my overnight bag which was holding my computer.

Everything I have fits in an overnight bag and one suitcase.

My roommates and I had all contributed to buying the threadbare furniture we'd had in our New York apartment. They were only items I'd partially owned, and I'd forfeited any claim to them when I'd left.

Not that any of the furnishings were worth splitting and moving to another place, but it was kind of pathetic that I could now put everything I owned into a carrier that I wheeled behind me.

"Good luck," Mary said sincerely as I reached her.

I peeked outside, and I noticed that my suitcase was being loaded into a black limo on the tarmac. "Thank you. For everything," I answered, grateful that I'd had somebody to talk to during the long flight.

I smiled at Mary as I moved toward the steps. I was immediately hit by a burst of warm, tropical wind as I moved down the stairs.

"I'm definitely not in New York anymore," I muttered to myself as I made my way to the car Dane's brothers had arranged to meet me here at the airport.

When I'd left New York, it had been well below freezing, and we'd just gotten a brutal winter storm. Being here in the Bahamas was like arriving in a whole new world.

Looking around curiously, all I saw was concrete because we were still on the runway, but I couldn't wait to see more of the island. Despite my nervousness, this job was going to be an adventure, and I wanted to savor every moment.

I hurried to the car as fast as my sensible heels would get me there. I decided almost immediately that the long-sleeved dress I was wearing was much too warm for the climate here. And the stockings I was wearing were already sticking to my legs from the humidity.

The warmth was *welcome*.

The humidity...*not so much*. Especially in attire that was meant for a cold climate.

I'd wanted to impress Dane by looking professional, so I'd dressed in a green wool dress that I'd found at a thrift store at Christmas, and matched it with a basic pair of low-heeled shoes.

As I approached the vehicle, an unknown male in a loud, flowered shirt got out of the driver's seat.

"Ms. Jordan?" he asked in a friendly voice.

I was taken aback by his politeness. Nobody called me *Ms. Jordan*.

I reached out to grasp the large hand he was offering. "Please call me Kenzie," I requested, smiling at him even though I was nervous.

The big bear of a guy had sparkling brown eyes and skin so brown that I suspected he was a native. When he spoke, I knew for sure he'd been born and raised in the tropical environment.

"I'll call you whatever you want me to," he answered in a laid-back Bahamian accent.

"Then definitely call me Kenzie," I said as I finally pulled my hand away from his strong grip. "Do you work for Mr. Walker?"

"I do," he confirmed. "I have been working for him as long as he's lived here on Walker's Cay."

"He named the island after himself?"

"Oh, no. He named it after his father," the big man answered.

I felt my heart clench as I thought about what had happened to Dane. "And what should I call *you?*" I queried.

"You can call me Theo. That's my name," he said jokingly as he opened the car door.

I looked into the back seat, knowing I'd feel awkward sitting behind Theo. "Can I sit in the front?" I queried hesitantly. "I'd love a front seat view of the island."

"Of course you can," he said magnanimously, moving his large body in a surprisingly agile manner as he jogged to the passenger door.

I took a deep breath and let it out, feeling more comfortable because Theo was so nice.

I hauled ass to get into the passenger side of the dark limo, hoping Dane was as kind as Theo was being to me right now.

I'm going to be safe. I'm going to have a great job.

The financial stress of the past two weeks was finally going to get better. Who cared if all I owned was in just one suitcase and a carry-on? I was going to be working as an assistant for a world renowned artist, and I'd do everything I could to be useful to Dane.

Truth was, I was so grateful for this job that I hadn't taken all that much time to wonder what it would be like to live on a private island with no people except my new boss. And it really didn't matter. I was a survivor. Always had been. I'd work any job I could find to keep myself afloat.

Honestly, I didn't want anybody to find me, and staying on an uninhabited island was as good of a place as any to hide.

Luckily, I'd scored a high-paying job, which was something I hadn't expected. But I swore that no matter what it took, I'd impress Dane Walker so he never wanted to be without a personal assistant—me in particular—ever again.

CHAPTER 2

Kenzie

"You for sure gonna burn that fair skin of yours, Kennie," Theo said with concern in his voice as he flew like a bat-out-of-hell down the road leading out of the airport.

I smiled, not bothering to correct him on how to pronounce my name. His lilting voice was relaxing, and the way he spoke was calming. "I'll get used to it, but I probably *will* burn first. We haven't exactly had much sun in New York."

Theo's driving didn't bother me. I was, after all, coming from New York City.

I sighed, knowing my blonde hair and fair skin wasn't the best complexion to have in a tropical environment. I rarely tanned, and if I did, it was *after* I'd already been burned to a crisp. I wore quite a bit of foundation makeup, and it had a pretty strong sunscreen, but the rest of my body would be fair game if I didn't protect it.

"Don't stay out long at first," he warned.

"I won't," I assured him. "Do you live here on the island?"

I was curious about Theo, and what he did for Dane. We were both employees of the island's owner now, and I was hoping we could become friends.

"Oh, no. I live on New Providence with my beautiful wife and my daughter. I use Mr. Dane's boat to get here and back home again every day."

I knew the capital city of Nassau was on New Providence, so he obviously lived in a more populated area. "He has boats?"

"Yeah. Several. I use one of the smaller boats to take myself here and back to Nassau."

"What exactly do you do for Mr. Walker?"

Theo shrugged. "Anything and everything. I'm his driver, property manager, handyman, and his friend. My wife comes out to the Cay a few times a week to clean that huge home of his, and to do general housekeeping."

"So he *does* live here alone?" I mused.

"Not anymore," Theo answered with a grin. "You're here now."

"I wonder how he'll feel about that. Does he have a guest-house for me?"

"No need. His home is enormous."

I had assumed I'd probably have to live in Dane's residence, and I wasn't quite sure how I felt about that. Although I'd always had roommates, I had always had my own place away from my work.

"What about a studio?"

"Oh, yeah. He has a big glass building for his art. He paints good."

I bit back a laugh. Dane's paintings were more than *good.* They were *extraordinary.*

I'd love to have Dane Walker as a mentor. I just hoped he'd let me sketch or paint with him on occasion, and possibly give me a few tips. I'd do my best not to bother him, but if he let me watch his technique, it would be fascinating.

I can't make a pest of myself. My number one priority is to help Dane.

Any dreams I had of bettering my art skills were secondary to doing my job, but a woman could *hope.*

I was quiet as we hit a road that appeared to skirt along the island's coast. "Wow. It's beautiful here," I muttered aloud.

The blue water of the ocean and the white sand beaches left me speechless. A sense of peace flowed over me as I stared at the beach, mesmerized by the azure waters, and the gorgeous sand. The land on the opposite side of the vehicle was just as stunning. The bright flowers, palm trees, and the green of the plentiful plants was one of the most incredible sights I'd ever seen.

"Very beautiful," Theo agreed readily. "I wouldn't want to live anywhere else."

I sighed. "When I left New York, it was cold and snowy. It seems almost surreal to be here now. It's so warm."

Theo chuckled. "It gets warmer."

I imagined it *was* a lot hotter during the summer, but at the moment, I was enjoying the mild winter in a tropical climate. Unfortunately, I'd never had the chance to see a lot of Los Angeles during my brief time in California, and I'd never traveled much outside of New England. New York had been my only real adventure, and *that* had turned sour really fast.

I soaked in the scenery as Theo navigated the winding road around the island.

"Can you tell me what Mr. Walker is like?" I asked hesitantly.

"Cranky most of the time, but don't let that scare you away. He's lonely, even though he doesn't want to admit it."

"How cranky?" I questioned nervously.

Theo shrugged. "Mostly, he doesn't have much to say. But once you get past the crusty exterior, he's a good man."

"Does he like company?"

"Don't know. He never has visitors," Theo said in a sad tone. "I think he'd like to have his brothers come see the island, but I don't think he ever asks them to come."

"They're the only close family he has," I mentioned thoughtfully.

I knew Paige and Sebastian were both worried about Dane. He hadn't made it to Denver for the holidays, and he hadn't left the island at all for quite some time. Paige had yet to meet Dane, but I knew she wanted to finally make the acquaintance of the one member of Sebastian's close family that she hadn't seen face-to-face.

Part of my mission here was to make sure that enough work was lifted off Dane so that he'd come to Paige and Sebastian's wedding, and I was determined to accomplish that task for my friend.

Seeing as every Walker was filthy rich, I found it odd that his family had never come to visit here. All they'd needed to do was jump into their private jet. I knew Paige would love it, and I couldn't understand how Trace and his wife could *not* enjoy a quiet vacation on the island.

"He needs his family," Theo said quietly. "He's been on this island alone too long. I'm here during the weekdays, but I'm usually off somewhere taking care of Mr. Dane's property. He paints alone all day. Being by himself that much isn't natural."

"Why does he hide himself away here?" I questioned.

"Says he likes his privacy, but he really doesn't. He was scarred after the accident that killed his father and his new stepmother, inside and out. I'm not sure what wound hurts him the most."

My heart fell when Theo mentioned Dane's injuries. "How bad is it?"

"Not all that bad anymore," Theo said. "He makes it much bigger than it needs to be. Over the years, they've done surgery and skin grafts to fix the worst of it. For sure, his body is marked in ways that will never be healed, but I think his heart aches worse than his body now."

For a moment, I could almost feel his pain as I imaged a man who hid himself away from the world. A loner, not by choice, but by circumstance. "I hope I can help him," I said wistfully.

"Oh, I'm thinking that you can. You seem like a nice woman," Theo answered in a mischievous tone.

"His scars won't bother me," I insisted.

"Then he might eventually come to accept you in his house."

I stopped looking at the island scenery and turned my head to look at Dane's caretaker. "What do you mean?"

"He ain't gonna like it."

"Like what?" I asked in a panicked voice.

"Mr. Dane isn't going to like the fact that you're here at first, but hopefully he'll get over it."

"Wait! He *knows* I'm coming, right? Trace and Sebastian told him?"

Theo shook his head. "He don't know anything. I guess his brothers thought it was better to send you here rather than to give Mr. Dane a chance to refuse you. Mr. Trace called me directly and asked me to come and pick you up. I told him I'd do it, but it wasn't my place to break the news to the boss."

My heart stuttered as my mind tried to deal with the fact that Dane didn't even know I was coming. He didn't know that Trace and Sebastian were sending him help.

The fact that nobody had informed Dane about me ticked me off, but those feelings were secondary to a fear I couldn't suppress. "What if he doesn't want me? What if he sends me home? I really need this job," I whispered hoarsely in a horrified voice.

Coming to work for Dane Walker had been my salvation.

Sadly, very soon it might become my ruination. If Dane Walker wasn't willing to let me stay and work for him, I wasn't sure what in the hell I was going to do.

CHAPTER 3

Dane

SEVEN YEARS AGO...

I was glad to get back to my island.

I'd just seen my brothers for the first time in almost a year, and even though I missed them, the meeting had been awkward for me.

Yeah, I'd enjoyed the holidays, and my brothers' company, but I *hadn't* liked the horrified looks I'd gotten when I'd gone to Denver to shop one day for Christmas gifts.

Mommy...he's a monster. Look!

The terrified voice of the child in the mall kept ringing through my head as Theo drove me back to my house. I'd arrived via helicopter. I'd eventually put up an airport, but most of my attention had gone into building my home.

Maybe I am scary to a kid.

The little girl's mother had scolded her daughter and hauled her away, mumbling apologies to me as they hurried out of the electronics store.

Still, I couldn't forget how frightened the child had been once she'd seen my face.

Granted, I'd just had some corrective surgery, and my mug had been covered in bandages. I probably shouldn't have left Trace's place, but I'd had a sudden attack of guilt once I'd realized I hadn't been off Walker's Cay to shop before arriving in Colorado.

"Glad you're home, boss. Your crazy puppy missed you," Theo informed me jovially.

That got a small smirk out of me as I rode in the passenger seat while my caretaker drove me home. I'd probably missed my potcake dog more than he'd missed me. Picasso, my young canine, had been my only real friend. The black and white menace with floppy ears hadn't given a shit that I was scarred up and broken. All he'd wanted was a safe home, food, and affection. In return, he gave me unconditional love.

I wished the world was that simple. Unfortunately, life with people was a lot more complicated.

"I'll be happy to see him," I finally answered, watching as my house came into view.

"My Emilee will be happy to give him back to you," Theo joked. "He's been whining since you left."

"I'm sure Emilee spoiled him rotten," I answered. Theo's wife was in the house with my crazy pup. She was a damn angel, and I doubted that she'd be happy to relinquish care of any creature.

"For sure," Theo agreed. "He's gotten plenty of treats."

Theo's answer cemented the fact that I'd come back to a very spoiled pup. Emilee loved animals, and she didn't exactly make them behave.

I exited when Theo pulled up to the front door, still amazed that so much had gotten done in such a short time. One year, and the house and studio were already constructed.

I slammed the car door and looked up at the work that had already been done to make Walker's Cay my home.

Yeah, I'd gone way overboard, but I was starting to realize that there was very little I *couldn't* do. I was too wealthy to exclude any possibilities.

Problem was, even after all of the work had been completed, I was *still* alone.

My visit with my brothers had been bittersweet. It had reminded me that no matter how much I built up Walker's Cay; it would never bring people here.

I shuddered as I looked up at all the windows upstairs, knowing the rooms would never be occupied.

Maybe someday.

I shook my head. My brothers obviously had no desire to visit, and there would never be anyone here except Theo and Emilee.

My chest ached as I walked into the house.

Jesus!

I *missed* my dad.

I *missed* my brothers.

I *missed* voices, and the sounds of the city.

I'll be fine alone. I'll get used to it.

Those words were my mantra. Maybe in the future, I'd finally convince myself that they were actually true.

CHAPTER 4

Dane

"I'm never going to be able to please everybody," I said grumpily as I tossed my paintbrush aside and examined the large canvas in front of me.

I'd been working on the painting for months. I was fairly satisfied with the piece. But I knew—just like I always did—that every painting I did was subject to individual interpretation. Some people would love the art. Others wouldn't. That was the problem with being an abstract artist. Two totally different individuals would have two separate opinions about what the picture said to them.

I stood and moved restlessly toward the house. As far as I was concerned, the painting was finished. I'd poured my emotions into the art on the canvas. It would be entirely up to the viewers to decide if the piece was relevant to their life...or not.

I rolled my shoulders as I walked, trying to get the knots of tension out of my upper back. I'd have Theo take the abstract and ship it to a gallery in New York City. No doubt I'd make good money from the painting, but at my level of wealth, the income meant very little. I'd doubled my net worth over the last several years, but it was a game, something that kept me occupied. The last thing I needed was more material wealth. Yeah, it had been nice to possess billions while I'd set up my place here on Walker's Cay. But I had no use for more money. I already had everything a man could want.

Everything except some company.

Sure, I had Theo and his wife to talk to sometimes, and they were both friends. But every once in a while, I wished I could have something...more.

There hadn't been a woman on the island since my brief relationship with Britney, and I'd learned my lesson well. Sometimes it was better to be alone. The woman I'd fucked for several months two years ago hadn't been company; she'd been a major pain in the ass.

She'd wanted to be with me only to get back at my brother, Trace, for dumping her. Not that I cared. I'd known from the start that Britney barely tolerated my appearance, and we never had sex in the light of day. The bitch had let me know when she moved out that she'd only hung around for the money I gave her, and the possibility of getting Trace back.

I'd known. I'd *always* known that she couldn't stand the sight of me. But I'd wanted some human contact so badly that I hadn't questioned the fact that she barely managed to let me fuck her. Britney had never been more than a high class prostitute. A very expensive whore.

Settling for what a woman would give me for money ended two years ago. Never again would I feel grateful for a screw. I could get myself off, and not worry about trying to please somebody who had no real interest in me.

"I'm better off alone," I rasped as I reached the front door of the mansion I'd built on the island. My solitary state had eventually become normal to me. I was resigned to being by myself on my island, even though it wasn't entirely by choice.

I turned before I entered the front door, my attention drawn to the vehicle that was pulling into the driveway.

Theo. What in the hell was he doing here?

The dark sedan, a vehicle that only came out if I needed to go somewhere off the island, made its way down the long driveway and stopped right in front of my house. These days, I rarely needed Theo to shuttle me from place to place. I preferred to drive myself now that my injuries were completely healed.

I was mostly curious and bemused at Theo's actions.

Until I saw *her.*

Not ten feet in front of me, I saw the female exit the passenger side of the automobile, struggling mightily with a carry-on bag and a purse.

"Damn it!" she said in a disgruntled voice as she yanked at the overnight bag that had gotten tangled up with the seatbelt. "Don't be a klutz now. Not now."

The small suitcase finally came free, and she stumbled back, trying desperately not to trip over her heels.

She failed miserably.

I flew forward instinctively, wanting to shield her from landing on the hard surface of the driveway.

My body was behind hers as she slammed into my chest. "Easy," I said in a raspy tone as I steadied her, my arms curling around her waist.

Jesus! She smelled like coconut and sin, and temptation was thumbing through my body just from feeling her sweet, curvy, warm form against me.

I froze, my cock immediately up, my body tense and ready.

Disgusted with myself, I let go of the female as soon as she had her balance.

"Mr. Walker?" she queried in a nervous voice as she slung both of her bags over her shoulder.

"That's me," I growled, my primitive instincts barely held in check as I scrutinized her, trying to figure out what had caused my volatile reaction.

Yeah, she was beautiful, and pretty adorable as she brushed her hands down her skirt, trying to get herself together. Straight, long, platinum-blonde hair flowed over her shoulders, and the delicate features of her face made her look a whole lot more innocent than any female could possibly be. She was petite, and had to tilt her head to look up at me with her baby blue eyes. It wasn't the *color* that hit me like a Mack truck, it was her *expression.* Her gaze was completely devoid of any disgust or dislike as she looked up at me expectantly, apparently waiting politely for me to say something more.

"I'm happy to meet you. I'm Kenzie. Your new assistant," she said in a breathless rush as she held out her hand in greeting.

"Your brothers sent her," Theo said as he stepped up beside her.

"No! Hell, no!" I grunted.

I stared at her outstretched hand, but didn't take it.

I was too damned outraged at the moment.

My brothers? Those bastards! They knew I didn't want anyone else on Walker's Cay, especially not a damn female.

"Take her back," I instructed Theo as I turned to enter the house. "I don't want her here. I don't *need* an assistant."

"You're being a jerk, man," Theo answered in a warning tone.

"My island. My rules."

"I'm taking her up to the blue room," Theo said, completely ignoring my orders as he took her suitcase from her, and followed me inside. "She came a long way to get here, and she needs a job. You're not sending her home right now."

"You actually helped my brothers," I accused as I turned around to glare at Theo.

"Yeah, man. Because I think they're right. Between your art, your actuary work, and your hobbies, you need somebody to organize you."

I hesitated for a moment, not sure what to make of the Theo I was seeing right now. He rarely argued about *anything*, and I didn't get why he was doing it now.

"With all due respect, Mr. Walker, your brothers promised me a job," the woman said in a steady, reasonable tone. "I quit the work I had in New York to come here."

"And why is that my problem?" I rumbled. "I had nothing to do with them hiring you without my knowledge. They fucked up, and I want you gone."

I watched as she tucked her long, blonde hair behind her ear anxiously. "Maybe not. But if you have any kindness, please let me stay for a while. This wasn't my fault, either, and I have nowhere else to go. I have five dollars in my purse. That's the only thing standing between me and homelessness and starvation."

Her confession was matter-of-fact, and it got my attention. I wanted to strangle my brothers for putting this woman into this situation. "I'll give you money," I told her.

"I'm not looking for a handout, Mr. Walker. I just want to be given a fair chance at the job I was hired to do. Maybe I don't have a lot of experience as a personal assistant, but I'm a hard worker, and I'll complete any task you throw at me. I'm an organizer, so I can help take some of the load off you."

Honestly, I didn't feel stressed by my workload. Well, I *hadn't*—until some drop dead, gorgeous, highly fuckable blonde had walked through my door. Right now, I was feeling downright overwhelmed.

"I don't need help," I snapped at her angrily, knowing I had to get away from her before my head was all fucked up.

Not once had she looked at me any differently than she would any other normal guy. She hadn't noticed my scars, and she didn't appear to be fazed by my messed up face.

It was a weird experience. I wasn't used to women looking at me like I was... normal.

"What if you *do* need it," she reasoned.

"I don't."

"At least let me try," she persisted.

"No."

I felt just like the jerk Theo had just accused me of being. I had to give her credit...the woman was spunky as hell, and I kind of liked that. She was fighting for a job, and she didn't seem to care what I looked like at the moment.

Not only was my face exposed, but I was shirtless, my old wounds readily exposed because of the warmth of the day. She was damn lucky I wasn't naked, but it hadn't been hot enough to shuck all of my clothing. I was still wearing an old, comfortable pair of jeans.

"Okay," she answered in a hopeless tone. "Theo, can I get back to the U.S. in the same plane?"

Yeah. I was an asshole. Looking at the devastated expression on the blonde's face, I felt like I'd just kicked a puppy to the curb. But dammit, why did I have to worry about her fate? Hell, I didn't even know her.

"I can take you back, Ms. Kennie," Theo answered her unhappily.

She pinned me with a disappointed gaze. "I wish I could say it was a pleasure, Mr. Walker, but it wasn't. I've always been an admirer of your artwork, and I was looking forward to getting to know you better. But I guess it's better if I just look at your pictures and try to forget how rude and unpleasant you are."

And scarred! Why in the hell doesn't she mention my scars?

Damned if she *still* hadn't mentioned my appearance or shown any type of reaction to the way I looked.

Her shoulders were slumped as she opened the door that I'd slammed closed earlier, during my fit of irritation...and fear.

There was something about waiting for the bomb to drop that had set me off, and caused me to have a negative gut reaction.

I admired this woman's spunk, and the last thing I actually wanted to see was for her to come to any type of harm.

As she went to exit with Theo following behind her, I said in an annoyed tone, "You can stay for now."

What the fuck? Why had *those* words come out of my mouth?

When she glanced over her shoulder with a hopeful expression, I knew exactly why I'd said them.

I couldn't send her back into the world with nothing.

I couldn't kick her out into a life that had no damn compassion. I'd experienced it myself firsthand.

And, I didn't want this female to suffer because my brothers had been complete assholes. Hadn't they thought about what would happen to her if I refused to have her on my island?

"Do you mean it?" she said in a breathless voice that had my cock harder than it had been since I was a horny teenager.

"Yes," I said through gritted teeth. "Theo, show her to her room."

It was going to be damn hard to give up my privacy. Being alone at least gave me some peace. But I was resigned to the fact that she wasn't going to take anything unless she worked for it.

"Thank you," she murmured.

"Just try to stay out of my way. I don't like to be interrupted when I'm working."

She nodded. "Understood."

I watched as she retreated upstairs behind a silent Theo, her heels clicking on the marble surface of the stairs. I tried to make my body relax as I continued to stare at her disappearing figure, ogling her attractive backside as she reached the top of the stairs.

"I'm fucked!" I whispered hoarsely as I lost sight of Kenzie, knowing that it wasn't just her body and face that mesmerized me.

I was attracted to her spirit, something that was *far worse* than just wanting to get laid. There was something about this female that made me want to get closer to her, and that wasn't a good thing.

I didn't get close to women.

I couldn't.

It had taken me years just to protect myself, so I sure as hell didn't need somebody to turn my world upside down. I was bound to be disappointed, and I had way too much failure and defeat in my past.

I shrugged my tense shoulders as I turned around to make my way into my office. I'd keep my distance. I'd make sure she didn't get to me. My sanity depended on it.

Still pissed off, I slammed my office door behind me as I entered, determined to call my brothers immediately and let them know I was never fucking talking to either one of them again.

CHAPTER 5

Trace

"**O**kay, spill it," my beautiful wife insisted as she entered my home office. "You're smiling in that devious way that makes me think you've done something extremely bad."

Like always, the sound of Eva's voice and her gorgeous smile made me grin at her from my office chair. "I did," I agreed readily. "Dane is so pissed off that he says he'll never speak to me again."

I knew he was just talking. My youngest brother would *eventually* talk to me. Right now, he was just releasing his anger.

It wasn't that Sebastian and I hadn't expected this reaction before we'd sent Kenzie to his island, but the ferocity of Dane's fury had shocked me a little.

My little brother generally didn't get angry, and the fact that he was seething was a good sign.

"What did you do to him?" Eva answered, sounding slightly alarmed.

"He's not happy about Kenzie arriving in his tropical paradise," I told her with a smirk, watching her take a seat in front of the desk with a frown.

"That's not good," she mused. "What if he makes her leave?"

"He won't," I answered smugly.

She cocked her head in the endearing way I'd come to love. "You can't know that. Maybe this will hurt more than it helps."

"I have to take that chance," I said in a more serious tone. "Dane needs someone to shake up his life. He's getting way too complacent about spending the rest of his life on his island alone."

"What if that's what he wants?" she argued.

"If I thought that was all he wanted, I'd never have sent Kenzie there. Do you really think he's happy?"

Eva was silent for a moment before she answered, "He seems...content. Maybe not happy, but okay with himself and his decisions."

"Is that enough?"

She shook her head. "I know you're right. I think he deserves so much more. He has to be lonely, but I guess I just don't want to see him destroyed because we interfered."

"I don't want that, either," I confessed. "But Dane isn't going to take any chances. His life has been too damn rough. If he's comfortable, then he'll settle for the life he has now."

"What did he say on the phone?"

"He sounds shaken up. He was on a roll with telling me off. I'm guessing he'll call Sebastian next, and I have no doubt that he'll see Dane's anger as a good sign, too. Honestly, I don't think he's as angry as he is afraid. He liked the way she confronted him, and he was babbling about her not really even noticing his scars."

Eva let out a relieved breath. "Thank God. All I want is for somebody to see Dane for himself. He's so talented, and he's attractive. Since he started laser treatments, his scars are improving even more, but he doesn't see it. Theo told me that it's making a big difference. Honestly, I'd like somebody other than all of his family to care about him, no matter how much money he has or how he looks."

"Money draws con artists," I told her reasonably.

She gave me a dubious look, "Like me?"

I shook my head, "Never you, love." I'd had to almost force the woman to marry me, and I'd known from the start that Eva had been sincere, something I'd never experienced before. That was probably why I loved her so damn much. Money or not, she loved me unconditionally.

She sighed. "I don't know Kenzie, but Paige swears she's the sweetest woman she's ever known, so I'm sure it's true. She has her own heartache that she's had to live through. I was hoping she and Dane would connect."

"I talked to her at length on the phone. I like her. If I was ever going to take a chance, I knew it would be with her. I have no idea if there will be some kind of love connection between her and Dane, but that wasn't what I was trying to do. My goal was for him to see that not all women are soulless vipers. If they can manage to be friends, I'd be happy. Maybe it would bring Dane out of himself. Maybe he'd get off the island more often."

"Sebastian really wants him here for his wedding," Eva said wistfully. "And I want to see him. It's been a long time."

"I do have a private jet," I suggested. "We could always go visit."

"I'd love that," she said in an animated voice. "I guess I've never even thought about going to see him. I'd feel like I was intruding. He's never actually invited us."

"I feel that way, too," I admitted. "But maybe it's time for us to just invite ourselves."

I'd never invaded Dane's privacy. I figured he wanted to be alone. But I was starting to wonder whether he'd just not asked us to come because he thought we'd refuse. I was beginning to regret giving him his space.

"Let's talk to him at Sebastian and Paige's wedding," Eva suggested. "I wouldn't exactly be sad to go visit a tropical island in the winter, and I'd like to see more of Dane."

"Same here," I agreed. "I just hope he gets to the wedding. He's been pretty busy for the last few years, and I have a feeling he's using that as an excuse. The longer he stays isolated, the more unlikely it will be that he'll continue to come visit. I can't handle that, Eva. He's all that Sebastian and I have left."

"He'll get here," Eva said confidently. "He isn't going to miss his brother's wedding. Maybe he skipped the holidays, but his brothers are only going to get married once. Well, I hope they only get married once, anyway."

"I don't plan on ever letting you go," I said firmly. "You're stuck with me."

Eva was my entire world, and I couldn't imagine my life without her.

"Happy to be *stuck*," she shot back at me with a charming smile.

"So, how long do we have until the wedding?" I asked my wife. "Has Paige set a date?"

"Not yet," she said. "But we're almost done planning, so it should be confirmed soon. Paige is considering relocating the ceremony since it's going to be so cold here."

My wife and Sebastian's fiancée had been planning the wedding for weeks, and I knew my brother was getting impatient. I knew my brother didn't give a shit where it happened. "It better be soon. Sebastian won't make it much longer."

Eva laughed. "He'll live. We don't need to hurry. They're already living together. It's not like she's holding out on him."

"Doesn't matter. He wants to make it official." I could understand his frustration. I'd had the same desperate need to make sure that Eva was connected to me. Maybe it was primal instinct, but it didn't feel right not being married to her. After all, I'd waited my entire life to find her.

Eva changed the subject when she asked, "What else did Dane say?"

I shrugged. "Most of what he was bellowing made no sense."

"Poor Dane," Eva commiserated.

"If he gets comfortable with Kenzie, his discomfort now will be worth it."

"I think it will be good for her, too," Eva said. "She hasn't had the easiest life, and maybe living on a tropical island will be a nice break."

"She's lived in the city all her life. I think it's going to be rather unnerving, actually."

"But it will be a respite. New York gets pretty old," she argued.

I knew the streets hadn't been kind to my wife, and there was nothing she loved more than hiking in the mountains. Even though we lived in Denver, we got away as often as possible.

"Do you need a break?" I asked, suddenly worried that I'd been neglecting her.

She stood and slowly made her way to my chair. I reached out and snagged her waist, pulling her down to my lap.

Holding Eva never failed to lighten my spirits. I had no idea how I'd gotten so damn lucky, but I'd stopped questioning my fate. I was just damn glad she'd married me.

"No. I don't need a break," she replied with a happy sigh, running her fingers through my unruly hair. "I like getting away, but we do it often enough. I have to be in a city to do what I love, and so do you."

I could argue that Walker Enterprises could pretty much be headquartered anywhere, but her studies in the culinary arts were a different story. Her talent required a lot of people who wanted to eat, and she was far better off in a place where people could appreciate her skills.

My wife didn't know it yet, but I planned on buying her the best restaurant in Denver once her studies were complete. She deserved a special place where she could create her own recipes.

"I don't give a damn where I am as long as I'm with you," I said hoarsely, tightening my arms around her waist.

"Ditto, Mr. Walker," she said playfully.

My heart skipped a beat as my beautiful Eva looked down at me with love in her eyes, an expression I'd learned to count on since we'd confessed how we felt about each other. "I love you," I said automatically, unable to keep my emotions confined inside my chest.

"I love you, too," she said in a husky whisper as she lowered her luscious mouth to mine.

All thoughts of my little brother faded as Eva flooded my damn soul. I'd worry about Dane later. There wasn't much I could really do, and I couldn't concentrate when I had Eva this damn close.

Whatever happened between Dane and his assistant had to be left to fate. I wasn't going to interfere anymore.

I just hoped that someday, my youngest sibling could be as happy as me and Sebastian. Nobody deserved it more than he did.

CHAPTER 6

Dane

I lived in a house with no mirrors.

On purpose, I'd avoided the presence of any reflective glass when the home had been decorated. It wasn't like I was a damn vampire or something. I was just a guy who hated the sight of my own face.

I rarely saw my reflection unless I was shaving—a task I'd just finished.

Looking at my jawline in the only mirror I had in the house, I called it good and flipped down the adjustable glass that I used in the master bathroom to take the hair off my face.

Okay, maybe I could have let the decorator put up mirrors in the other bedrooms, and I would probably be open to getting some—if I ever had visitors. But right now it was just me, and I hated looking at myself.

I gazed down at Picasso's soulful dark eyes as he looked up at me from his position at my feet. "Yeah. Okay. *You're* here," I muttered to my dog. "But I don't think you want to check yourself out in the mirror."

Picasso cocked his head in a way that had always perplexed me, like he understood every word I said, even though I knew he didn't.

I went into the walk-in closet to get a clean shirt, pulled it over my head, and asked the mutt, "Do you want to go to the beach?"

The canine was up in a flash, and whining to be taken out to the water.

I was pretty sure Picasso understood the word "beach." Or maybe he just knew that we started almost every day with a walk out to the water.

I watched, slightly amused, as he shot out the door. I followed at a slower pace.

Going about my daily routine kept me sane. I'd have coffee first, then I'd retreat to my studio. Really, all I had to do was work on my art. It wasn't like I really had any other pressing matters right now.

I wondered what Trace and Sebastian were doing, then tried to resist the urge to call and find out.

I'd only been home from my annual holiday visit for a few weeks now, and I was already feeling the oppressive silence of the large residence.

Occasionally, I'd give into the urge to talk to Sebastian and Trace on the phone, and then I'd end up feeling more alone than I could handle. So I avoided their calls until I *had* to talk to them.

It was easier that way. I didn't want to hope for something that would never be reality.

After I finished prepping the coffee, I leaned against the sink waiting for it to finish.

Really, was living on a private island so damn bad? I had my freedom. I had my dog. I could pursue anything that interested me and work on my art.

I had boats now, so I entertained myself with fishing and scuba diving.

I'm fine being alone. I'll get used to it.

I tried to banish my brothers from my mind as I poured a cup of coffee and sat down to read the world news, trying not to think about how much I wished that I had somebody to talk to about what was happening around the globe.

Like I did every morning, I just scanned the news by myself.

Just like every other day.

I was always alone.

CHAPTER 7

Kenzie

I collapsed on the bed in the most gorgeous room I'd ever seen with a sigh of relief. Theo had finally finished telling me where I could find everything in the suite, and had retreated, so I was alone for the first time since I'd been picked up at the airport.

Dane had almost sent me away, and I shuddered to think about what might have happened if I had to try to start all over again.

I'd be homeless.

I'd have nowhere to go.

I'd have nowhere to run.

This job opportunity had meant everything to me. I thought it would be my chance to build up my resources and plan my life. I needed a new start so badly, and I'd been desperately hoping that working for Dane Walker would be the beginning of something different for me.

Now, I knew it was going to be just one more battle for survival.

I didn't want to have to move every time my location was discovered. I'd been doing it since I'd hit adulthood.

I lay on my back and looked around the enormous bedroom. It was tastefully decorated in a light, bright, beachy décor. The *blue room* was actually an *aquamarine* color. Splashes of bolder navy blue and other deeper colors made the bedroom fun and relaxing.

There wasn't anything fussy or pretentious about the space. But it screamed *luxury* anyway.

I'd seen the attached bathroom when Theo had brought me upstairs, and I knew that the colors and theme had been carried throughout the space. The bath was the same color, and I love the bold accents.

The only really strange thing I'd noticed was the surprising lack of mirrors. Luckily, I had a large makeup mirror in my suitcase, but the fact that an amazing suite like this lacked reflective glass was rather...odd.

There was a lovely sitting area and desk on the other side of the room, and I knew I was going to love having my own TV. Sharing a space with several other women meant I rarely got to watch what I wanted on the television. Not that I'd had much time.

"No slacking," I told myself sternly as I sat up. I was here to do a job, and I *was* going to accomplish as much as I could immediately.

I started putting away my clothes, unwilling to believe that my stay would only be temporary.

I have to stay here. I need to stay here.

After changing into a pair of jeans and light shirt, I told myself I was ready.

Even though I wasn't thrilled about having another interaction with Dane, I *was* ready to get to work. I couldn't stand to be idle. I was fairly certain it wasn't in my DNA. I'd spent my whole life being busy, very rarely taking the time to kick back and relax.

I'll be fine.

Dane Walker had definitely not left me with a good first impression, but I'd have to get over my fear of running into him. I was here to *help* him.

Unfortunately, he was more than a little intimidating. He looked like he was in his mid-twenties, about the same age as me. Not that it helped to know we had something in common. The tension between us could practically be cut with a knife.

I'm attracted to him. Really attracted.

Now *that* was a problem.

There was no way I could look at his massive body and not feel slightly *daunted*. He was ripped, but I had a feeling that it wasn't from lifting weights or working out. Dane had sun kissed skin, and the appearance of a man who worked a lot outside. His skin was naturally tanned by the sun. So I was betting he was incredibly active around the island.

His chocolate-brown stare had been unnerving, but I couldn't deny how much it had gotten to me. He had strong features, and they were topped off by his unruly jet-black hair.

Yeah, he had some scars, and I'd wondered how he'd gotten them, but they weren't something that would put anybody off. My heart ached for whatever had happened to him, and I assumed that he'd gotten those marks from the accident that had killed his father.

I went downstairs to explore, trying to get my bearings in the mammoth home.

On the first floor, I found a living room, a family room, and a chef's kitchen that I was dying to check out. I wasn't a *great* cook, but I did know my way around a kitchen.

I walked by the theater room, looking at the indoor pool and spa for a moment before I kept moving on.

Finally, I reached his office.

To my dismay, I found that it was already occupied.

"Mr. Walker?" I asked hesitantly as I passed through the open door.

"What do you want?" he asked unhappily.

"I'm your assistant. I meant to ask *you* what you wanted."

"Nothing. Working hours are over."

Thank God he'd donned a shirt. It made looking at him far easier to do without drooling over his heavily muscled form.

"What exactly *are* my working hours?" I asked, hoping he wouldn't say I had to leave.

"Since you're my assistant, I guess they're whatever I want them to be," he stated in a bemused tone.

He wasn't looking in my direction. He was standing in front of the French doors with his back to me, apparently lost in thought. Jesus! I did like the view. The man had the tightest ass on the planet. "Okay," I said obligingly.

I was pretty sure he was trying to get rid of me, but I lingered inside the room. It didn't feel right for me to just leave.

"Tell me why a beautiful woman like you ended up here?" he demanded.

I stared at the broad shoulders that were encased inside the stretched cotton T-shirt. "I needed a job," I said honestly.

Dane turned to me, and then took a seat at his desk. His expression was still broody, but he motioned for me to sit down in the chair in front of his desk.

"Why did you need a job?" he pressed.

I moved to sit down, considering what I wanted to reveal about my disastrous personal and professional life, feeling like a loser for messing things up so badly. "I lost my job. I worked at an art gallery in New York."

He lifted an arrogant eyebrow. "Which gallery? And why did they fire you?"

"I didn't say they *fired* me," I protested.

"Did they?"

"Yes," I said in a defeated tone. "It wasn't *they*; it was *him*. I worked at Keith Maxfield Fine Art."

He nodded. "I do business with him."

"I know. I saw your painting in person for the first time when I went to work there."

"Tell me what happened," he demanded. "I'm your employer now. I have the right to know."

I let out a nervous sigh. Dane was right. He *should* know my work history, even though I wasn't technically his employee. I'd actually been hired by his brothers. But I knew I was rationalizing.

I made it as simple as possible. "He'd deny it, but Keith asked me out a number of times. I said no. He tried to force himself on me. I kicked him in the balls. The next morning, he fired me."

I hated to think about that day. It had been one of the worst of my life. I would have just walked off the job and never gone back if I hadn't desperately needed that position. Had I known Keith was going to fire me, I would have left without having a dismissal on my work record. Unfortunately, I *had* needed my job, so I'd stayed, hoping Keith would recover from having his balls handed to him and leave me alone.

Dane leaned back in his chair, assessing me. "That motherfucker tried to assault you?" he asked in a hoarse, guttural voice.

"Yes."

There was an eerie silence between us until he finally answered, "First thing tomorrow morning, you'll be contacting the gallery and letting them know I won't be giving them any more of my work. I don't do business with guys like him."

I nearly choked on the big lump in my throat as I stared at Dane in shock.

His order had been matter-of-fact, but I had no doubt that he meant what he said. "You believe me?"

"Do I have reason not to think it's true?"

I shook my head, my heart pounding heavily in my chest. "No. But I'm nobody. Maxfield is a big gallery."

"Until you give me reason not to trust you, your word is good with me," he answered.

My eyes watered as I took in what he'd just said. I had just been a woman in the lowest position somebody could have at the gallery. Yet, Dane believed me. Just like that. It made my chest ache with gratitude that he had taken me at my word. "Thank you," I said in a low, emotional tone.

"For what?" he asked.

"For believing me. Most people would take Keith's side. Especially his clients. He's pretty powerful in the art world."

"I don't give a damn about how well he can throw his weight around. All he is to me is a peddler who can sell my pieces. I don't need him."

Dane was right. He *didn't* need Keith. Any other gallery would kill to exhibit his work. "I know a few that are still up and coming," I said haltingly. "They'd love to have any pieces you'll give them. I have a friend. An old roommate. She's a female, but extremely knowledgeable in abstracts."

He shrugged. "Fine with me. Contact her. I have a painting that's ready to be sold."

"Oh, my God. She'd be elated," I told Dane excitedly.

My happiness soared as I thought about telling Stephanie that Dane Walker was actually putting a piece into her fledgling gallery. She'd worked her tail off, but the art world in New York was a hard enterprise to crack. Artists wanted the most prestigious galleries, and Steph wasn't quite at that level right now.

"Like I said, it doesn't matter to me," he grumbled.

"What *does* matter to you?" I queried. "I don't want to screw this job up."

"I have no idea what to give you to occupy your time," he answered roughly. "I've never had an assistant. I do everything alone."

"Why?"

"Because I prefer it that way," he said in a disgruntled tone. "Let's just get this out of the way now. Then you can stop pretending that you don't see my messed up face. I have scars that people don't want to see. I know it, and I try to stay out of the public eye. That's why I live here."

I gaped at him with disbelief. I opened my mouth, then closed it again. Did he *really* think his scars were so unsightly that he had to hide himself away from the entire world?

"You do have scars," I replied carefully. "But they aren't that bad."

Dane snorted. "They suck. Let's get real. My mug isn't anything that anybody wants to see."

I felt sad as I watched him basically mock himself. It had taken an enormous strength of character for Dane to survive and thrive after his accident. He'd experienced a great deal of loss at a very young age. Yet, he'd created magnificent paintings that had skyrocketed into the world of art. "I want to see them. I don't think your face is messed up at all," I said, wondering what he'd make of my comment after I'd blurted it out. It wasn't that I actually *wanted* to see the marks that had caused him so much pain in his past. But they made him more unique. How could anybody look at Dane and not see enormous strength? "It must have been hard to handle things with so much bravery when you were badly injured and then lost your father that young."

He let out a strangled, humorless laugh. "Brave? You think I'm brave?" he questioned. "I'm a fucking coward. It wasn't difficult to buy myself a private island because I was born rich. The only thing I had to do was stay away from people."

"Easier said than done," I observed. "Loneliness is enough to drive a person crazy. So yes, I do think you have a lot of courage. Most people would want somebody to talk to about what happened. They'd want to be taken care of."

With Dane's wealth, he could have hired a gazillion employees to be at his beck and call. Obviously, he hadn't handled his injuries that way at all.

"I don't talk about it," he snapped. "What's the point? It is what it is. I can't change the past."

I stood, knowing I was probably crossing some kind of line. I could see how tense he was, and I didn't want to keep trying to convince him that he was wrong. Nobody knew better than me how it felt to feel rejected and outside of the norm. "Not everybody cares about your money *or* your appearance," I said as I walked slowly to the door. "I think you've just met far too many who do."

He'd obviously had some bad experiences after his accident. His self-protective instinct was pretty strong.

Dane glared at me as I turned around at the exit to the room. "Really? What do you know about being unattractive? You're fucking beautiful. You could have easily been a model."

His words made me visibly flinch, and my stomach began to churn. "That doesn't mean my life has been easy," I defended.

"At least you don't have to hide on this goddamn island. You chose to be here."

I nodded. "I did. But didn't you choose it, too?"

He felt stuck here. I could sense it. For some reason, he seemed to think he *needed* to be isolated.

"I suppose I did," he admitted in a husky voice.

"Nobody is holding you prisoner here except yourself," I informed him as I left the office and closed the door behind me.

I felt his pain, and I want to reassure him that he was so much more than just a body and a face. Granted, he had an incredibly nice body and he *was* attractive, but his talent—and his compassion— were the most remarkable things about Dane.

He believed me when nobody else had.

He was apparently not going to throw me out of his house without letting me try to do the job I was hired to do.

He created art that touched people on a gut level.

I sighed and walked slowly back upstairs.

Someday, if I could only stop hiding and running *myself*, maybe I could take my own advice about not feeling like a prisoner. It was difficult to tell someone else they were wrong when I wasn't following those rules myself.

CHAPTER 8

Dane

FIVE YEARS AGO...

"No. No. No. You have to feel your art, boy," Carlo told me. "You aren't *feeling* it."

Carlo Benning might be one of the most highly regarded artists of his time, but at the moment, I wanted to turn away from my canvas and punch the shit out of him.

The only thing that stopped me from taking a swing was my respect for the painter. "I *am* feeling it," I grumbled.

Carlo was on an extended stay on the island, teaching me to improve my art. Granted, his visit had cost me a whole lot of money, but I liked to think we'd become friends during the last several months.

"The feeling is *not* there," he protested. "What do you feel when you're painting?"

I shrugged. We'd been through this routine before. "I feel like I'm trying to make a good piece of work."

"It is not enough," he answered. "What you feel has to be projected onto the canvas."

What I felt, what I was always feeling, was lonely. A permanent darkness seemed to have taken up residence in my soul.

"Darkness. I feel darkness," I admitted.

The artist threw a gesturing hand toward the easel where I was working. "Fear. Darkness. Despair. Whatever it is that you're experiencing can be transferred to your art. When you can accomplish that, you'll be successful, boy. You have raw talent, but no emotions."

I wanted to tell him that I wasn't a boy. Far from it. I was a guy who had grown up pretty damn fast. I had emotions, but most of them were so twisted that I didn't understand them, and I could hardly put them into my work.

I turned back and looked at my painting. I knew what I wanted to portray, but Carlo was right. As of now, I wasn't seeing what I wanted.

Problem was, I wasn't sure how to make it show on the canvas.

Doggedly, I picked up my brush, determined to find a way to communicate with the world while I was still inside my own bubble.

What did I want to say?

What did I want people to know?

"I don't know much about the world," I answered earnestly. "All I know is here."

"Then tell them about your life on the island. Emotions are universal, boy. Everyone feels the same pain, the same darkness, the same joy."

I frowned at my painting, realizing that it said almost nothing about anything important. Maybe Carlo was right. Maybe my emotions on canvas could be my connection with the outside world.

After a few bold strokes with my brush, I considered the fact that my mentor was leaving tomorrow. I had to get things together now.

Yeah, I could pull another artist I admired to the island with the promise of money for his personal teaching. And I probably would. I had a lot to learn. But even though Carlo drove me a little bit crazy, it had been nice to have another person around.

I'm fine being alone. I'll get used to it.

I let those familiar words sink into my heart.

Maybe someday, I'd believe them.

CHAPTER 9

Kenzie

"Good morning, Mr. Walker." I greeted my new boss with much more optimism than I actually felt.

I moved to his desk and set a cup of coffee on it.

Black.

No cream.

No sugar.

Theo had been by while I was making coffee, and he told me how Dane liked it.

I couldn't believe he was functioning without his caffeine. I was completely addicted, and the first thing I did every morning was suck down as much coffee as I could get.

Of course, maybe my coffee intake had something to do with being completely sleep deprived.

For the first time, I actually felt rested. I'd slept eight hours last night, waking up feeling like my head was clear.

"Thanks," he answered, sounding distracted as he focused on his computer screen.

"You're welcome," I replied, sitting down in front of his desk with my own full mug, and a notebook in my hand.

I planned on making notes about what he wanted me to do, and get started on any work that he had outstanding.

"You can go," he remarked absently.

Oh no, you don't! You're not just dismissing me for a second day!

"I wanted to get a list of instructions from you," I said. "It would help if we could meet every morning."

I arranged my cotton sundress around my legs. Since Dane didn't seem to be much on formal attire, I'd dressed in a casual blue and white sundress with floppy sandals. I didn't have a ton of clothes, and I generally dressed casual except when I'd been at the gallery. I'd worn one of the two professional outfits I had yesterday.

Finally, he looked up from his computer and handed me an envelope. "Here," he said in a grumpy tone.

I took it, hoping it was a list of the things he wanted. It would be so much easier for me to know what he expected.

"What's this?" I questioned as I drew out the contents of the envelope.

"A check," he answered in a brusque tone.

"For what? I haven't done anything yet."

"It's an advance on your salary. No woman should be without some cash."

I looked at the check, then at him, but he'd already turned back to his computer screen. He'd given me the equivalent of a few months of pay, and it touched me that he'd even thought about the fact that I had no money.

I was torn between gratitude and shame.

"But your brothers hired me," I informed him gently.

"You're mine now," he answered huskily.

I let his words sink into my consciousness. For some reason they made me feel warm and safe. It didn't matter if Dane had only meant that I was going to work for him directly. I still savored the words of belonging *somewhere.* It was a feeling I hadn't experienced much in my life.

"Thank you," I said gently. "That's really kind."

"Believe me, I'm *rarely* kind," he answered in a guttural voice.

I ignored his self-deprecation. He'd been nice to me, so I didn't believe for a minute that the man didn't have a decent heart. It might be well hidden, but it was there.

"Maybe Theo could take me to Nassau some time," I said hesitantly, not knowing how Dane felt about me leaving the island. "I could use some clothes."

Everything I had was thrift store bargain bin. I was good at making something out of nothing.

"I'll cover your clothes," he offered as he kept tapping away at the computer. "It's not like you asked to be stuck in a tropical environment."

"No. I'm fine," I sputtered, surprised that he'd made such a generous offer. He hadn't wanted me here, and now he was offering to cover everything from my cash poorness to my wardrobe.

"It's no big deal."

Yeah. Actually, it was a *big deal* to me. Other than Paige, nobody had ever offered to do anything nice for me in years.

"The check is fine. I'll work hard to earn it," I told him, and meant every word I said.

It was obvious that Dane had decided to give me a chance, and I wasn't about to take that trial for granted.

"I think you should take some time off," he suggested. "Sleep. Eat. You look tired and you're way too skinny. You're in the perfect environment to relax a little."

"I'm here to work," I protested. "If you tell me my working hours, I can relax on my time off. Tell me what I'm allowed to do. Can I use your pool?"

He shrugged. "Of course. Your work hours can be from ten a.m. to noon."

I laughed, hoping he was joking. "I was thinking more like nine-to-five."

"Nine-to-two," he said emphatically.

"Dane, that's—"

"If you keep talking, I'll fire you." He finally looked up from his screen to shoot me a warning glance. "I work during the morning and early afternoon. I usually work on my accounts early. I taught myself to be an actuary, figuring out the risk and benefits of investments. Then I work on investing into the ventures that I like. After that, I catch the late morning and afternoon light to paint in my studio. I don't work late. I take off to the beach to surf or dive."

"Can I use your studio after hours?" I asked breathlessly.

"You paint?" he asked.

I nodded. "I'm not very good, but it's a passionate hobby."

"How do you know your work isn't good? It's good if you feel better after you release your emotions on canvas. There is no right or wrong way to express yourself."

"Says the guy who gets more than a million per piece," I answered with a smile. "Not that you don't earn it. I've admired your stuff for several years."

"I was trained by some of the best," he said nonchalantly. "I couldn't attend college, but I brought the artists that I admired the most here to the island to study under them. We all start somewhere. It's a never-ending progression. As artists, we never feel like we're skilled enough, which is why we keep trying."

I felt good that he'd included me in the artist crowd, even though I wasn't talented enough to deserve it. "My first love is actually making pottery. I do paint and sketch, but I'd much rather be making something useful."

"Then keep on doing it," he suggested, his dark eyes softening as he encouraged me.

"It's not that simple. Equipment costs money. But I'll go back to it someday."

"I'm sure you will," he concurred.

Flustered, I turned my attention back to my notebook. "So tell me what duties I can take off your shoulders."

"Honestly, I'm not *that* busy," he said reluctantly.

"Then why am I here?" I was confused.

"I skipped going to Denver for the holidays last year. I told my brothers it was because I was so busy," he said.

"But you really aren't?" I questioned, starting to understand why there was so much miscommunication between the brothers.

Dane had things he didn't share with his siblings.

"I have a lot of pieces that I want to complete, but I'm not really pressed for time. I don't do commissioned pieces. I give the stuff I'm satisfied with to galleries when I finish them."

"I know. The galleries hate that," I verified with a smile.

Nobody knew when they were going to get a Dane Walker painting, and it had driven my boss crazy.

"Fuck them," he said. "I don't send my work out for money. Did you contact your old boss yet?"

"Not yet," I replied. "But it will be the first thing on the list." I sat my coffee down on his desk and wrote the item down, then looked at Dane again. "What else?"

"You could do the communication between me and the galleries I work with. Contact your friend, and let her know she can take Maxfield's place. I'm sure they'd appreciate a much nicer voice than mine," he considered.

"Okay," I said happily.

He caught me up on the pieces he was currently wanting to put on exhibition, and I took copious notes. Then he talked about what he planned on doing in the future, and I took *more* notes.

When we finished, I finally asked, "Why did you lie to your family?"

He was silent, glaring at me from his seat behind the desk. "You're getting a little too personal," he warned.

"That's why I'm your *personal* assistant," I said with humor in my tone.

"I'm not always going to tell you what I'm thinking. I'm not used to spilling my guts, except when I'm painting," he informed me with a pained note in his voice.

"I'm not asking you to do that. But if I'm really going to be an asset to you, I do need to understand some things."

He was quiet for moment, appearing to consider my words. After a tense silence, he said, "I didn't feel like going. Trace and Sebastian are hooked up and happy now. Nobody needs me to ruin the party."

God, Dane sounded so much like me. I felt exactly the same way about inflicting my presence on anybody who was happy.

"They *wanted* you there," I protested. "Paige was looking forward to meeting you."

"Some other time," he mumbled.

"I thought you liked Eva," I said.

"I do," he reassured me. "It's just...awkward."

"Because they're a couple now?" I understood what he was saying. It was uncomfortable when everybody around you is with somebody and you aren't. I'd been there myself.

"I don't know," he answered tersely. "I just didn't feel like going."

He'd obviously had a serious case of the holiday blues, or maybe the constant isolation was just getting to him. "I get it. I really do," I commiserated.

I moved back to my objective, feeling him out about duties I could take over. Even though he wasn't overwhelmed, he could definitely use a personal assistant, and I was determined to be the best I could be at making his life easier.

"Thanks," I told him as I finally rose from the chair. "I'll start with this." I looked down at my notes, knowing I'd have enough to keep me busy for the rest of the day.

I walked toward the door, then turned back to him again. "Where am I working?"

He pointed toward a door on the other side of his office. "There's a small office connected. I was pretty sure I'd never use it, but I had the builders include it anyway."

The door was hidden behind a massive plant, and I didn't see it until I moved beyond his desk. I rearranged the overgrown greens, and then pushed the door open. "Oh, my," I muttered in a gut reaction to the room.

Dane's office was very masculine, and this space was feminine in comparison. It was light and bright, and the doors leading outside gave me a stunning view of the beach.

"It will work, right?" he grunted from behind me.

I glanced at the white desk and chair, thinking that it was probably the most calming atmosphere I'd ever had the privilege of working in.

The office was obviously an add-on in case he married, so I had hope that he wasn't completely cynical. The space was definitely built with a possible woman in mind.

"Who did the painting?" I croaked, mesmerized by the seascape that took up a large portion of one wall.

"Me." Dane had risen from his chair and was right behind me.

The powerful watercolor was nothing like Dane's usual work.

He didn't do watercolors.

And he *definitely* didn't do whimsical.

But the piece was both of those and more.

I stared at it, still entranced by the powerful, mesmerizing image. "It's beautiful," I murmured, knowing the words weren't nearly enough.

"Not one of my best," he rumbled. "But I was in the mood to do something different."

"It worked," I answered in a hoarse whisper. "It definitely worked."

"Glad you like it. Have a good day. I'm going out to my studio soon."

"Okay," I agreed distractedly, still staring at the piece on the wall. "I'll get to work."

The door closed quietly behind me, signaling Dane's exit. I had to force myself to sit down at my desk and quit gawking at the unusual work on the wall.

Granted, the watercolor wasn't Dane's signature work. He did powerful oil abstracts that generally got a gut reaction from the viewer. The watercolor was subtle, but no less beautiful in a completely different way.

It was no less powerful than his abstracts. The dark, powerful painting hit me right in the gut.

I glanced at my notes, trying to get myself back on track. Then, because I couldn't help myself, I got up and rearranged the desk until all I had to do was turn my head to look at Dane's painting.

Satisfied, I picked up the phone to call my ex-boss and let him know he'd never receive another painting from Dane.

It was the most gratifying and empowering phone call I'd ever made.

CHAPTER 10

Dane

"*I* think we're going to get a pretty good storm, Picasso," I mumbled to my dog as I absently scratched his ears. I was sitting on the beach with the mutt, watching the angry waves churn into the sand.

As of now, it was simply a tropical storm. One thing I'd learned about living on a Caribbean Island was that I always had to keep an eye on the weather.

Not that I was actually in danger.

I had a state-of-the-art storm shelter underground, and it was nearly as large as my residence. So far, I'd weathered up to a category two hurricane in comfort. It had escalated fast, and I'd had no chance to evacuate. But I wasn't stupid. If I had to leave the island for a monstrous storm, I would.

It sucked that my next teacher, an incredibly talented water-color artist, wasn't going to get to the Cay today. I'd been looking forward to talking to somebody other than my dog. But it wasn't going to happen. He'd be delayed until the weather cleared.

The water was mesmerizing, and I suddenly wished I had the skills to immortalize it on canvas.

Seascapes weren't something I painted. Well, until now anyway.

Why can't I do something different? I can feel the volatility of the ocean. Couldn't I capture it with my brush?

There wasn't a single thing stopping me from learning different types of art. Maybe I'd rarely feel like painting in various mediums, but I could do it as a hobby. Fuck knew I had nothing but time.

I'd had those thoughts before, which was why I was going to try to learn a new kind of way to make images from watercolor. Maybe I wouldn't be feeling it often, but it would be nice to learn something different.

I rose from my spot on the sand and signaled for Picasso to follow me. I was starting to feel the strength of the storm, which meant I needed to get my ass—and my dog's—underground.

With any luck, we wouldn't be confined for long. Theo and Emilee were seeking shelter with her family, so I wouldn't even feel anyone else's presence for at least several days.

I'm fine being alone. I'll get used to it.

Those words ran through my mind automatically now.

I was pretty sure I was starting to believe them.

CHAPTER 12

Dane

"*F*uck! I can't concentrate," I said with disgust, tossing my brush down next to the painting I'd been working on.

I couldn't put my emotions into my work when all I wanted to do was go find the beautiful blonde working for me.

About the only thing I could feel right now was lust, and I had no fucking idea how to slap *that* on a canvas.

I started to clean up, resigned to giving up for the day.

Kenzie had been here one week, and she'd managed to send my world into goddamn chaos.

When I got up in the mornings, I looked forward to seeing her when I got downstairs. More often than not, she had breakfast ready and the coffee done. Even though it wasn't something I'd asked of her, she did it anyway because she liked to eat.

And I was more than happy to partake. I couldn't cook worth a damn, and it *was* pleasant to actually have a hot breakfast.

We'd started eating together, and it was too damn cozy. Kenzie was sharp, smart, and funny.

Unfortunately for me, she was also gorgeous, and she smelled like coconut with a hint of flowers after a good rain. Not the overbearing odor of some pungent perfume. Nope. Her fragrance was sweet, but light. A scent I could get used to needing to smell every single day.

I have to stop craving her presence!

I was fucking addicted to her already, and the tantalizing sweetness that was part of her personality.

Sure. She could occasionally be stubborn or sassy, but I was getting used to it. If I wanted to be truthful, I'd admit that I actually liked it.

Kenzie treated me like she would anyone else, and she never seemed to notice the fact that I wasn't perfect. Her friendliness was disarming, and I didn't like being without some kind of weapon.

There was no fucking way I could be mean to her. Well, not consciously. I'd wanted to keep her at a distance, but I couldn't. Not completely. She had just wheedled her way into my life when I wasn't looking.

Breakfast.

Office time.

Dinner.

It wasn't enough, and I was constantly wondering what she was doing. Even though I hadn't wanted an assistant, she actually had taken away a lot of work that I didn't realize had taken up so much of my time.

Probably because I'd *wanted* it to keep me busy.

I had more time to spend on the beach or to hike the island. Some of the things I'd slowed down on were now suddenly possible again. Hell, she'd even talked me into teaching her some of the skills it took to be an actuary, and she picked it up incredibly fast.

More! I wanted more.

She hadn't really seen the island, and even though we'd settled on work hours, she spent more time in the office than we'd agreed.

She needs a break. She needs to eat better. She needs more pleasure in her life.

She needs...me.

Okay, maybe she really *didn't* need me, but I liked to think that she did.

I could show her the island. I could show her the beach. I could teach her everything she didn't already know.

I clenched my fist around the brush I was cleaning, trying not to think about the fact that what I wanted the most was to see her in my damn bed.

Naked.

Moaning.

Pleading for me to make her come, then screaming when I did.

"Fuck!" My dick was as hard as iron, and being around Kenzie drove me bat-shit crazy. "Why did I have to be attracted to her?" I mumbled irritably.

Really, wanting her had probably been inevitable. My need to fuck her had been swift and immediate, and it was growing stronger every day that I spent in her company.

She was definitely a woman to be admired. Kenzie had worked hard just to keep herself afloat because she'd had no chance to go to college. She'd taken some art classes, but that had been mostly for fun. Just like me, she was pretty much self-taught in everything that she excelled in, and things hadn't been nearly as easy for her alone as it had been for me.

I had no idea what it was like to be poor. I could only imagine how hard her life had been. I'd been filthy rich since the day I was born. But she'd been working like crazy since she was old enough to drive, and it had to wear on her. But if it did, she didn't show it. Every day, she was positive and upbeat, something I wasn't exactly used to, but it wasn't totally unwelcome.

I just didn't exactly know how to handle someone like her.

The women I'd known had been privileged, just like me, or they'd been an expert at getting the money they wanted through manipulation.

But Kenzie, she wasn't like that. She seemed happy just to work for me and spend time on my island. As of yet, she didn't seem bored, but she might get there eventually if she didn't stop doing nothing but work.

I wanted to give her everything she'd never had, but I knew she wouldn't lightly just take it—like every other female I'd known. She was...different, but not in a bad way.

"I like her," I admitted to myself, the statement ringing out in my studio.

That was the problem. I *did* like her, and it put me into one hell of a fix.

The more I liked her; the more I wanted her.

Honestly, I was hoping I'd *stop* liking her so damn much. My balls were turning as blue as the damn ocean.

I can't fuck her.

Not only was I afraid she'd leave, but I was worried that she'd flinch away from me. Yeah, she appeared to be totally unconcerned about how I looked, but that didn't mean she wanted me all over her.

For some reason, I couldn't even try to make her a money deal for sex.

Number one: I knew she *wouldn't* sell her body.

Number two: I didn't *want* to buy it.

I wanted her willing and eager, and that thought was a complete fantasy. A beautiful woman like her wanting somebody like me? Nope. It wasn't happening.

It didn't seem to matter how much I told myself Kenzie was just an employee. My dick thought otherwise.

I finished cleaning up my workspace, then exited my studio, restless as hell from being unable to focus on my work.

Getting rid of the temptation was impossible. I'd known from the moment she'd given me hell about not delivering on promises that I wanted to help her. I just wasn't sure how to do that and keep my sanity.

I walked to the house, telling myself that I wasn't going to allow myself to go into the office since I was certain that Kenzie was still there.

Not surprisingly, my ass went *straight* to my home office, like Kenzie was a homing beacon and I was a fucking lost ship.

I pushed the door of her office open, not exactly shocked to see her gorgeous ass in the chair, and her gaze intently on her computer as she clicked her mouse.

"Kenzie?" I said.

She startled, looking up as she realized I was in the room.

"Yes, Mr. Walker?"

Her beautiful eyes were trained intently on me, and it made me swallow hard, like I was a horny teenager who'd been caught checking her out. "I was going to hit the pool. Do you want to come with me?"

Fuck! Why in the hell had I said that?

Guilt rocketed through my system as I saw her face light up. I hadn't offered to have her share any real activities with me because I was afraid I'd end up down on my knees and begging her to put me out of my damn misery.

"It's only one fifteen," she said as she gnawed on a pencil she'd picked up from her desk.

Oh, shit. Now I'd fantasize about where else that luscious mouth could be right now. "Doesn't matter. I'm knocking off for the day. Get off the computer. You've been at this long enough."

"I—"

"Don't argue," I demanded. "Go put on your swimsuit and I'll meet you at the pool."

Kenzie had worked hard since her first full day here. If she started to do a task, she found another that she could take over.

Little by little, she *was* making my life easy. Maybe too easy. Other than my art, I had very little to keep me from thinking about her all damn day.

"If you're sure it's okay," she said longingly.

"It's fine. I asked you, didn't I?"

"Yes," she said as she stood up. "You did. And I'm not going to turn you down."

Oh, she'd definitely *turn me down* if she knew what I *really* wanted to do.

Because I wanted to do *her.*

Pretty damn desperately.

"Go," I replied, anxious to get myself to the pool as a distraction. Of course, that really wouldn't work very well if I was taking my greatest temptation with me for a swim.

I'm a dumbass!

"Okay. I'll just be a minute," she said as she scurried away, presumably to change her clothes.

"I'm so fucked," I said aloud once she'd left the office. But I was also relieved that she agreed to come along.

As I wandered outside, I had to wonder why I wasn't really all that upset with myself about making Kenzie the offer.

CHAPTER 13

Dane

THREE YEARS AGO...

 amn, I wish you didn't have to go back," Trace told me as we got ready to part ways at the airport in Denver.

My private jet was waiting. I'd finally gotten a full airport on the island, and it was more than capable of landing and housing my aircrafts.

I knew my brother was telling the truth. He probably wanted me to stay, but there was no way that was going to happen.

The holidays had been pleasant this year. I was out a good year from my last surgery, and there were no bandages in sight.

Of course, I'd made sure that Theo and Emilee had done my Christmas shopping, just as I had in the previous years since I'd run into that frightened child at the mall.

I wanted to tell Trace that he could always come visit the Bahamas.

I had enough space.

But the words wouldn't come out of my mouth.

My oldest brother had a busy life here in Denver, and Sebastian was starting to do nothing except party his life away.

I wasn't busy like Trace. I wasn't trying to manage an international business.

And I had no interest in Sebastian's party lifestyle.

But damn! I still wanted to see my brothers more often. Living alone on Walker's Cay was slowly driving me crazy.

Say it! Tell him you want to see him more often.

"Yeah, I wish I could stay a little longer, too." The words had flown from my mouth automatically.

"Don't be a stranger," Trace grunted as he gripped me in a bear hug.

I briefly hugged him back as I answered, "I won't."

I would. I knew that I would.

"Call me when you get back to the island," he insisted, standing back so I could leave.

Sebastian had left the day before, so there wasn't much to say except goodbye.

I lifted my hand as I walked toward my jet, forcing myself not to look back.

My brothers had their lives, and I had mine.

They were nothing alike.

I'm fine being alone. I'll get used to it.

I shrugged off our parting as soon as I got into the aircraft.

It seemed that I was finally succeeding in convincing myself that my mantra was the truth.

Someday, I'd be okay with my solitude.

I just hoped that day came soon.

CHAPTER 14

Kenzie

THE PRESENT...

*W*hen you lived in the same house with another person, there came a time when hiding some of your vulnerabilities became nearly impossible.

"It's time," I said to myself nervously.

I'd known, from the first day I'd come to work on the Cay, that Dane would eventually know the real me. Living in the same home was personal, and I couldn't be on guard every moment of the day.

I turned away from the mirror I'd been using, and went to the closet to grab a casual cover-up. I donned it over my one-piece bathing suit, knowing it hid very little since it was light and almost transparent.

I didn't want to hide anymore, but I was terrified to show Dane who I really was beneath my façade.

If anybody would get why I hid, Dane would.

I couldn't say I'd never have to run again in the future. But that was a different issue.

This problem wasn't really a big deal. Or so I told myself. If he didn't want to look at me, then I'd go back to being an assistant who never did anything but work when the boss was around.

Honestly, I desperately wanted to make the island a place where I could be myself, and that wasn't going to happen without taking a risk.

I was tired of being afraid, and being in this tranquil place made me wish things could be different for me.

"Here goes nothing," I muttered to myself as I opened the door and took the steps to the lower level of the house.

I stepped into the pool area before I could stop myself, turn around, and go back to my room.

"About time," Dane rumbled from the middle of the pool. "I thought you'd backed out on me."

"I didn't," I called from the water's edge. I shrugged out of my pink cover-up and dropped it on a lounger.

"Is this deep?" I asked.

"That's the shallow end. Don't dive from there," he warned as he easily treaded the deeper water.

Don't look back, Kenzie. Just jump.

I took a leap of faith, one of the hardest things I've ever done since I didn't trust anybody, and hopped into the water.

The pool was heated, but the shock of the water still took my breath away.

I surfaced close to Dane, and swiped my drenched hair back from my face. "Oh, my God. That was colder than I thought it would be," I said breathlessly.

"I don't like it too hot," he said in a deep, guttural tone. "I have the hot tub for that."

He did. The spa was across the room. "I like it," I admitted. "I guess I just wasn't ready for it."

I finally turned my head, lifted my chin, and stared directly at Dane.

Our eyes locked, and the tension in the air became nearly unbearable.

My heart raced as I watched his expression. Surprisingly, his features shifted into an expression I hadn't expected.

He's...angry.

It wasn't difficult to pinpoint how he was feeling. The outraged fury was there in his dark eyes.

"What in the fuck happened to you?" he asked in a husky, dangerous voice.

I flinched as he moved forward in the water and grabbed my wrist as I lifted my hand to my face.

Maybe this was a bad idea. Maybe I shouldn't have taken a chance.

"What do you mean?" I asked, confused.

His nostrils flared as his gaze searched my face and my upper body, the only areas he could see clearly above the waist-high water.

"Who hurt you?" he rumbled.

I realized what he was asking. "Somebody I didn't know."

"I'll kill the bastard," he said, his furious expression earnest.

"It was years ago," I admitted, my eyes glued to Dane's face.

He let go of my wrist and lifted his hand to my face.

Dane traced the large mark on my cheek, and then the scar on the opposite side of my face.

Time moved in slow motion as the tension between us grew more and more intense.

My body was vibrating with tension, waiting to see if Dane was going to accept me as I was.

It was the first time he'd touched me, and the simple feel of his hand on my skin made my heart skitter.

"Tell me," he demanded as he continued to gently trace the scars on my face like they were still new and painful.

I took a tremulous breath, and let it out slowly before I started to speak. "I went to California when I was eighteen to interview for a modeling job. I'd been working as a model during my teen years, mostly small stuff that came up in Boston, and minor teen pageants. Silly stuff, really, but it brought me to the attention of a reputable modeling agency."

My stomach churned as Dane's stare continued to impale me, and I continued, "My parents were both drug dealers and criminals. They didn't much care what I did, and I forged their names to have consent for me to keep up my small modeling jobs when I was younger. If I didn't, they would have taken every penny I earned, and I had to eat."

Those had been tough years, and I'd had to scramble for costumes and to pay the fees. That was how I'd learned to make something from nothing.

"They didn't feed you? They didn't fucking take care of you?"

I shook my head. "No. I pretty much raised myself. They were rarely around, and when they were, they were stoned and drunk out of their minds. I liked it better when they weren't there, but I had to find a way to feed myself and take care of some of the expenses. They rarely paid the bills."

I'd been a grown up for as long as I could remember, the latchkey kid who had needed to make her own money somehow.

"Fuck! Where in the hell was social services?" he growled as he finally lowered his hand from my face to caress the minor scars on the skin of my shoulder and chest.

I shrugged. "Nobody knew what was happening, or they didn't want to know."

"Your neighbors—"

"Everyone in my apartment building were addicts, Dane. They didn't give a damn about what happened to some unknown kid. They couldn't get their own shit together."

Fire was shooting from his beautiful dark eyes as he looked into mine. "That's fucked up!" he exploded.

I shot him a sad smile. Somebody like Dane Walker would never know what it was like to live through a childhood and adolescence like mine. He'd fought his own demons, but he hadn't done it without two pennies to rub together. Not that I was saying he'd had things better than me. He'd suffered his own pain. But our circumstances had been...different.

"It *was* fucked up," I agreed. "But I adapted. I knew if I could succeed at a career in modeling, it would be a way of stepping up in the world. I wanted to go to college, and I couldn't do it without making some serious cash. I wanted something better than I had. And if modeling was the only way to get out of living in poverty, then I'd use that road to save up some college money."

"How did you get these scars?" His tone was deep and husky.

"In California," I told him, my body trembling from the continual, gentle touch of his fingers. "When I left Boston for California I was eighteen, I was grateful that it might be the break I needed. I needed to get out of Boston, and start living my life. All I wanted was to be successful at *something* back then. I wanted to stop living hand-to-mouth. I couldn't afford the pricier areas of L.A., so I settled for a studio apartment in a much less expensive area. I'd been in crappy neighborhoods my whole life..."

"Keep talking. Tell me everything," he prompted.

"I came back from my interview pretty happy. I was sure I'd be picked up by the modeling agency. My interview had gone really well. But when I got to my apartment, there were two men there, stoned out of their mind."

"You walked in on them?" he guessed.

I nodded. It was true. I couldn't tell him the whole truth about my past. Not now. Possibly never. But I could share what happened to me in California. "I didn't see them until it was too late. I fought as hard as I knew how, but I was no match for two men with switchblades."

I closed my eyes as flashes of that incident intruded into my brain.

The fight.

My overwhelming terror.

And my certainty that I was going to die that day.

"Open your eyes, Kenzie. Now. Don't let the memories get to you," Dane commanded.

My eyes popped back open, and I was suddenly staring into the comfort of Dane's compassionate stare.

I swallowed hard before I said, "I lived. But I had the scars, so that was the end of my modeling career."

"Why?" he muttered. "You're still so fucking beautiful that I can't stop looking at you."

My heart clenched inside my chest, a squeezing pain that brought tears to my eyes. "Not beautiful enough," I answered. "I eventually learned how to cover my scars with makeup. I'd learned a lot about covering up imperfections during my teen years. But it wasn't good enough. The camera would still see my flaws, especially back then when they were fresh. The marks weren't completely coverable."

I usually wore clothing that would cover the scars on my body, but I had never been able to work in the modeling field again.

"They aren't that bad," Dane protested.

"They've improved over time," I told him. "But the world wants perfection."

"So what happened after California?"

"I moved back to the East Coast. It was a world I was familiar with. I took any jobs I could get to stay afloat."

"What about your parents?"

"My mother died while she was serving her sentence, and my father is still incarcerated. They were responsible for killing a guy during a bad drug deal. They took a plea deal and went to prison." My parents were murderers, and I rarely told anybody the truth about what had happened to them. I preferred to say they were gone, which they were. I preferred to leave out the information that my father killed a man, and he was still behind bars.

"And your attackers?" he asked in a low, dangerous voice.

"Dead," I told him truthfully. "They raided another apartment the next day to look for money. The owner killed them both."

I let out a sigh of relief, glad I'd come clean with *some* of my past. I just wasn't sure how he'd process it. I was the scarred up kid of two convicted murderers. How could anybody process that without some kind of suspicion that I could be as bad as my parents?

"I guess that saves me the time of tracking them down," he answered in a disgruntled voice, like he was disappointed that he couldn't get revenge himself.

"That part of my life is over," I informed him softly. "I was hoping I could start all over again here on your island."

I was *also* hoping I'd never have to go on the run again, but I chose not to mention that.

"You can," he said in a gentler tone. "Any damn thing you want is yours. Just name it."

My body was beginning to scream with need, but it wasn't clamoring for anything Dane *owned.* It was pleading for him to touch me more. "I'm happy here right now," I confessed. "For the first time in my life, I actually feel safe."

"Good," Dane grunted. "You're going to stay that way."

Not once, from the time I'd entered the pool, had Dane looked at me with anything other than an out-of-control protectiveness that I coveted. But in between those emotions, I could feel that sizzle of a gathering storm between us.

My fingers were itching to touch the massive amount of tanned skin of his chest. In spite of any scars he might have, Dane was beautiful to me. There was something so ruggedly handsome about him that I craved his touch.

"Are you going to kiss me?" I whispered breathlessly.

"I shouldn't," he rasped as his hands came to rest on each side of my face.

Disappointment flooded my being. "I suppose not."

Dane was a billionaire, and my employer. The last thing I wanted was to risk this job. Now that he accepted me, scars and all, I didn't want to leave his island.

I risked revealing my imperfections because I'd had a feeling that Dane would understand. His acceptance and protectiveness was more than I'd hoped for.

He looked at me with desire in his eyes, a reaction that was unexpected. Yes, I'd wanted him to be able to deal with my flaws. But knowing that he wanted me despite my imperfections was almost more than I could handle.

"But fuck if I'm not going to do it anyway," he warned as he tilted my chin, right before his mouth crashed down on mine.

CHAPTER 15

Dane

TWO YEARS AGO...

"*I*'m so sorry, Mr. Dane," Theo told me. "Picasso just got away from my Emilee when she was taking him for a walk. The car hit him before she could do anything to save him."

I should have never gone home for the holidays this year.

Sorrow at the fact that my potcake dog, Picasso, was gone forever flooded my soul.

My fur ball was the only thing that really made this island bearable. Picasso had loved me unconditionally. He hadn't cared that I wasn't perfect.

Dead? No! Just. Fucking. No!

"We can get you another dog," Theo suggested.

I shook my head. The enormous lump in my throat kept me from speaking.

I'd returned to the island from my Denver holiday trip only to find out that the only other permanent resident here, my faithful potcake, had been struck by a vehicle in the capital city while he stayed with Theo and Emilee while I was gone.

I'd never see my faithful mutt again. "I don't want another dog," I finally rasped to Theo.

We were headed home from the airport, and knowing I wouldn't see Picasso when I got to the house was fucking killing me.

It would be a hell of a lot lonelier here without Picasso.

I didn't want a replacement, like he'd been a piece of furniture. My canine had been my friend and companion for the last six years. I wasn't ready to let him go.

I yanked at the seatbelt, feeling like it was choking me.

Potcakes were plentiful in some parts of the Caribbean. They roamed around as strays, and made a nuisance of themselves when they got overpopulated.

But Picasso had been far from annoying for me. When Emilee had brought him to me as a pup, I'd felt the connection with the playful black and white bundle of energy.

He'd needed a good home.

I'd needed the company.

It had been a perfect match for us...until he was gone.

Goddammit! My dog had been raised on this quiet island. He hadn't recognized the dangers of traffic.

"You sure you don't want another?" Theo queried remorsefully.

"Yeah. Picasso was special," I answered coarsely.

I was fucking heartbroken over a dog. Maybe that made me kind of pathetic. But I didn't give a damn.

Theo and Emilee didn't really see the animals as a blessing. Potcakes were everywhere, and generally kind of a pain in the ass for the locals.

I was alone in my grief, but the last thing I wanted was another dog, like Picasso had been interchangeable with any other potcake.

He wasn't.

He'd been my friend.

Suck it up, Walker. Twenty-four-year-old men don't cry over a mutt.

I coughed to clear my throat, and started asking Theo about other things that had nothing to do with my pet.

I'd deal with my grief when Theo and Emilee left to go home.

I'll be fine alone. I'll get used to it.

As the familiar chant rushed through my brain automatically, I convinced myself it was true.

It was easier that way.

CHAPTER 16

Kenzie

*D*ane devoured my mouth like he owned it, and that ferocity fueled a fire that was already raging inside my body.

I'd only had one guy in my life, a quick teenage affair that had soured most of my desire for another physical relationship. Not that I'd really had the chance after the attack. I was too afraid to let any male know me, to find his way into my heart. Most men wouldn't want me when they saw my scars. But Dane... Oh, God, he was so much different than any man I'd ever known.

But Dane's fiery embrace was different, unlike anything I'd experienced. He was a *man* who knew exactly what he wanted, and he'd plunder until he got it.

I wrapped my arms around his neck, and pressed my body into his with an inward sigh of satisfaction. His rock-hard body cradled mine perfectly, and I clung to his muscular back, sensation invading me and landing squarely between my thighs.

I wanted him. I needed him so desperately that no other thoughts could penetrate my fog of lust to get to my common sense.

"Dane," I said in a stunned tone when he finally pulled his mouth from mine.

"Fuck! Theo's here," Dane growled.

It took me a minute to process what he said after I heard the subtle sounds of somebody's presence in the kitchen.

Theo had made a run for groceries, and he was obviously back and putting the supplies away.

My body screamed in protest as Dane let go of me and backed away.

I wanted to be back in his protective hold again, but my common sense finally returned. "I don't want him to see us this way," I confessed. "I like him and Emilee, and the last thing I want is for them to think I'm sleeping my way into your good graces."

He shot me a wicked grin that felt like a punch in the stomach as he answered gruffly, "If I was fucking you, there is no way you'd be sleeping."

I wanted to climb my way up his strong, chiseled body after he uttered those confident words. "Maybe I wouldn't be sleeping," I said absently, my brain still muddled.

"Shit! I wish I kept the water a hell of a lot colder," he said with a masculine groan of pain as he dove toward the deep end of the pool.

I let out a shaky breath that I hadn't known I'd been holding, watching Dane as he cut through the water effortlessly.

Dunking my head, I hoped that my body would catch up with my common sense sometime soon.

I mounted the pool stairs, grabbed a towel and my cover-up, then made my way quickly upstairs.

My body was still shaking with need when I got to my room.

My reasoning ability recovered long before my body did.

I didn't see Dane until the following morning. Both of us had kept our distance, and I'd decided letting my guard down had been an enormous mistake.

Maybe it had been the right thing to show him who I really was. He was my boss. And we had to live in the same house. I couldn't keep hiding my own scars. But letting him kiss me had been a completely different story.

I was vulnerable whenever he touched me, and that scared the shit out of me. I was a survivor. I knew better than to let myself feel that much.

Being alone for most of my life had taught me that the only person I could count on was myself. Paige had been the only real friend in my life. Others had been transient and short-lived friendships, and some just casual friends.

I couldn't be counted on to be there for anybody, so I avoided any kind of real intimacy or connection most of the time out of necessity.

I'm not sure whether I would have shared my history with Paige had I not been her roommate for so long, and had slowly learned to trust her.

I sighed as I poured water into the coffee pot and switched it to the *On* position.

Maybe I'm so drawn to Dane because we're so much alike.

Both of us had experienced profound loneliness on a scale that most people would never understand. We both had scars, but the physical marks were far less painful than the emotional ones.

Dane hid out on his island.

I hid in plain sight.

Even on the streets of New York, which were shared by millions of people, I'd always felt lonely.

I tucked my hair behind my ear as I wondered when I'd meet up with Dane that day.

"You're nervous," Dane drawled from the entry to the kitchen. "You only start fidgeting with your hair when you're feeling edgy."

I turned to watch as he advanced into the room. As usual, he was breathtakingly handsome in a pair of jeans and a navy blue polo that hugged every toned muscle in his upper body. I cursed the fact that he was in such good shape, and that the sound of his deep voice sent shivers down my spine.

Yes, Dane had scars, but nothing that made him less attractive. If anything, it seemed to add to the mystery of the man.

"I guess I never noticed," I said before I turned my head back to the coffee.

I couldn't stand to look at him without somehow wishing we were naked, hot, sweaty and satisfied.

"Why are you so uptight this early in the day?" he questioned as he leaned against the sink right next to me.

I shook my head. "I'm not. I was thinking."

"Bullshit," he countered, folding his muscular arms in front of him. "Maybe I haven't been around people a whole lot in the last seven or eight years, but I've watched you long enough to know your body language."

I opened my mouth to tell him that nobody had ever cared enough to watch how I reacted, but I closed it again, knowing I couldn't give away too much of myself. It made me feel raw and vulnerable, and I couldn't afford to experience those kinds of emotions.

I forced myself to draw a deep breath and let it out slowly. "Okay. I'm a little jumpy I suppose. Things got out of hand yesterday, and I'm sorry about that."

He turned and opened the cupboard, then grabbed two mugs and set them on the countertop. "I'm not," he said in a husky voice.

"I'm your assistant," I argued.

"Who the fuck cares," he said. "It's just you and me out here. It's not like there are any employees, other than Theo and Emilee. And I know they sure as hell don't really care what we do. There's no etiquette book on what two people alone on a private island should do."

"I care. I need this job." I finally turned to look at him.

His eyebrow rose in challenge as he stared at me. "You think I'd fire you?"

"I hope not." The words just slipped from my lips before I could stop them.

"I won't," he grumbled, then his eyes narrowed. "Why in the hell are you wearing a ton of makeup again?"

Hiding my scars was a habit when I was working, and maybe I'd felt too bare this morning. "It's appropriate."

"No, it sure as hell isn't," he answered. "Get rid of it. Your scars are barely noticeable, and it's hot as hell here. In the summer, that stuff will be running all over your clothes."

He had air conditioning, but I had to admit I wasn't quite used to the humidity of the tropical environment. "Is that really something you want to see?" I asked defensively.

"Yeah. I think I do," he answered as he poured coffee into both mugs.

"Why?"

"I have no fucking idea. You're beautiful either way. But I prefer to see your skin rather than caked on makeup. It's not you."

He wasn't joking when he said the coverage was excessive. To make my scars completely invisible it took a lot of time, effort and a whole lot of makeup. I used layers, each one thicker than the last. "Nobody ever really sees the real me."

Dane grasped my upper arm and pulled me forward, then swung his body around to trap me against the counter. "I see you, Kenzie," he growled. "I notice every single thing about you. I know your nervous habits, your likes and dislikes, and I know when you aren't telling me everything. I know you've always handled stuff on your own, but you don't need to do that anymore. I'm here to help if you let me."

Our eyes locked, and I could see the sincerity in his gaze. I wanted to trust Dane, but my need to stay alive was still so close to the surface that I wasn't sure I could. "Thanks," I uttered.

"Will you let me?" His stare was penetrating, leaving me bare and vulnerable, exactly what I was trying to avoid.

"I'm fine," I insisted. "You've given me a good job, a nice home to live in. That's more than enough."

"It's nothing," he answered. "You have to put up with my sorry ass. You should probably get combat pay."

I bit my lip to keep from smiling. "You aren't so bad."

Honestly, Dane was probably one of the nicest people I'd ever had as a boss. He'd been encouraging in his own gruff way, and he was teaching me things I'd never had the chance to learn before.

Yeah, he *had* kissed me, but I was fairly sure I'd been begging him to do it with pleading eyes. He wasn't the type to come on to a woman if she didn't *want* his attention.

"I'm attracted to you," I blurted out before I could temper the statement.

"Yeah. I don't really get that," he said in a confused tone.

Unable to stop myself, I reached out a finger to trace his scars.

He flinched, but then let me touch him. "There's more to you than just your superficial appearance," I mused. "I know you think your scars are ugly, but they really aren't. They're just part of who you are, and your experiences with life."

"My life experiences suck."

"Mine, too," I said softly. "Maybe that's why I love your painting so much. I could feel a kindred spirit, I think."

He reached up and grasped my hand, and then held it against his cheek. "How's that?"

"I could feel the despair and anger in your paintings, but I also felt a tiny sliver of hope."

"The *hope* part was probably painted by accident," he informed me.

"No, it was not," I protested. "It was there."

"Buried deeply inside the anger and despair," he said teasingly.
I shrugged. "Sometimes. But it was still present."

His grip went to my wrist, and he slowly pulled my hand
down. "The things that happened to you weren't fair, Kenzie. At
least I had a childhood until my father died. I came up privileged
and spoiled. But my dad gave me a good foundation. I just never
had a chance to put it to work in the real world. But that was my
choice. You didn't get to choose much of anything. And when
you finally got free of your parents, you ended up in the hands
of some of the worst motherfuckers in existence."

Dane entwined our fingers, and I don't think he even noticed
that he was still clutching my hand in a death grip.

"I had Paige," I argued. "Her friendship made me believe that
not all people were bad."

"They *aren't* all bad," he agreed. "But I'm probably the biggest dick you'll ever meet. And I can't stop my attraction to
you, either. I've probably wanted you almost from the moment
I saw you. Trying to make you leave was a knee-jerk reaction to
wanting you."

"We can't act on the attraction," I said desperately.

"Who is going to stop us?" he asked. "Kenzie, nothing bad is
going to happen if we do."

I didn't entirely believe him. I'd spent my whole life waiting
for the hammer to come down, waiting for something bad to
happen. And it almost always did.

I yanked at my hand, suddenly uncomfortable with the conversation. "We can start over," I suggested as Dane finally released
my hand. "We can just forget what happened yesterday."

He shook his head. "Not possible. I've wanted you in my bed
since the first time I saw you."

"Is that why you decided to let me stay?" I asked in a tremulous voice.

"No. I let you stay because somewhere deep inside me,
there probably is still a part of me that wants to be fair and help

someone who is trying as hard as you are. It just felt like the right thing to do."

"Do you regret it?"

It had only been a little over a week, but I hoped he didn't have any misgivings now.

"I don't. You're starting to make yourself irreplaceable."

My heart clenched. "Good. I want to be useful."

He reached up and tipped my chin up so he could look directly into my eyes. "You're more than useful, Kenzie. Don't ever forget that."

I wasn't used to any kind of compliment, so his words threw me. "I'll go and wash the makeup off. You're right. It does bother me, especially here."

It was a mask I was used to wearing, but it didn't feel all that necessary anymore on Walker's Cay.

I'd effectively managed to cover myself this morning, a move that I hoped would put some distance between Dane and myself. Unfortunately, it had done the exact opposite. He knew what I was trying to do, and he seemed determined to bring my walls down around my feet.

He looked hesitant for a moment, like he wanted to say or do something, then he let go of my chin. "Fine. I'll cook."

"Please don't," I pleaded. "I'll be back in a minute."

"What? I can manage to fry some bacon or something," he protested.

I raced toward the stairs, hoping he wouldn't really get started before I got back. Dane had tried to *help* me in the kitchen once or twice. It hadn't turned out so good.

"Don't start without me," I called over my shoulder.

My heart skipped a beat as I raced up the stairs, almost certain that I'd actually heard Dane Walker laugh.

CHAPTER 17

Dane

*I*wasn't sure why in the hell I'd switched the painting I was working on, but I had more focus on what was in front of me now.

It was another seascape, in oil this time, and something I hadn't really practiced since my mentor, a master at sea paintings, had left the island to go back home.

I was more comfortable with oils, but I wasn't so sure about the subject of my work. I didn't do real pictures. I did abstract emotions. But for some reason, working on the perfect sunset over the ocean drew me.

Strangely, I was learning that I could pour emotions out on canvas with any subject. The scene I was painting was dark, the ocean churning with waves and a burnish brightness of the setting sun over a dark and angry sea.

Hell, that was kind of the way I was feeling. Kenzie was the light, and I was the tempestuous ocean. All I really wanted to do was sink down into her like the setting sun.

"Shit!" I cursed, realizing that everything I was painting depicted what I wanted in real life. "She's driving me crazy."

Kenzie had left the kitchen this morning and washed off all of her makeup, an action that had my complete approval. Her skin was beautiful and perfect, her nearly invisible scars a symbol of how much she'd been through in her past.

I told her life hadn't been fair, and it was especially true in her case. How did one person live through her shitty childhood, and equally crappy adult life?

It wasn't hard to believe she'd had modeling aspirations. She was fucking gorgeous, even with the blemishes on her face. Washing off the makeup did nothing to curb my urges to pin her up against the wall and take exactly what my cock was clamoring to get.

I wanted her to experience hundreds of kinds of pleasure, all of them taught by me.

"I'm never going to survive this," I told myself as I stood in my studio examining what I'd done so far on my current project. "She'll kill me."

I knew I sure as hell wasn't going to be able to stop touching her. Knowing she felt a similar attraction didn't help me, either. All it did was make it harder not to try to get her into my bed. I wanted more than just her body. With Kenzie, I wanted every part of her, and that scared the hell out of me.

Seeing her every day, having another person I liked to talk to was slowly beginning to change me. Whether that was good or bad was still undetermined. But it *felt* good. It *felt* right having Kenzie here, and I wasn't going to ignore something that had helped me start to regain my sanity again.

So much time on the Cay alone had been starting to get to me. Hell, maybe I'd started to lose my mind a long time ago, but I hadn't really given a damn because I hadn't wanted to be vulnerable.

"Dane?" a hesitant voice called softly from the door of my studio.

I turned to see Kenzie standing at the door, backlit by the bright sunshine. "Yeah?"

She smiled at me as she said, "Steph is ready to take your last painting. I just need you to sign the contract."

"I'll do it when I get back to the house," I agreed.

"Okay," she muttered, then turned to leave again.

"Wait!" I demanded.

"I don't want to disturb you," she said.

Damned if that sweet, feminine tone didn't get my dick harder than it already was just from seeing her beautiful face.

"You're not bothering me," I confessed. "I think I'm done for the day."

Once I saw her, I didn't want to *unsee* her. Kenzie was an addiction, and I never seemed to get enough of her uplifting presence.

Seeing her smile had just made my damn day.

"Can I see it?" she asked curiously, waving her hand toward my current work.

"Yeah," I consented. "I still have a lot to do. I was working on something different, but I'm not in a place where I want to finish it, so I'm working on another canvas."

She moved closer, and the scent of coconut and heat invaded my nostrils. I breathed in deeply, then let out the air slowly, savoring the smell of Kenzie.

"Oh, my God. It's…amazing." Her breathless expression made me want to reach out and wrap my arms around her waist so I could feel her soft, curvy body plastered to mine.

"I'm hoping I'll see another sunset like last night," I told her. "I didn't take a camera for pictures."

"I love it," she said as she cocked her head to examine what I'd done. "It's raw and beautiful."

"Then it's yours once it's done," I stated.

Maybe having some of my work would give Kenzie some kind of security. I didn't give a damn what she did with it. If she needed the money someday, she could sell the stupid thing.

She gasped. "No, Dane. I could never accept that kind of gift. Your paintings get at least seven figures. And this one is unique."

"I don't give a damn about the money. I never have. Keep it, or sell it. I don't care. But I am giving it to you as a gift. When's your birthday?"

She hesitated before she answered, "Next month. The sixteenth."

"Mine, too," I confided. "The fifteenth. I'll be twenty-six. So you can take it as a birthday gift. How old?"

"Twenty-six," she replied.

"I'm one day older than you are."

"I'm not taking your painting," she denied. "It's incredible enough that I get to look at them."

She'd take the painting, and any future work she wanted. But I didn't feel like arguing with her right now.

"Do something with me?" I asked in a tone that sounded more like a command. "Let's celebrate our birthdays together."

I could argue with her about the paintings later.

"Sebastian called. He and Paige are getting married the day before your birthday. Paige wants me to stand up with her as her maid of honor."

"Do you want to go?" I asked.

"Yes. I'm really honored that she wants me to be in her wedding. Sebastian wants you to be in it, too."

She frowned, emphasizing the small crinkle between her eyebrows when she did.

I let out an exasperated sigh. "Okay. But we go out after and celebrate. It's a damn miracle that you made it to your twenty-sixth birthday."

She let out a startled laugh. "I guess maybe it is. Thank you so much. I don't want to miss my best friend's wedding."

I knew she was sincere. Kenzie was the type of woman who would be there for a friend, even though life hadn't been particularly kind to *her.*

"It's not like I wasn't going anyway," I shared.

"But you thought about skipping it," she answered.

"How did you know?"

"Because the longer you avoid something, the harder it is to fix. You haven't seen your family for over a year."

"I'll see them at the wedding," I grumbled.

"It's going to be a gorgeous ceremony," she said excitedly. "Eva and Paige have been planning this for weeks."

"Did you want to be in on the planning?" I hated to think I was keeping her away from something she wanted to do.

She shook her head. "I already see it because Paige and I conference with video online."

I was relieved. I didn't want to have to be there early, but if Kenzie really wanted to go for the planning, I'd do it. There wasn't much I *wouldn't* do to see her smiling like she was right now.

"Will your jet make it to Hawaii?" she asked uneasily.

"Of course. Do you want to go to Hawaii?" I was confused because I thought we were talking about Denver and the wedding.

"The wedding is being planned there. Since it's still going to be cold in Denver, Paige decided to have the ceremony in Maui."

"Sebastian will probably like that," I told her. "It's one of his old hangouts."

"Do you like it?"

"I haven't been there since I was a kid. My dad used to take me scuba diving all over the world. I started when I was eleven. I was a junior diver before I certified when I turned fifteen," I told her, my chest aching over the hobby that my dad and I had enthusiastically shared. They were good memories, but not necessarily easy to recall because I no longer had my parent to share it with.

"Do you still dive?"

I smirked at her. "I'm in one of the best dive areas in the world on a private island. Yeah, I go out as much as I can."

"I've always wanted to learn," she told me in a wistful voice.

"Then I'll teach you."

"You will?" She looked dumbfounded.

"Can you snorkel? We might want to start there and work you into scuba diving when you're comfortable."

"I have a confession to make," she said solemnly.

"What?"

"I can't really swim very well."

I shrugged, filing the information away so that I was always near her when she was in the water. "Then we make you a stronger swimmer before the snorkeling."

A childlike excitement lit up her expression. "Really? I'd love that."

"Can you work the time into my busy schedule?" I told her with a grin.

"Yes, Mr. Walker," she shot back at me with humor in her voice.

Holy hell. I was pretty sure I'd do just about anything to keep her smiling like she was right now.

Kenzie had occasionally appeared kind of melancholy and uptight for a few days after she'd arrived on the island. I was guessing that the prospect of not having a job had dented her optimism. I didn't ever want to see her tense and worried again.

I wasn't prepared when she suddenly leaped forward and careened into my chest.

Luckily, my reflexes were quick, and I snaked my arms around her. And dammit, she felt so fucking good that I didn't want her to pull away again.

"Thank you, Dane. Thank you so much," she whispered loudly next to my ear.

"Not like it's exactly difficult or a hardship to go diving. We're kind of surrounded by water," I teased.

"I know you aren't thrilled about traveling, but you'll love the wedding. I promise."

Her tone was so earnest that I didn't want to disappoint her, so I didn't say anything.

To be truthful, I probably *would* love the trip to Hawaii if she was there next to me. Her needs were rapidly becoming more important than my fear of the outside world.

I gritted my teeth as her sensual body rubbed against mine. Shit! What I wouldn't give to be doing this *without* clothing between us. I wanted to explore her incredible body, and take my time doing it.

"I really don't mind all that much," I said as I buried my face in her hair. The feel and the scent of her drove me crazy. Maybe I was a closet masochist, but I couldn't let her go.

"You were always planning on going," she accused as she pulled her head back to look up at me.

"I was," I confirmed. "My brothers are probably only going to get married once. I want to be there. I'm shocked that Sebastian has settled down at all."

"Paige loves him," she said. "I hope he's good to her."

There was no doubt that Sebastian was going to treat Paige like she was a queen. He adored her, and I knew he'd put his past behind him. "He was a player. But since he met Paige, I don't think he's even thought about another woman. He's reformed."

"I'm the last one to talk about past mistakes," she shared. "As long as he sees what he has now, I'm good with that."

"Nothing that happened to you was your fault, Kenzie," I assured her.

"I feel like an idiot at times. I'm going to be twenty-six and I haven't accomplished much."

"Don't," I rumbled. The last thing I ever wanted for Kenzie was regret. Her life had sucked until the present, and I was going to make damn sure she never knew another unhappy day in her life if I could avoid it.

Much to my displeasure, she pulled away from me. "I'm sorry I interrupted you."

I shrugged. "You didn't. Like I said, I'm done for the day."

"Can I use your studio for an hour or two?"

"Of course. I told you that you could." I thought for a moment before I added, "But only if you let me see your work."

I didn't care about her technical skills. I wanted to see her doing something that made her happy.

"I don't have anything with me that's even started. I'm mostly just doing sketches right now."

"I have the perfect place for you to start," I said as I started to clean my brushes.

"You do?" she answered, sounding confused.

I washed my hands and dried them with a paper towel. "Let's go. I have something to show you."

I took her hand and led her to the house, hoping I could make her smile one more time today.

CHAPTER 18

Kenzie

*T*o say I was astonished by what Dane had to *show* me would have been an understatement.

He led me to the back of the house and pulled me into a room I'd never seen before, an enclosed porch that I assumed he never used. I'd actually passed over the room myself when I'd explored the house, thinking that the closed door was a closet or storage area.

It was a fairly large space, and it was beautiful. It was air conditioned, but someone had thrown open a few of the many windows so the sound of the ocean was clear inside the room.

"I didn't know this room was even here," I told him as I entered, stopping so abruptly that Dane slammed into my back.

"I never use it," he commented as he steadied me. "I have the other huge porch areas, so I guess I haven't needed it until now. What do you think? Can you work in here?"

It took me a minute to understand what he meant.

I looked around, finally noticing that the room was set up for pottery making. And it was equipped with the latest and best equipment. My experience had come from working on an old pottery wheel and with aged kilns and processors at a local rec center in Massachusetts.

"This equipment is incredible," I muttered as I walked around the room and ran my hand over one of the pottery wheels.

"It's yours," he rumbled from behind me. "Theo and I set it up, but it may need somebody more skilled to figure it all out."

"You even have the equipment to make bisque items," I said, still marveling over the volume of equipment he'd brought in. "And they can be painted."

"I can paint some for you, but I'm not sure my work is exactly what you want on pottery."

I laughed. "I'd have pottery worth way too much money for me to be comfortable eating or drinking from it." Maybe I wasn't quite certain what a piece of pottery would cost with Dane's mark, but it would be a display piece only. "How did you know what to buy?"

Honestly I was stunned that he'd put a pottery room together when he was never going to use it.

He shrugged. "I just bought whatever they told me might be useful for a pottery room."

I let out a startled laugh. "It looks like they sold you an entire store."

"I wanted to make sure you had everything you needed. Do you like it?"

I turned to face him. "It's amazing. I honestly don't know what to say."

Thank you didn't seem like enough. What touched me the most was the fact that Dane had done this simply to make me happy. Who does things like that? I didn't need any of the stuff, but I was itching to try to make some pieces now that he had the pottery room.

I couldn't even pretend that he'd done this for any other purpose than to make me more content on the island, and I wasn't sure how to handle that. I didn't know how to handle *him*. I'd never really worried about making myself happy. Hell, I'd never gotten past staying alive. What could I say to somebody who had done something expensive and probably time-consuming simply because he thought I might like it?

"Don't say anything," he suggested. "Just tell me if it has everything you need."

"I can't believe you did this for *me*," I answered honestly. "Nobody has ever gone to this kind of trouble just for me."

Tears welled up in my eyes as I continued to stare at him.

"Oh, God. Don't fucking cry, Kenzie," he pleaded in a husky voice.

"I can't help it. Why did you do this? I'm just an employee."

"You said you like to mess with pottery. And what's wrong with doing something nice for an employee. Not to mention that you're more than an employee to me, Kenzie."

"I do like to putter around with pottery. But you didn't *need* to do this." I felt guilty, and I certainly didn't feel worthy.

"I wanted to do it," he protested.

"Thank you," I said as a tear leaked from my eye and fell onto my cheek. I didn't want him to think I was ungrateful. I just wasn't sure how to handle this whole thing very well. "I'll be in here every chance I get."

"Make time," he insisted. "You can start knocking off earlier."

I smiled at him, a broad grin that I couldn't hold back. "I don't need to do that. I have plenty of free time. I've felt like I'm on vacation. I'm only on one job, and my hours are way too short in my opinion."

Like he didn't give me enough time off already? I'd never worked so few hours before. My work days were usually seventeen hours long. And pretty much every day was a work day. Working for Dane an average of six or seven hours a day was like a holiday for me.

"You've worked way too much in your life already. It's time to learn to play a little, Kenzie."

I had no idea what it would be like not to work almost every waking hour of my day. "I'm not sure I know how," I admitted. "Working short hours here is giving me a serious case of guilt considering how much I'm being paid. I like staying busy, Dane."

"Stay busy with something other than my work," he demanded.

"I'm paid to deal with your business," I teased.

"Then maybe I should change your job title. What if I said I need a companion, and that's going to be part of your job?"

The last thing Dane needed was somebody to be pestering him all the time. He worked hard at weighing the pros and cons of his investments, the risks and possible rewards. Then he went on to work on his art. His days weren't exactly short. "I'd say you were lying."

I watched his throat move as he swallowed hard. "I'm not lying," he said flatly. "I like having you here."

His words were the sweetest compliment I'd ever had. "Nobody has ever really wanted me," I said hesitantly, emotions expanding and threatening to boil over the walls I usually put up to shield them.

He moved closer, so close I could feel his warm breath on my face.

"I want you, Kenzie. I don't *want* to want you, but I'm not going to lie to you *and* myself. I think you already know how I feel. Hell, I can't be in the same room with you without my dick getting hard."

Unable to stop myself, I wrapped my arms around his neck, sighing as I threaded my fingers into the coarse, thick hair on his head. "I feel it," I admitted. "I wish I didn't, but I do. It's always going to be dangerous because I'm your assistant."

"My assistant-slash-companion," he corrected. "And no matter what happens between us, I'm not planning on firing you."

His arms came quickly around my waist, holding me like I was something precious.

Maybe he had good intentions, but how did you live in the same house with somebody in a working relationship after you've had sex with them?

Knowing I needed my job was *almost* enough to make me back away from him. But I couldn't. Being close to Dane, being held by him, was so damn intoxicating that I couldn't give the opportunity up.

His hand ran up and down my spine in a comforting, possessive motion that made me feel like I'd found peace exactly where I was at the moment.

I lay my head against his shoulder, feeling defeated. "You might not be planning on it, but if we have sex, it will end up awkward."

"I'm pretty sure that at some point, you'll end up in my bed, Kenzie," he grunted.

"I...can't," I said in a breathless voice, knowing that his prediction was probably true.

How long would I be able to deny how much I wanted him?

"I think you *can*. Honestly, I don't think either one of us can resist the temptation anymore," he contradicted, not giving me time to reply before he lowered his head and kissed me.

His intent was clear, and I shuddered as I finally felt his mouth fuse to mine. My blood turned white-hot as Dane demanded that I surrender to him, and I gave way without much thought.

I couldn't think.

I couldn't reason.

All I could do was feel what he was doing to me, and I responded with a moan that was stifled by his mouth.

I can't do this. I can't.

Somewhere inside of me, my brain was screeching to be heard, but the warning voice was so quiet compared to the roar of need silencing it that I paid no attention.

All that mattered was Dane, and the fact that I craved the feel of him.

I let out some kind of feral sound as he broke off the kiss to trail his sensual lips over the sensitive skin of my neck. My short nails dug into the nape of his neck, then started clawing at his T-shirt clad back.

I needed something more, anything substantial that would put me out of my smoldering damn misery.

"Dane. God, I need you." The words slipped out of my mouth before I could censor them.

"I'm here. I'll give you whatever you want," he growled. "Just don't tell me to stop."

His hands stroked down my back and landed on my jean-clad butt.

Dane's warm breath wafted over my neck, and then to my earlobes.

I tried to push my body harder against him. I wanted to feel that rock-hard body as close as he could get.

"You're the most beautiful woman I've ever seen," he said huskily. "Leaving you alone is impossible. I can't be in the same room with you without wanting this."

"Me, either," I confessed, my breath coming hard and fast from my lips.

When he lifted my T-shirt and started to pull it over my head, I didn't protest. In fact, I held up my arms so he could discard the item. My bra came off immediately after, and I almost purred when we met skin-to-skin from the waist up.

Dane was shirtless, which was his habit when he was working in his studio. It was torment to see his chiseled, smooth chest and abdomen, and not want to touch him.

He was right. I was going to fail no matter how much I knew I needed to protest. I was beyond protecting myself, which had never happened to me before. Right now, I wanted Dane more than I wanted to survive. Either that or I trusted him enough to know he'd never hurt me.

I wanted to whimper in protest as Dane moved away from me, but his focus was on something else.

"Step out," he commanded gruffly as he lowered my jeans and panties down my legs.

I lifted my feet one at a time until he'd discarded my pants, and I stood before him naked.

I felt so exposed that I faltered for a moment, but my hesitation didn't last long.

I looked down at him with hungry eyes, shuddering when I saw the heat in his gaze.

"I've dreamed about this," he rasped as he rose, his hands skimming over my body reverently as he straightened. "But seeing you like this is so much better than my imagination."

"I ache," I said in a tormented voice that cracked as his fingers toyed with my throbbing nipples.

"I'll make it better," he promised.

"I'm nervous," I confessed. "I've only had sex with one guy, and that was back in high school."

"Forget about him," he said in a muffled voice as he nipped at the sensitive skin on my neck. "I've already forgotten about any other woman except you."

Somehow, it didn't matter if Dane saw my imperfect body. I knew he still wanted me, scars and all.

He moved back and traced the white line of the mark on my chest, a knife wound that had barely missed my heart.

"I hate this," he mentioned angrily. "I hate that those motherfuckers ever laid a hand on you...period."

"It's over," I moaned as I reached for the zipper of his jeans, frenzied to get him as naked as I was right now.

"Don't," he warned in a low and guttural tone. "My patience is already gone."

"I don't need patience," I protested. "I just want you."

I didn't recognize the needy woman who was fervently groping for Dane's cock. I wanted to feel him. I wanted to know that
he was just as desperate as I was.

His body tensed as I finally found what I wanted. A feeling
of power coursed through my entire body as I recognized how
violently Dane reacted to my touch.

In full makeup, with my scars hidden, men had come on to
me occasionally, but nobody had ever understood me or accepted
that I was flawed.

None of them had known me at all.

Dane really did *see me*.

But he still wanted me—regardless of the marks on my body.

And the sensation was intoxicating.

"I want to touch you," I whimpered, frustrated with any kind
of material that separated us.

"Goddammit, Kenzie. I want to take this slow. I can't do that
when you're touching me."

And I wanted it wild and passionate. With Dane, there was
no other way.

I let out a short squeal as he picked me up and carried me
to a couch in a small sitting area in the corner of the room. He
stopped at the door on the way, and flipped the lock, preserving
our privacy.

A small portion of my brain was trying to make sense out of
what was happening, but it was drowned out by the carnal desire
that was causing my body to pulsate in anticipation.

He lowered me onto the couch, and then quickly stepped
out of his jeans and boxer briefs, tossing them to the side as he
crouched next to me. "I want more," he said darkly. "I need you
to forget anything but me."

Like I *could* think about anything else when he was touching
me? That would never be an issue.

I was already primed and ready, but the moment Dane trailed his hands over my body, and then lowered his head to suck on a diamond-hard, ultra-sensitive nipple, I was completely lost.

I *did* forget everything else but the feel of his hot mouth on my breasts, and his hand delving between my thighs.

"Touch me," I pleaded, letting my legs part to let him in.

"I'm taking my time, baby," he said, his teeth clenched from holding back. "I'm not rushing this."

I released a short moan, knowing I wasn't going to get the instant gratification I craved.

My head fell back against the pillow, and my back arched as Dane swooped down to catch my other breast, the intensity of his grip on my nipple nearly unbearable. The sting of his insistent nips landing right between my quivering thighs.

It was hard to miss the sharp intake of his breath as his fingers brushed against my pussy, and then found entrance only to be greeted by the wet heat that was waiting for him.

"Christ! You're so fucking wet, Kenzie," he said in a harsh tone.

"I can't help it," I said, barely recognizing my desperate cry.

"I don't *want* you to help it. I want you just like this."

I wasn't even going to pretend to know exactly *what* he wanted. Dane was overwhelming every one of my senses, and I couldn't really put two thoughts together.

I knew I was completely gone when he stroked a finger through my drenched folds, and it glided over my clit.

I was lost, and I wasn't sure whether I'd ever find myself again.

At that moment, I didn't even care.

All I wanted was him, and to hell with the consequences.

CHAPTER 19

Dane

"Do you really think anybody would want you?" Britney said with an evil laugh. "You're scarred. You dress like some kind of transient. You're pathetic next to your brother, Trace."

I'd known, even while I was in Denver, that Britney was going to eventually arrive on the island to pick up her clothes. We'd parted in Denver, but there was no way she was going to give up her expensive wardrobe I'd funded, or the other things I'd given her. I'd just hoped that it would take a while for her to perform that particular errand.

But it hadn't.

She'd arrived in the Cay the same day that I'd gotten back from the holidays in Colorado.

Now that her things were packed up and ready to go, I knew I wasn't going to be able to avoid her. If I tried, she'd find me.

"It's over, Britney. Just go."

Unfortunately, she'd already hunted me down until she discovered me in my studio. I had no idea why she needed to tear me down just because I wasn't Trace.

Hell, I'd known that she never really wanted *me*. I'd just paid for the privilege of using her body, and the price had been pretty damn high. But I'd craved human contact. I'd been perfectly aware that she'd been using me for my money. I just hadn't quite comprehended that she was using me to get back at my brother, Trace, for dumping her.

Had she really thought that my brother would take her back? Britney was a viper, and I was glad Trace had Eva now. What I'd never really understood was why my sibling had been taken in by Britney's false charm in the first place.

"Oh, I'm *leaving*," she said vehemently. "I just wanted you to know how much I hated every fuck with you."

"Why?" I asked nonchalantly. Not that I really cared, but it seemed like the obvious thing to ask.

She elaborated. "I suffered through it every single time. Your scars made my skin crawl. It isn't even worth it. The money you gave me was pretty sad."

I'd shelled out tens of thousands of dollars on her for the short time she'd been on the Cay. Whatever I gave her, it was never enough. I was kind of doubting any man would *ever* have enough money to satisfy Britney, and I felt sorry for the next poor bastard she decided to drain.

"Go, Britney. I'm trying to work."

Honestly, I was just glad she was leaving my island, and that she would never get my brother's attention again.

She'd threatened Trace.

She'd tried to break up his relationship with Eva.

And she'd thoroughly used me to get the money she coveted.

Not that I hadn't known that.

I'd just been desperate enough to let her hang around.

Now, I preferred to be alone. I knew just how empty it felt to be fucking a woman who hated looking at me.

"Work!" she screamed in a shrill voice. "That's all you ever care about."

"Did you want me to care about you?" I questioned, knowing the answer to my question before I even asked.

"No! This whole experience was bad enough. I hated being forced to sleep with you."

I shrugged. "You could have left at any time. You definitely weren't unwilling."

"You know I need money. Trace left me high and dry."

"So our money was interchangeable?" I asked.

I could practically see the steam coming out of her ears as she retorted, "You'll never be Trace."

Nope. I'd never be my older brother, but she should have known that from day one. I wasn't as polished or as educated as my older brother, and I sure as hell didn't look like him. I was scarred. Trace was not.

"I'll send you a check," I said flatly, wanting nothing more than to see the back of Britney. Maybe there had never been any emotions between us, but her insults were starting to jab at my insecurity.

She pointed her nose in the air. "Good. It won't make the sacrifice I made less difficult, but the money will help."

I watched as she whirled around and left the studio.

Christ! I was glad she was gone. What had I been thinking when I'd decided to let her hang around?

Had I been hoping she'd change?

Maybe I'd just wished she'd be tolerable for a while. I'd wanted some kind of distraction, some sort of companionship. And yeah, maybe I *had* wanted to get laid, but the price to my sanity had been way too high.

I'll be fine alone. I'll get used to it.

This time I knew those words were completely true. Getting off hadn't been worth the emotional price I'd had to pay in the form of Britney's constant complaining and criticism.

Her words had touched a nerve, even though I didn't want to admit it.

Screw getting laid. I could get myself off with a lot less hassle. I'd never be with another woman again unless I really wanted her and she felt the same way.

I was pretty sure that was *never* going to happen.

CHAPTER 20

Kenzie

THE PRESENT...

*H*is heated mouth on my pussy was like a thousand tiny shocks inundating my body all at once.

It was powerful.

It was overwhelming.

And I was consumed by a desire so strong that it was actually as terrifying as it was pleasurable.

"Dane!" I screamed, still stunned by the fact that he was devouring me like a starving man.

Pleasure shot through my body, and I was consumed by Dane and what he was doing to make me experience a primal desire that I'd never experienced before.

"Please," I begged helplessly, my entire being focused on my need to hit a pinnacle and find my release.

At the moment, nothing else existed except Dane and his wicked tongue.

My back arched from sensation overload, a feeling of euphoria that I couldn't contain.

My orgasm hit me in pounding waves that I couldn't stop if I wanted to.

I spiraled back down slowly, my breath coming hard and fast as I finally relaxed on the couch, completely spent.

"Oh, my God," I rasped as I pushed my hair back from my face. "What just happened?"

Dane finally lifted his head and turned toward my face. "You came?" he suggested with humor in his tone.

"That's never happened to me before," I explained in a breathless voice.

My high school experience had been brief and unremarkable. Mostly, it had assured me that I wasn't missing much by staying away from sex. My partner had been inexperienced, and it had been a rather painful encounter.

Dane scooted until he was next to me and kissed me, and I wrapped my arms around his neck and clung to him as I tasted myself on his lips.

I felt shaken and vulnerable now that my conscious mind was re-entering my body.

What in the hell had I just done?

My body craved more with Dane, but I was starting to realize just how dangerous that desire could be.

As Dane raised his head, I mumbled, "This shouldn't have happened."

He frowned at me. "Why?"

I sat up, my emotions raw as my racing thoughts told me just how perilous my situation was at the moment. I was in danger of losing my heart to a man who generally preferred to be alone.

"You're my boss," I explained shakily, using our work relationship to justify my emotions, even though I knew there was far more to my fear than just employment.

He touched me in a way that left me completely exposed, and I wasn't used it.

I couldn't tell Dane how I felt, how really afraid I was of falling in love with him.

Just like him, I was accustomed to being alone, fighting all my battles on my own. Trusting someone and letting myself begin to rely on him could be disastrous.

"Be with me, Kenzie," he demanded in a low, guttural tone. "Sleep with me every night. Let me show you just how good it can be to have a man who fucking worships your body."

My body? What about the rest of me?

I swung my feet to the floor, forcing Dane to move back.

It was scary just how much I wanted to give in and follow down the path we'd just barely started.

I craved him so badly that my body was trembling from withdrawal once he'd backed off.

"I can't," I finally responded, my lips barely able to form the words.

Maybe I'd get instant gratification if I did what he wanted, but in the long run, I'd end up devastated. I knew Dane had the power to destroy me as well as give me pleasure.

"I'll raise your salary accordingly," he suggested.

My heart clenched as I got to my feet. His words had just ripped my heart from my chest. He wanted me, but obviously as another business arrangement. "I don't sell my body," I answered tersely as I gathered up my clothes.

"I know that," he answered. "I shouldn't have even suggested it."

Problem was, he *had* wanted a business transaction, and it hurt worse than I ever could have imagined.

Dane Walker was the kind of guy who could buy almost anything he wanted, so naturally, he'd assumed a poor woman like me would jump at the chance to get more money.

"I made a mistake," I told him as I held my clothing in my arms in front of me like a shield.

"Kenzie, I didn't mean—"

"I think you meant it," I told him. "But I can't accept. That's not what I want."

"What do you want?" he questioned in a graveled voice.

I wanted more than he'd be able to give me.

Tears threatened to pour down my cheeks and I turned away. I sprinted to the door and flipped the lock open, trying to salvage my dignity.

"Don't go!" he said sternly.

"I'll see you for work in the morning," I said flatly.

I didn't wait another moment. I flung open the door and raced out of the room. Theo was on the other side of the island, and I wanted to get upstairs in case he came back to the house.

I took the stairs quickly, determined to get to the privacy of my suite before I cried.

"What in the hell was I doing?" I panted as I closed the door to my bedroom and leaned against it. "Dane is my boss, and having sex with him will never be enough."

I moved to the couch and sat down, my legs quivering with fear.

How had I lost complete control? Had it been the fact that he'd been so thoughtful about the pottery room?

If I was truthful, my emotions had been all over the place since the moment I'd arrived here. Dane had always been a threat to my heart. Day after day, I'd become fonder of him until it had blossomed into something else entirely. It had occurred so quickly; I'd never been able to recognize exactly what was happening.

Now, I was screwed. I'd given in to desire, which was something far different for me than it was to him.

He wanted sex.

I wanted something more.

"It's dangerous to want more than a person can give," I whispered to myself.

Dane had made a life for himself here on his island. Maybe he was hiding, but he seemed to prefer it that way.

Somehow, I *had* to put him back where he belonged—as my boss. Otherwise, I knew I'd suffer nothing but heartache.

No matter how many walls I'd put up, Dane was able to make them crumble.

I took a deep breath as I stood up, determined to shower and try to get myself together again.

In order to survive, I *had* to stop looking at him in any other way except as my superior, the person I answered to for *work only*. It was the only way I had of protecting myself and my now fragile emotions.

I'd learned a very long time ago that the only person I could ultimately trust was myself. Nobody wanted me to survive more than I did.

I startled as I walked around the corner toward the shower. I set my clothing on the vanity, my eyes drawn to what was in front of me.

Mirrors. I suddenly had a reflection of myself right in front of me.

Someone, almost certainly Theo, had mounted two circular mirrors over the sinks of the double vanity earlier in the day.

I studied my face in the reflective glass.

I looked like shit.

My hair was tangled and wild, and my eyes were puffy and terrified.

"Get it together, Kenzie," I encouraged myself.

Despite his scars, Dane Walker could have almost any woman he wanted. He was still hot, and he was a member of one of the richest families on the planet.

I looked away from my image, not wanting to see the longing that was still present in my eyes.

Yeah, maybe Paige had captured the Walker of her dreams, but my friend was beautiful, and she had a Harvard education.

I'd barely graduated from high school, and I'd taken some art classes for fun. I was damaged from my past, both physically and mentally, and I was pretty certain those wounds would never heal.

I turned on the water and stepped into the shower before I finally let my emotions out in the form of monstrous sobs of mourning for a love that could never actually exist.

CHAPTER 21

Dane

*I*t had taken everything I had not to tear off after Kenzie. But I gritted my teeth and put my jeans back on, and then plopped down on the couch.

What in the hell had I been thinking when I'd offered her money to sleep with me? Jesus! Maybe a money arrangement was the only thing I'd ever known for adult intimacy. But Britney had been about getting my rocks off.

Kenzie was different, and it screwed with my head that I'd hurt her.

I hadn't done it on purpose. The offer had been made out of desperation. Now that I'd touched her, had the privilege of watching her come, I was addicted.

Dumbass! I knew Kenzie was nothing like anybody I've ever known.

I'd just blown any chance I'd had to gain her trust. She didn't have to tell me that I had. I could see the disappointment and betrayal in her beautiful eyes.

"It's going to fucking haunt me," I said in a loud and disgusted voice.

Kenzie reminded me of a wounded animal, and I hadn't healed her. I'd acted like a wolf who was just waiting to prey on a vulnerable creature.

I put my head in my hands, feeling defeated.

There was no way I could set back time and take the offer back. I was stuck with my fuck-up.

Problem is, I didn't really want her for money at all. I'd made a promise to myself that I'd never do that again, but I'd forgotten all about how it felt to have a woman let me use her body for money.

It sucked.

But in a moment of desperation, I'd caved and resorted to the only way I knew to have a female in my bed: I'd offered her money.

Kenzie isn't just another female.

Hell, I'd known that since the moment I'd set eyes on her. I wasn't going to deny that I wanted her, but it wasn't just sexual.

I ran a frustrated hand through my hair and then rested my head against the back of the couch, staring at the ceiling, wondering how I was going to get Kenzie to forget all about my stupidity.

I hurt her. I'd seen the naked, vulnerable, wounded look on her face, and it made my damn chest ache with remorse.

Pretty much everybody except Paige had disappointed Kenzie, and the last thing I wanted to be was just another person who she thought only wanted her for one thing. Truth was, I wanted her for almost everything.

I wanted to have breakfast and coffee with her every morning.

I wanted to be in the same room as she was just because it made me happy.

I wanted to be the one she came to whenever she needed to talk or just to have somebody who cared about her close to her.

I wanted to be everything for her.

But I'd turned into the one that she had to run away from because I offered her money for sex.

"I didn't mean it. That's not what I want," I said, so pissed off that I hated myself.

I don't sell my body.

Her words had been like a slap alongside my head. I'd treated the woman who meant so much to me like a common prostitute. And I detested myself for doing it.

Kenzie had jerked me out of my solitude in a good way.

And I'd repaid her with one of the biggest insults a person could ever get.

I can go to her. I can apologize. Tell her I didn't mean it.

However, I'd held back for a reason. Words meant nothing to Kenzie. She'd been hurt too many times to believe whatever came out of a person's mouth. Actions spoke louder than words, and I was going to have to prove to her that I could keep my hands to myself. I needed her to know she had more value than just her body.

It was clear that she wanted to be alone. Not that I could blame her.

I'll leave her alone, but it won't be easy.

My best option was to try to be a friend before I became her lover. Really, I wanted her trust more than I wanted to fuck her. Okay, maybe it didn't *seem* like her trust was a priority because my balls were blue, but I wanted all of Kenzie, and most of all, I needed her to know that I was her safe haven, the guy who would never hurt her.

I wanted to call Trace and ask him what he would do if he was in my position, but I stifled the urge. It wasn't like there was a gaggle of women on the island. He'd make one conclusion, even if I asked it hypothetically, and he'd be correct since Kenzie was the only female on the island. Besides, Trace would never blow it like I had.

As I thought about the wild-eyed look of panic and pain I'd seen on Kenzie's face, I knew I was going to have to play it cool.

Much as I wanted to go see if she was okay, I *had* to back off and give her time and space.

"I'm sorry," I said to the ceiling since there was nobody around to listen to me. Kenzie had given me her trust, and when she panicked, I wasn't there to calm her fears. Instead, I'd acted like a spoiled rich bastard who could buy what I wanted.

There were things she wasn't telling me, but I'd let her decide when and what she wanted to reveal.

I stood, knowing I was going to have to make sure she was okay. I wouldn't back her in a corner; I just had to know that she was all right.

I left the pottery room I'd set up for her, cursing myself again for being a prick as I sprinted up the stairs, stopping in front of Kenzie's door on the way to my room.

The only thing I could hear was the hum of the shower, and the faint, muffled noise of running water.

She's okay. She's in the shower.

My heart was pounding in my ears, and I had to fight back the compulsion to talk to her.

It was Kenzie's move. I'd given up the right to insist on any-thing when I'd said something incredibly stupid.

Move on. Give her space.

I was never really sure how I'd found the strength to turn away from her door and walk down the hall to my own bedroom.

My gut ached like I'd taken a sucker punch as I entered my suite.

I dropped my clothes as I made my way to the shower, stunned as I turned the corner and saw my own reflection.

The first thing I saw was my scars.

Moving closer, I examined the markings. Yeah, they'd defi-nitely faded, but they were still on full display. I could see every one of them since I was buck naked.

Were they as bad as they used to be? No

Could I still see them? Oh, hell, yeah.

I touched the scar on my abdomen where they'd done surgery on my internal organs to stop the bleeding. I touched a few more surgical scars before I moved to my face.

It was possible that no children would run away in fear, but the markings and burns that had occurred were glaringly obvious to me.

"I had a woman who didn't care if I was scarred, and I screwed things up," I rasped, still angry with myself.

I turned away from my reflection, pissed off that I'd even stopped to look at it in the first place.

My imperfections were never going to go away.

My scars would never disappear.

I went to take a shower, hoping that getting myself off would relieve some of my tension and erase the memory of Kenzie's reaction to my offer to make her nothing more than a glorified prostitute.

It didn't work.

Her hurt expression haunted me.

In my mind, I probably deserved it.

CHAPTER 22

Kenzie

*I*t took me a few weeks to finally get my emotions completely contained.

Dane was suitably distant, a fact that had both crushed me and made me grateful at the same time.

I was grateful because the more I was able to get my emotions in check, the easier it was to deal with him on a work basis.

However, I couldn't stop wanting him, so I was crushed when he had turned cooler and broodier.

We had a working relationship, and I never stepped over that line again.

I was the perfect personal assistant.

I didn't put my nose into his business unless it directly affected his art.

After work, I usually didn't stick around the house. I explored the island, sometimes wandering farther down the coast to find a nice spot to work on drawings of whatever caught my attention.

Very seldom could I be in the pottery room Dane had set up for me. I'd tried, but every time I entered that space, I thought about what had happened between me and Dane.

I couldn't think about *that* without giving in to a depression I didn't want to experience. I'd completely lost my head that day, something that just didn't happen to me. I always had to be on high alert, and I didn't *ever* completely give myself over to anybody. It was a mistake I couldn't afford to make.

Since I didn't really want to spend time in his studio, either, I'd spent the majority of my time sketching images of things I'd like to paint.

Until today.

I was going to be forced into his company for days, whether I liked it or not, since we'd already landed in Maui for Paige and Sebastian's wedding.

It had been a long flight, and I was exhausted by the time we finally checked into our rooms. I wasn't sure if it was emotional or physical, but just being near Dane was...difficult.

"Maybe I could get a room of my own," I told him in my professional voice that I'd been using for the last few weeks.

Granted, we were in a *suite* at the resort, the same hotel where Paige and Sebastian were holding the ceremony. But it just felt awkward to be stuck in the same space as Dane.

"I booked the suite intentionally," he countered. "It's easier to have us here together. It's not like I'm asking you to hop into my damn bed. You have your own bedroom."

I *did* have my own sleeping area, and the last thing I wanted was to sound ungrateful. There was no way I could have afforded accommodations like this grand suite. I would have found the nearest cheap hotel, and those didn't exactly look common in Maui. "I'm sorry," I told him in a clipped voice, a tone certain to push Dane away. "It's a beautiful room. I just don't want to intrude on your privacy."

Actually, I didn't want to be near him because I was afraid I'd lose my professional cool and beg him to fuck me, but I wasn't about to tell him that.

"You aren't intruding," he rumbled as he flopped on the couch with a drink he'd made for himself from the bar. "I want you to be here."

I didn't know what to say to that comment, so I left it alone. It had been a while since Dane had mentioned anything personal. Of course, it could be that he wanted me nearby to do things for him. Maybe it wasn't meant as a personal comment. I was, after all, his personal assistant. "I can't wait to see Paige," I said, changing the subject.

There was plenty of square footage in the suite. I just had a hard time being so damn close to him *all the time*. It was my hang-up, not his. And I *did* want to be in the resort for convenience. We had a few days of preliminary activities before the actual ceremony.

"Sebastian texted. They'll be back shortly. He took Paige out to pick up some things she needs."

"Do you want me to unpack your stuff?" I asked like a good personal assistant.

"Hell, no. We aren't here for that long. And I'm perfectly capable of putting away my own damn underwear."

"Are we joining Sebastian and Trace for dinner tonight?" Paige was having a quiet dinner with just her parents and family.

He was silent for a moment before he spoke. "Yeah. I guess."

I knew he didn't want to go out, but he was participating for his brothers' sakes. He hadn't seen them in over a year.

"They'll be happy to see you," I answered as I went over to the bar for something to drink.

We'd had a long flight, and I was pretty sure that Dane was as tired as I was, but he wasn't going to ditch his family.

"It's a small affair," I mentioned, taking a seat beside the couch after getting myself a drink of water.

I was hoping to make him feel comfortable. It was obvious to me that he was feeling like a duck out of water. Maybe I recognized it in him because I was feeling that way myself. I hadn't gotten personal since that day in the pottery room, but it was almost impossible for me to ignore his fear of being out in public.

"It's in a restaurant. Too many people around."

"Dane, your scars don't matter. They're not even very noticeable." I wondered if he'd ever bothered to look in the mirrors he'd finally installed in his home. Theo had told me that he'd put mirrors up in all the bathrooms, so I presumed that included Dane's bathroom too.

"Bullshit! I see them perfectly from my bathroom mirror."

Okay, so he'd looked.

He continued, "And they aren't something I can cover up."

"Like I do?" I questioned in a hushed voice.

"I'm not judging you," he answered brusquely.

"I'll leave my cover-up behind if you try not to think about your scars," I offered. I hadn't tried very hard to hide the blemishes on my face. Dane accepted them, and so did Theo and Emilee. I did a light, natural makeup most days, but not the pile of makeup that I used to use to hide.

"It doesn't matter what you do. You're fucking beautiful."

I sighed. Even though Dane kept his distance, he didn't hold back on the compliments. "And you're handsome," I informed him. "Your scars won't make a damn bit of difference to most people."

"I'll try," he grunted. "But no promises if I start to scare little kids."

He'd shared his experience about the little girl he'd run into years ago while he was Christmas shopping. He'd mentioned it briefly a few days ago when we were getting ready to leave. It had made it difficult for me to keep my distance, and I hadn't known what to say. I'd nearly lost my appearance of being *just* his assistant when he'd shared how he'd felt years ago. "You were wearing a ton of bandages," I reminded him. "It wasn't your scars. It was the mass of gauze that made you look like a scary monster to her."

He shrugged. "Whatever."

The easiest way to show Dane that he wasn't going to draw attention, other than women who would probably be eyeing him as a prospective lover, was to keep taking him out.

I was hoping that once he was desensitized, he'd lose his desire to stay holed up on his island all the time.

Luckily, Paige had plenty of things planned.

I swallowed the last of my water and stood. "I have to press my dress for dinner tonight. I wish I had something a little dressier. Maybe I should have gone with Theo to Nassau."

Thanks to Dane, I had money. I'd spent very little on the island, so the majority of his generous advance check was still in my bank.

"Do you want to go find something? I could probably use something a little nicer myself. I have my tux for the wedding, but I didn't bring anything that's appropriate for all the things that Paige has planned."

Even though I'd informed him that there would be preliminaries, I don't think he'd been ready for the amount of time we were going to spend out of our rooms.

My heart skipped a beat. I couldn't believe that Dane was actually offering to take me out in public. He didn't have to. He was volunteering. Considering how much he hated being in public, I couldn't ignore his invitation. "I'd like to," I admitted.

"Then we'll go," he answered, the muscle ticking in his jaw from tension. "We can kill the time before dinner."

Before he could change his mind, I gathered up my purse and sunglasses. "I'm ready."

He rose from his seat, and then picked up his own dark sunglasses and slid them onto his face.

I began to walk toward the door, only to have Dane grasp my upper arm. "I never meant to hurt you, Kenzie. I swear."

His simple touch made my heart dance. I wanted to give up the fight of being nothing more than an assistant, but my logical brain curtailed that train of thought.

I knew he had never meant to injure me. He wasn't that type of guy. But that didn't mean we weren't worlds apart.

Yes, it had hurt when he'd treated me like nothing more than a prostitute but that pain wasn't what had kept me away from him.

Dane was dangerous to me, and I was used to protecting and saving myself.

"I know you didn't," I said, my voice little more than a whisper.

"I hate this relationship," he rasped as his hand tightened around my upper arm. "I hate the fact that I can't just talk to you about anything that comes to mind. I miss what we had before I completely blew it."

"Being friends?" I questioned.

"You being yourself," he corrected.

"I was stupid," I revealed. "I should have never let anything more happen between us. We come from very different lives."

"Yet, we're very much the same," he grumbled.

He was right. Dane and I had faced different but similar struggles. If nothing else, I *did* want to be his friend. But how could I manage it without crossing the line? I had no willpower when it came to him. "We understand each other," I admitted.

"Then can we stop this shit and feel free to talk about anything we want?"

Could we? I honestly wasn't sure. But maybe if we got close as friends, I could shake off the torment that was threatening to drive me insane.

"I'll try," I agreed reluctantly. We both needed companionship, and our relationship had been so much more pleasant in the beginning when we were less guarded.

I can protect myself and mange to be friendly.

At least, I wanted to think I could.

"That's all I ask for right now," he said in a relieved tone.

"It's all I can give."

Dane let go of my arm and headed toward the door as he said, "Then I guess I'll have to be satisfied with that for now."

I let out a relieved breath. "Let's go find something nice at the stores," I said, trying to sound upbeat.

I was excited to be in Hawaii for the first time, and I wanted to see everything.

As we stepped out the door, I could only hope that I hadn't made a very big mistake.

CHAPTER 23

Kenzie

Even though Dane had given me a very generous advance, and I had money in my bank account, I cringed at the prices in the shops at the resort.

I'd rarely bought new clothes. Most of them came from a thrift store, and I got creative with those items. So not only was I buying something new, but I was looking at spending a small fortune for a dress I might never wear again.

The thrifty woman in me shuddered as I looked at the prices on the dresses in the designer stores.

I didn't do dressy restaurants or parties, so I hardly knew the etiquette on what to wear.

Dane had followed behind me through several shops, waiting patiently as I covetously eyed the beautiful clothing.

"Are you going to buy some stuff, or are we just looking?" he said, his tone a mix of irritation and humor.

"I'm looking," I said defensively.

What was I hoping to find? Maybe something on clearance, or at least on sale. I hadn't seen a discount price anywhere.

Everything was full retail, and more than I'd previously spent on rent for a good six months.

"You haven't seen a single dress that you like?"

"I've seen some," I said evasively.

I was doubtful that he even had to look at prices, and didn't have a clue how much a dress cost.

"Then buy them and let's get the hell out of here," he replied.

Dane had been tense, but he'd been so good about letting me look from store to store.

"I think I'm good," I said in a falsely cheerful tone. "I think I have enough stuff. I can just wear something I brought with me."

I really *had* wanted a few nice things, but I just wasn't willing to spend *this* crazily. My frugal instincts were too strong to piss my money away on something frivolous. I was too sensible to throw caution to the wind.

Dane frowned at me. "Then why are we here?"

"I think we should go look at the men's shops for you." I reluctantly let go of the garment I was fingering.

"Not until *you* pick something."

Unfortunately, he had that stubborn look that told me he wasn't going to accept my excuses, so I told him the truth. "I can't spend this much on one dress."

"You won't. I told you I'd pick up your clothes."

"Not happening," I told him. "I'm not letting my boss absorb the cost for my personal clothing. You already let me tag along with you so that I didn't have to pay airfare, and I'm staying with you in your suite."

He shrugged. "I want you to have something nice. I want to buy stuff for you."

His voice was so sincere that I wanted to cry. Dane did things just to make people happy, and his offer touched me. "I appreciate it. I really do. But I can't do it. Besides, I'd be terrified to wear anything that was this expensive. I'm more comfortable in my old stuff. Let's go check the men's store."

I led the way, and Dane had no choice but to follow me.

He caught up with me as soon as I left the store. "Wait, Kenzie. I don't want to leave here without getting you something you wanted."

I stopped abruptly as his strong hand curled around my upper arm.

"I'm sorry," I said remorsefully. "I had no idea that all the clothes would be so pricey here. I guess I should have known since this is an expensive resort."

He swung me around gently so we were face-to-face as he replied, "Look, I don't know how it feels to be poor, but you don't have to sacrifice anything to let me buy for you."

"It feels humiliating," I answered honestly. "I can't remember getting a new clothing item in my entire life. I got really good at revamping old thrift store clothes. Paying my rent and eating were more important than new apparel."

"Then why don't you let me buy them?" he asked, obviously perplexed.

I took a deep breath and let it out. "I may be poor, but I still have my pride, Dane. I've always taken care of myself."

He released my arm, but he didn't move away. "Yeah. And what I'm saying is that you don't *have* to completely take care of yourself now. I can help. I *want* to help."

I shook my head as I turned and headed back to where I'd seen the men's stores, Dane walking beside me since there was more room.

"I'm fine," I assured him. "I can put something together from what I brought. It's not like it was that important. Paige knows I don't have money to buy the fancy stuff."

"Stubborn female," he grumbled.

"Stubborn *male*," I retorted, my heart still swelled by Dane's offer.

I knew there were no strings attached to his offer, but I still couldn't accept. But it was so damn sweet that he just put himself out there that way, never expecting a damn thing in return for his generosity.

We entered the men's store, and he counted heavily on my advice. I gave my opinions willingly, thrilled when he picked out everything I liked. I might have no idea what was trending in men's fashion, but I knew what made him look even hotter than he already was.

He met with a personal shopper to get some of the accessories he needed, and asked for the merchandise to be delivered to his room. I waited outside so I could absorb the beautiful weather.

It seemed like he'd been gone for hours when he finally arrived back to the bench I'd been occupying.

"We're all set. Let's head back to the suite," he said, sounding relieved that this outing was over.

I fell into step beside him on our short walk back to the beachfront room.

"Not one person even looked at you funny," I observed. "Are you convinced that your scars are no big deal?"

"Nope," he contradicted. "I just got lucky that nobody looked all that close."

I released an exasperated breath. "The reason nobody cares is because they aren't that visible anymore." I hesitated before I asked, "Why did you put mirrors up in your house?"

"Because I wanted to see myself," he said vaguely. "And I didn't think it was fair to you not to have them. It's inconvenient."

"I have scars," I reminded him.

"Not like mine."

My scars were very similar to Dane's: old, healed and hardly noticeable. Granted, I'd escaped by covering mine in a pile of makeup for my jobs, but that didn't mean I thought they were completely unsightly. I'd just wanted to survive in a world where beautiful was the best way to look if one wanted unskilled employment. Nobody wanted to see a scarred receptionist.

The difference between me and Dane was the fact that I hadn't been traumatized over my scars when they'd been fresh and more noticeable. He had, and it had ingrained the rejection in his mind. His recovery time had been horrendous and painful, while mine had been shorter and less complicated.

I hadn't lost my only parent in my incident. I'd grown up alone, while Dane felt like he'd been completely abandoned. He'd associated his loss with his scars, and it had done a number on him.

"We don't always see what is," I explained as I kept pace with Dane. "What we see in the mirror is *our* truth, but it isn't what other people think."

"Then I hate my goddamn truth," he grumbled. "It's fucking ugly."

"Only to you," I said. "Do you want to know what I see?"

"Probably not."

I smiled as I looked at his profile. "I see a gorgeous guy who had to survive some horrible emotional and physical trauma at a young age. I see somebody strong, attractive, and worth knowing."

"Your vision is screwed up," he said with a humorless laugh.

"No, it's not," I denied. "You're the one who isn't seeing yourself for who you really are, Dane."

"Then why did you run away from me?" he asked hoarsely.

Is that what he thought? That I'd run away from him because I wasn't attracted? He had to know better. "It had nothing to do with *you*," I said gently. "It was all me."

"I offered you money for sex," he reminded me.

"Yeah, that pretty much sucked. But I knew you well enough to know that you didn't really mean it the way it came out. Or at least I hope you didn't think of me in that way."

"I didn't. I swear. I'm just used to paying for everything I get."

In many ways, his statement was sad. Nobody should have to pay for everything, especially somebody who wanted to be intimate. "I would have never taken your money. I think you know that. But it isn't really the reason I couldn't be with you."

"Then why?" he persisted as we boarded the elevator that would take us up to our suite.

Because my life is a shit-storm. It always had been.

How could I explain to a guy like Dane that most of my existence had been spent running, just trying to stay alive?

When we were alone in the elevator, I answered, "I've always had to do everything alone. I'm not used to being that close to another person, and I don't know how to believe in anyone. It's not that you're not trustworthy. I just don't...trust. My life depends on me taking care of myself, and not putting myself in a bad situation. I can't afford to make a mistake."

"And you see me as a mistake?"

Frustrated, I told him, "I'm not sure you can understand. I've never caught a break, Dane. Survival was just damn hard work almost every minute of my day. I didn't have time to sketch or go for a walk on the beach. I had no time for my art. I can't even swim. I never needed to, even though I lived close to the coast."

Yeah, I'd told him I didn't swim well, but the truth was, I really couldn't swim at all.

He sent me a puzzled stare. "You never had *anything* good in your life?"

"Nothing," I answered emphatically. "Not until I came to work for you."

My life had changed since I'd come to the Bahamas. I had time off. I had a nice place to stay. I ate regular meals. I had a somewhat normal life.

And Jesus, Dane had no idea how amazing that was for me.

"You have no family?" he queried as he motioned for me to exit the elevator.

"None worth talking about. Most of them are in jail or dead. I told you that my father and mother were junkies and career criminals."

He unlocked the door of the suite before he said, "How in the hell did you even survive?"

"Because I thought I had a way out. I thought I was going to make decent pay as a model. I didn't want to be like them." My eyes spontaneously manifested tears, and I had to swallow the lump in my throat.

I wanted to go to my room, but Dane stopped me with a halting hand on my arm. "Don't run away, Kenzie," he requested in a low, growly voice. "You should be proud that you survived. You should hold your head up because you wanted to make something out of your life instead of pissing it away with drugs and crime."

"I don't know where I belong," I confessed with a sob.

"You belong with me," he answered. "You just don't understand that yet."

I swung around and faced him. "Why would you ever want somebody like me?"

"Because I see in you everything that you see in me," he explained. "Hell, do you think I see what *you* do when you look in the mirror? I don't. I see a woman so damn strong that she managed to beat back the odds of becoming just like the rest of her family. You didn't take the easy way out."

I hadn't. I knew that. But I'd also wanted to experience what it was like to not be wanted by the police like my parents had been. My motivation had been pretty strong after growing up in the roughest area of Boston.

"I wanted something different for myself, but I found out just how much the world wanted me to stay in my neighborhood. Getting out was nearly impossible without some job training or a profession."

"All you needed was one fucking break," he said, his nostrils flaring in anger.

I shrugged. "I didn't get it. Maybe if I hadn't been attacked when I went to California, my life *would* be different. Maybe I would have made decent money as a model, which would have made college possible for me. But I try not to think about what could have been. I had to deal with reality."

"Reality sucks," he rumbled.

"Sometimes it does," I agreed. "But *you've* given me my break, Dane. Don't you see that? That's why I didn't want to screw things up by trying to have another kind of relationship with you. It could turn out badly."

He was silent as his predatory stare stayed focused on my face. "It has nothing to do with me. You made *yourself* valuable, Kenzie. And not just for your face or your body, although I can't deny I want that, too. You've single-handedly taken over and organized my art business, and my life. I didn't have my shit together when you got here. I just like to think that I did."

"You really think I'm doing a good job?" I asked hesitantly.

"Yeah. I do. I would have fired you if I didn't think so. Hell, I wanted to fire you in the beginning, but you were so damn efficient that I couldn't. You may not have a college education, but you're pretty damn smart and organized."

I smiled at him through the tears that were trickling down my cheeks. "Thanks. That means a lot to me."

"If I'd known that, I would have told you sooner."

"I know it now."

He finally released my arm and freed me. "You have a hell of a lot more value than you think."

I nodded. "So do you."

A knock on the door silenced both of us.

"The clothes," Dane mumbled as he went and opened the door.

I gaped as several guys with moving dollies entered one after another, and Dane directed them into our rooms.

I followed, surprised when half of the packages were delivered to my bedroom.

I was silent as the men left, standing in my room, half afraid to see what Dane had purchased.

And why the stuff had been delivered here.

I approached the bed and lifted the lid on one of the boxes, shocked when I saw several apparel boxes inside.

After pulling them out one by one, I opened the lids.

"Oh, my God," I gasped as I realized that every item had been one I'd loved from the stores.

"Don't say no," Dane said from the doorway.

I turned around, still holding the adorable black cocktail dress I'd found in the last box. "Why? You know I can't accept."

"But you want to," he said. "For fuck's sake, take it."

Yeah, I did covet the items he'd bought. I couldn't deny it. "How did you know what to buy?"

"I noticed a certain look on your face every time you stopped near an item you wanted. You looked like a girl staring at the candy you couldn't afford. I took a saleswoman back to the stores to gather the merchandise with me."

I looked inside the collar to the dress. It was my size. "And how did you know what would fit?"

He shrugged. "I looked after you'd looked for your size in the beginning. Probably before you'd found the price tag."

The black dress was an item I'd really wanted, and I *had* looked for my size. "Dane, this is way too much. It's practically a whole wardrobe."

"It's a couple of dresses and some accessories," he contradicted. "Don't say no. If you want to argue, you *are* my employee. I bought Theo and his family a new car for Christmas. I'm generous with valued employees. And this really isn't much."

Listening to him try to rationalize buying me clothes was kind of amusing. "Theo has worked for you for years."

"Does it really matter, Kenzie?" he asked huskily. "I wanted to do it."

I could see the pleading stare he was sending me, and I wasn't immune to it. As much as I wanted the items, that wasn't what made me decide to swallow my pride. More than anything, I didn't want to hurt Dane by refusing his thoughtfulness. "I don't know how to say thank you for all this," I told him in a shaky voice.

"Then don't," he suggested as he reached into the pocket of his jeans. "And as long as we're at it, I have a birthday present for you. I want to give it to you early."

I took the small box from his hand and opened it. "Oh, my God, Dane," I said, my voice catching as I stared at the most exquisite set of earrings and pendant that I'd ever seen.

He plucked the gorgeous necklace from the box. "It's an aquamarine. It reminds me of the ocean and your eyes. It's our birthstone."

I was pretty sure there were diamonds surrounding the large, drop pendant, but I didn't comment. Knowing Dane, the chain and everything else was white gold. How in the hell was I supposed to react to this? Nobody gave me gifts, and I was pretty overwhelmed. "It's the most beautiful set I've ever seen," I murmured as he put the chain around my neck.

"I know you're thinking about it, but you can't *not* take a birthday gift," he said in a warning voice. "It will look nice with your dresses."

Nice? Seriously? The jewelry was gorgeous. The pendant was large, but not so big that it wasn't classy. The long chain left the stone and the surrounding diamonds nestled right above my breasts. My fingers shook as I took the earrings and put them in at Dane's urging.

As I stood in front of the mirror to look at the results, tears were coursing down my face at such a rapid rate that I was nearly blinded. I blinked them away and stared at the woman in the reflective glass, stunned by the way the earrings and necklace glittered and shined.

"They suit you," Dane said from behind me. "They do match your eyes."

Our gaze met in the mirror, and locked tight. "I left your gift at home," I confessed. "All I got you was a stupid art book."

His eyes grew warm as he said, "I love art books."

I nodded slightly. "I know. I wanted you to have it for your collection."

I'd asked Theo to pick Dane's birthday gift up for me when he was in the capital city, and it was wrapped up and under my bed at Walker's Cay.

"Thank you," he said sincerely. "No one has ever bought a book for my collection except me."

I held the stone of the necklace in my hand as I answered, "It's nothing compared to this."

He shrugged. "It's not a contest, Kenzie. And your gift will mean a lot to me."

"Not as much as this," I argued.

Nobody had ever done anything like this for me.

A sob escaped my lips, but I didn't try to smother it. I started to cry, then turned and threw myself into Dane's arms a blabbering mess.

He held me for an undetermined amount of time, not seeming at all anxious to let me go.

CHAPTER 24

Kenzie

"**S**o how are things really going with Dane?" Paige asked me as we freshened up in front of the mirror in the lavish powder room later in the evening.

Everything about the restaurant we'd gathered in that night reeked of money. Even the bathroom was classy.

I'd missed my best friend so much. I hadn't seen her since I'd left our shared apartment for New York, right before Paige had moved to Denver to work for Walker.

She looked so happy now, something I was grateful to see. She honestly loved Sebastian, and the joy that exploded between the two of them was nearly palpable.

"The job is good," I hedged. "I'm so grateful to you and Sebastian for setting it up."

"How good?" she said as she shot me a quizzical stare in the mirror.

What could I say? I couldn't tell her I was madly in love with her almost-brother-in-law. "Just…good. His island is incredible. You should visit sometime."

"Do you like him?" she asked.

"Very much," I answered honestly. "He's a good man."

"Come on, Kenzie. I see how he looks at you. And you aren't exactly indifferent."

"How?" I asked as I turned my stool around.

Paige swung with me until our backs were to the mirror. "I don't know Dane well, but I can see how much he cares about you. He never even looks at anybody else. His attention is on you." She reached out and gently touched the pendant Dane had given me. "Is this from him? It's beautiful."

I shook my head. "It's not like that, Paige. We're...friends. And the earrings and pendant are a birthday gift. You know my history. Dane and I understand each other."

"You're *not* just friends," she said emphatically. "I'm in love with Dane's brother. I recognize that look on your face."

I sighed. "Okay. Yeah. I like him. He's attractive, and he's unattached. But I'm never going to go there. I like my job too much."

Paige laughed, a booming, amused sound that rung through the tiny room. "Yeah, that's what I thought, too."

"Weren't you afraid?" I asked, knowing Paige had probably risked losing her job if things hadn't worked out with Sebastian. The difference was, Paige had an education. She was a Harvard grad attorney. She wouldn't have lost her livelihood entirely.

"I was. Look, I know how you feel, but I'm worried about you. You have to open up and trust somebody eventually, Kenzie. Sebastian broke me down little by little. He proved to me that he could be someone I trusted. But I think you're even harder to convince."

"I trust you," I shared.

She rolled her eyes. "Yeah. And it took years. You know it did."

Paige was right. It *had* taken me a long time to tell her everything about my past. "It did," I admitted. "But you know how my life has been. It's never included a guy."

"I understand why," she explained. "And I wouldn't want you not to protect yourself. Cynicism was actually good for us back in

Cambridge. It kept us from getting distracted from our goals, and not allow anybody to hurt us. But if you pass up an opportunity with the right guy, it could really hurt."

"I think I might have already done that," I said unhappily.

"Did he make a move on you?"

"Third base, I guess. But we never hit the home run."

"And was it everything you hoped it would be?"

"He's so much more," I confessed. "But it's dangerous to sleep with your boss. You know that."

Paige chuckled. "Don't I know it. I thought the last thing I wanted was to have sex with Sebastian. But sometimes your heart won't listen to your head."

"Things worked out for you, but you were in love."

"Aren't you?" she queried. "Even a little bit."

I should have known that Paige would apply a crow bar to my emotions. "A lot," I answered simply.

"He feels the same way," she said excitedly. "I can see it."

"I let him buy me some clothes," I grumbled.

"And you look fantastic," Paige exclaimed.

My black dress and stiletto heels did look good on me, and it gave me a confidence boost. As Dane had predicted, the jewelry set off the little black dress perfectly. "I refused at first. But Dane is a hard guy to say no to."

Paige frowned. "Why do you want to?"

"You know why. I'm scared, Paige. Nothing has ever really worked out the way I wish it would."

"I know," she said sympathetically. "But that doesn't mean it can't change. Dane isn't really worldly. He's been on that island since he graduated high school. He's never had the chance to become an asshole."

"He's not. He's talented," I defended. "He's smart and he's kind."

"Then you have no reason *not* to trust him," she argued. "The only woman he let into his life crapped all over him. So he has good reason not to trust a female."

"Dane had a girlfriend?" I asked breathlessly.

"I'm not sure you could even call Britney a *girlfriend*. She was more like a leech. All she wanted from Dane was to pay Trace back for dumping her. She found out where Dane was, and she used him to try to get Trace back. I think she wanted his money, too, since she made a career out of sucking guys dry for funds to keep up her expensive lifestyle."

"Did she live with him?" I asked, my heart breaking from the fact that anyone had used Dane.

"For a while," Paige said. "But Trace says that Dane knew she was using him, so he wasn't that attached."

I asked her more questions, and Paige provided answers, telling me the whole story about the Christmas that had ended his relationship with Britney.

"He didn't deserve that," I said in an angry voice. "How could she deliberately use a guy like Dane? Maybe he knew she didn't love him, but that doesn't make it right. Somebody like that isn't good for him. He needs somebody who cares about him. He deserves that and more."

Paige stood up. "I agree. Maybe somebody like...you."

"I'd make him happier than she did," I said confidently. At least I adored him.

"Then do it," she teased.

All joking aside, I *knew* I could make Dane happy. But I didn't know how long it would last. I was just too afraid to try, and then end up failing.

I was silent as I put my lip gloss back in my purse.

"I guess we should get back to the table," I said regretfully.

"Think about what I said?" she answered. "Kenzie, I'm not in a bad situation anymore. I'll always make sure that you're okay. I love you, and you're my best friend. We've always been there for each other, and I'll always be there for you, whether you want it or not."

I nodded as I fell into step behind her. I wasn't going to ever take anything from Paige, but the fact that she offered to always have my back touched me.

I knew that I'd think about what she'd just shared, and it would continue to make me angry. Dane was any woman's dream guy, and it pissed me off that some bitch had used him for revenge and money. Who did that?

"Was she pretty?" I asked hesitantly as I followed Paige out the door of the lavatory.

"She was," my friend answered. "But not as gorgeous as you."

I snorted. "I think you're biased."

We couldn't have a private conversation with everybody around, and we were both quiet as we sat down again.

Four men rose as we returned to the large table, and it was rather charming. Dane pulled out my chair and sat me down again, his brother Sebastian doing the same for Paige.

I glanced around the table as all the guys sat back down again, noting that although I was a modern woman, I couldn't hate the manners that the guys had been taught growing up in Texas.

Sebastian was sitting by Paige across from us. I'd met Trace and Eva earlier, who were seated on the engaged couple's right hand side, and they obviously had the same loving type of relationship that my friend had with Sebastian.

I hadn't known that Gabe and Chloe were also coming, but they were a lovely couple. They were seated next to Dane, and he'd introduced Gabe as his cousin. Another filthy rich Walker who seemed head over heels in love with his wife. I was beginning to think that when a Walker male fell, he went down pretty damn hard.

"Everything okay?" Dane asked as he put his mouth near my ear.

"Fine," I whispered back to him.

"I didn't know what you wanted, so I ordered you a girlie drink," he shared.

I bit back a giggle. "What's a girlie drink?"

"Something with fruit juice and whipped cream," he said. "Paige likes them, so I was hoping you would, too."

I was good with whatever he ordered. I rarely drank alcohol, but I thought it might help get rid of my nerves.

This wasn't an environment I was used to, and although the couples were all really nice, I was afraid I'd do something socially wrong. "Okay," I told him with a smile.

Dane looked so handsome in semi-formal clothing. He was wearing a sport jacket, dress pants, and a white shirt that he'd left open at the collar. He looked like he belonged here with his brothers and cousin. It probably wasn't unusual for him to look confident in his surroundings. He might live on an island now, but he'd grown up in a very wealthy world in Texas.

"Relax," Dane said in a hoarse whisper that nobody else could hear. "Nobody here is going to bite you except me, but only because you look so beautiful."

I actually felt my skin flushing from the compliment. I tried to release the tension from my body so I could enjoy the evening.

Paige caught my eye as she smiled, her gaze moving from my pink cheeks to Dane's cozy position.

I shook my head, trying to silently tell her that it didn't mean anything.

To my surprise, she winked at me before her attention was drawn back to her fiancé.

CHAPTER 25

Kenzie

I wasn't drunk, but I was pretty uninhibited as Dane and I made our way back to our suite after dinner.

"That was an amazing dinner," I said brightly to him as we pulled up in front of our tower in the limousine. "I don't think I've ever eaten that well."

"It was seafood," Dane said in an amused voice.

I nodded as he helped me from the car. "But it was fabulous stuff."

Dane chuckled as he took my hand to guide me to the suite. "Ms. Jordan, I do believe you're drunk."

"I'm not," I denied. "I'm just happy."

"And what makes you so merry tonight?"

I sighed after we walked into the elevator. "My best friend is going to marry the man of her dreams. She deserves that."

The doors clanged shut, and Dane didn't let go of my hand as he replied, "Don't you deserve that, too?"

"Someday, I hope I find someone who loves me that much. But right now I'm just glad that Paige is so happy. She's my best friend."

"And what kind of man would make you happy?" he asked.

"He'd have to love me," I considered.

"Is he rich?" Dane grumbled.

I shook my head so strongly that it made me a little bit dizzy. "Not necessary. He just has to have a job."

It would be glorious to have two incomes to support a household. But wealth wasn't necessary. In fact, I'd probably just proven that I wasn't completely comfortable with it.

"And what does he look like?"

I stared at him. "I think he looks just like you—in my dreams anyway."

"Is that so?" he said in a guttural voice as he put one hand on each side of my head, essentially holding me captive.

My confidence fueled by alcohol, I looked directly up at him. "Yep. He's one hot guy."

"Kenzie," he said in a warning voice. "What are you saying?"

"Nothing. Just that if I had a guy, I'd want him to be just like you." The logic made perfect sense to me.

"And if you had the real thing?" he asked in a harsh tone.

"I can't have you," I said with regret.

"Bullshit," he countered. "Who says?"

"I do. I think you'd break my heart," I shared earnestly.

"Kenzie, I'd *never* hurt you."

"Maybe not knowingly," I explained. "But I'd never want us to end."

The elevator door opened, and I pushed on his chest as I saw an older couple waiting to enter.

Dane reluctantly let me go, but snatched my hand as he led me toward our room.

Once inside the suite, he didn't appear to be ready to relinquish his hold on me. He immediately pinned me to the closed door, his voice husky as he said, "If you want me, I'm all yours, Kenzie."

"For how long?" I asked boldly.

Jesus! Alcohol was making me bold. But at the moment, I didn't care.

"As long as you want," he answered.

I didn't have a chance to ask any more questions. His wild-eyed stare disappeared from my vision as his mouth swooped down to capture mine.

There was no holding back. Not only was I less cautious because of the girlie drinks, but I was also tired of holding back my emotions. A whole lot of longing was escaping my soul, and I had no desire to stop it.

He kissed me like I was the only woman in the world, the only one he wanted.

I opened to him, and I let him wipe away any inhibitions I had with his passion, responding to him like a flame that had suddenly become an out of control wildfire.

I wrapped my arms around his neck, letting myself drown in sensation. The feel of his hard, hot body against mine was an aphrodisiac that I couldn't resist.

"Dane," I said in a voice full of longing as he released my mouth. "I want you so much. I can't *not* want you anymore."

"I don't want you not to want me," he growled next to my ear. "Jesus, Kenzie. I need you so damn bad that I can't think about anything else. You're driving me fucking crazy. I wanted to pound the hell out of any guy who even looked at you in this dress tonight."

"Nobody looked at me," I argued.

"Two different guys were trying to decide what you looked like naked," he answered angrily. "I wanted to beat the hell out of them both."

"Why?"

He pulled back and impaled me with his dark eyes. There was a torment on his face that I wanted to stroke away as he answered, "Because you're fucking mine. I didn't want those bastards looking at you like you don't belong to me."

"I didn't want either one of them. I didn't even notice. I was too focused on you," I confessed breathlessly. "All I've ever really wanted was you."

"I have to know that you're going to feel the same way when you're sober," he said in a graveled voice as he picked me up and carried me into my room. "I'll go fucking crazy if you don't."

"I'm not drunk," I said.

"Maybe not totally," he agreed. "But you're definitely impaired. I won't take you this way. I want you to know who's fucking you. I want you to be totally aware of whose name you're screaming when you come."

My body reacted immediately to his blunt statements. Heat flowed between my thighs, and my core clenched with desperate need. "I'll know exactly who you are."

He put me on the bed as he went to search for my nightgown. Disappointingly, he helped me undress, only to cover me back up with my pajamas.

"Don't leave me," I said as he turned off the bedside lamp, plunging the room into darkness.

"You'll thank me for it tomorrow. Believe me, it's killing me, but I don't want a one-nighter, Kenzie. I want *you*."

I wanted to yell for him to come back as he left the room. I wanted to know what he meant by saying he wanted *me*.

My heart ached with a pent-up yearning so painful I felt like I couldn't breathe, and it took forever for me to finally fall into a troubled sleep.

CHAPTER 26

Kenzie

I was used to being alone, but I was terrified of being in Southern California. This was unknown territory for me, and I wasn't crazy about the neighborhood I'd ended up in because of my budget.

But it wasn't like I wasn't used to living in a crappy area.

I'd get out eventually. I had to hang onto that.

Relief flowed through me, a sudden burst of happiness that I normally didn't experience, because my interview had gone well for my first adult modeling job.

I was desperately hoping the agency would take me on. I wasn't going to be able to survive well if I didn't have work.

I'll find something, even if it isn't in modeling.

I'd been surviving my entire life, and I'd keep on trying. It would pay off eventually. It had to.

I hurried to my new apartment from the nearest bus stop, hating the fact that it had taken me so long to get home. The long trip had landed me back in my neighborhood after dark.

I'll find a better place after I get working.

At the age of eighteen, I already had work experience. Surely somebody would give me a job. I didn't care much about what kind of work I could find. I just needed something to earn me money while I tried to launch my modeling career.

Maybe then I could attend college, and get a normal career, something that would last after I was too old to model anymore.

I entered the old apartment building and trudged up the stairs, bone tired from traveling back and forth to the modeling agency. I'd lost count of how many buses it had taken to get there and back, and I'd walked for miles from the nearest bus stop.

All I could think about was getting something to eat, and collapsing on the tattered couch I'd gotten from the thrift store. My furnishings weren't much, but they were mine.

The moment I walked into the apartment, I knew something was wrong. Stuff I'd put into the kitchen drawers were now on the floor, and the small space that I'd left tidy that morning looked like it had been ransacked.

A chill ran up my spine, and I'd learned to listen to my instincts. I turned around to run out of the kitchen, but I wasn't fast enough.

Two enormous bodies dressed in black tripped me up, and I ended up on the floor completely winded.

I rose up quickly, trying to save my ass.

Neither of them said a word, but one of the men reached for my arm, and he snagged it as I went flying by him. The other one pulled out a switchblade that was horrifyingly large.

"Please, don't…" I begged as he lifted his arm. I was only eighteen. I wasn't ready to die. I'd worked too damn hard to stay alive so I could have a better life.

I was unable to speak as the blade sliced through me over and over again.

Pain.

More pain.

Then agony.

Horror.

And finally, the blessed relief of blacking out.

Before I closed my eyes, I told myself I'd survive.

I'll make it. I just have to find the strength to keep trying.

Turns out, I was right. I *did* make it through. But I didn't know the price I'd pay later when my dreams were completely destroyed.

CHAPTER 27

Kenzie

THE PRESENT...

I woke up screaming, and completely unaware of where I was for a few minutes after I'd forced myself to shut the hell up.

Shivering from the aftereffects of my nightmare about when I'd been attacked, I pulled the blanket over my body, trying to warm myself again.

It had been a long time since I'd had that particular nightmare, but it caused the same emotional overflow that I'd always had whenever the horrific dream had popped up in my sleep.

"I'm okay," I panted. "I'm safe. It was just a dream."

"Kenzie!" Dane bellowed as he entered the bedroom.

"I'm here. I'm fine," I told him, knowing he'd probably heard me scream. Paige had once told me that our neighbors could hear me when I had one of my nightmares.

"What happened?" he asked as he sat on the side of the bed and turned on the lamp.

I squinted, but was grateful not to be in complete darkness. "Just a nightmare," I answered, trying to force myself to forget the horrific images of my near death experience.

Dane was dressed in a pair of black pajama bottoms, and nothing else. There was nothing more I wanted to do except wrap my arms around that hot body and find whatever comfort I could.

I suddenly remembered what had happened between Dane and I the night before.

God, I wished his words had been true. I wished he really wanted me, because I sure as hell wanted him.

"What were you dreaming about?" he asked gruffly as he slipped underneath the covers, forcing me to move over.

His arms came around me, and I was immediately warmed. He threw off body heat so tempting that I burrowed into his chest and wrapped my arms around his neck. "The attack," I admitted. "I have nightmares about it occasionally."

"Jesus, Kenzie. I wish I had been there for you," he said, his arms tightening around me protectively.

Warm and safe, I finally relaxed into Dane's hold, grateful that I had him here with me right now. "I think you were probably busy recovering from the plane crash."

It was funny how Dane and I had so many parallel experiences. Judging by the date of his accident, I was pretty sure we'd been in the hospital at the same time. But my recovery hadn't taken nearly as long as his.

"I was," he agreed. "But I still wish you hadn't been all alone."

"Me, too," I told him.

It would have been nice to have somebody special in my life, but I was convinced I was cursed when it came to men and my love life. I'd had one brief, adolescent relationship in high school that hadn't ended well for me. And after that, I'd never trusted any guy enough to want to start anything more than a casual acquaintance.

"Do you want me to stay with you?" he asked, not sounding at all certain that he wanted to go.

"Yes, please," I answered instantly.

Dane was here, and I wanted him to stay here so I didn't have to think about my dream.

"Tell me about it," he insisted.

"It's always the same," I explained as I laid my head on his shoulder. "I remember coming home, and then being attacked. I was hoping the dreams would be less terrifying by now, but all I can remember is that terrible feeling that I was going to die before I had a chance to live."

"I felt the same way," he commented. "When we had the plane crash. I knew we were going down, and I wasn't sure if anybody could live through that kind of accident."

"You did," I reminded him, my hand automatically running down his chest and to his ripped abdomen. I wanted to feel him, and assure myself he was okay.

His fear had to have been enormous when he discovered his dad's jet was going to crash, and I was grateful that he'd made it out.

"What was it like for you when you woke up and realized you were still alive?" Dane asked.

"It was so painful that I can't remember thinking much of anything," I confessed.

"Me, either," he confessed.

My heart clenched at the thought of Dane waking up after he'd been burnt so badly. The burns on his face couldn't have been too bad. Regardless of what Dane thought, his chest and abdomen bore a lot more burn scars.

"Were you scared?" I questioned curiously.

"Fucking terrified," he confirmed.

"Me, too. I guess I never realized just how alone I was until there was nobody in the hospital for me to talk to."

"No friends? Hell, at least I had my brothers, even though my dad was gone."

"Nobody," I informed him. "I was a loner. I never let anybody get close to me. It was the only way I could protect myself."

He stroked my hair in a comforting motion as he replied, "You're not alone anymore, baby."

"I know. And it scares me."

"Don't be afraid of me," he requested.

"I'm not. Never have been. Yes, you pissed me off in the beginning, but somehow I knew you'd never intentionally hurt me. I wasn't feeling that craziness that people have when they're dangerous."

"Instinct?" he questioned.

"Gut instinct," I confirmed. "I developed a good one when I was young. I should have listened to it when I got to California. But I needed a place to sleep, and I didn't want to waste any of the funds I had."

"So you moved into a dump," he concluded.

"Yes. My instincts were screaming, but I wasn't listening. I wanted to succeed too much."

"There's nothing wrong with wanting to have a better life. I just wished you'd had more money. But I'm starting to understand how desperate you were."

"After I paid for my first month in my crappy apartment, I only had fifty dollars to my name."

"Christ! You can't live on that."

"I had no choice. It's always been *sink or swim* for me, so I was trying to learn how to navigate in a very big pond."

"You're so fucking brave that I feel like a coward. I took my money and moved somewhere that nobody could hurt me. I had the funds, and I never even appreciated it."

"It's not your fault," I pointed out. "You came from a rich, healthy family. I wish it could be that way for everybody, but it's not. I think if I'd had the money, I would have wanted to escape and lick my wounds for a while. I might have done the exact same thing you did."

"I doubt it," Dane answered in a raspy voice. "You fight for what you want. I was born into it."

"Stop doing that," I demanded. "I hate it when you put yourself and your actions down. You're enormously talented, both with your art and the skills you've learned to evaluate the risk and rewards of investments. You didn't have to do anything, Dane, but you did. You have the money to just seek whatever pleasure you want, but you chose to become a better, smarter person."

"I would have been bored if I'd just done nothing with my time."

"Because of who you are," I explained. "You want to stay busy and never stop caring about being productive, even when you don't have to."

"Why do you care about what I think about myself?"

"I just...do." It wasn't a very good reason, but I couldn't really tell him how much I cared.

Unconsciously, I started to move my hand that was still on his abdomen, a sign of how much more I wanted from Dane.

"Maybe I should go," he said.

"Why?"

"Because if you keep touching me, I'm not sure that I can keep myself from pinning you to this damn bed, and fucking you until you're screaming my name."

I didn't stop touching him. In fact, I just explored even more. "Don't go," I requested.

I couldn't bear it if he left me again. Maybe I'd once pushed him away, but I knew I couldn't do it anymore.

I didn't *want* to do it again.

Paige had been right. I needed to start letting people into my life. I'd always be cautious, but I was tired of not letting Dane in. He meant too much. He was too big of a temptation.

Somehow, I was going to have to learn to let go of my fears when the situation was warranted. And Dane was definitely somebody I couldn't shut out anymore.

Problem was, I'd blown my chances to be closer to him.

I'd have to be the one to convince him that I was sincere.

Finding out that a woman had hurt him practically made my damn heart bleed. He hadn't deserved what she'd done, but I wanted to be the one to show him just how much he had to offer.

I wanted to be the only one.

Even if the relationship didn't last, I knew he'd never intentionally hurt me.

I'd nearly died eight years ago, but I'd never really learned how to live.

Not yet.

But I wanted to.

I moved my hand down his body slowly, taking my time to get to what I wanted.

Dane was rock-hard and ready as I finally pushed my way into his pajama bottoms and wrapped my fingers around his cock. "God, I want you inside me, Dane. So badly that it hurts."

He grabbed my arm, ready to attempt to stop me. But I wasn't giving in.

"Are you still drunk?" he rasped.

"I was *never* so drunk that I didn't know what I wanted. I knew what I was asking for last night."

"Don't do this to me, Kenzie. I don't know if I'll be able to stop."

"Don't stop," I suggested as I shook off his hold. "I want to be close to you, Dane. As close as we can get."

"Thank fuck!" he answered. "Don't change your mind."

I felt guilty about what had happened between us before, but I knew I wasn't about to run again. I wanted to see what it felt like to be with the incredible male who was currently in my bed. I couldn't ignore the way desire gnawed at me every single time I saw him.

I rose up and swung a leg over his body until I straddled him. I hated taking my hand away when I had everything I wanted in my grasp, but it was the only way I was going to get what I needed.

I pulled the nightgown I was wearing over my head and tossed it on the floor.

With anyone else, I wouldn't be so bold. I couldn't even imagine *wanting* anybody else. But I wanted to show him just how serious I was, and that I wasn't leaving until we'd hit a homerun or two. Maybe three.

"Fuck! You're so beautiful that it kills me to even look at you," Dane rasped. "I've wanted to see you like this almost from the day we met. I wanted to see that look on your face that said you wanted me as much as I want you."

His hands went to my breasts, pinching each nipple, and sending my body into a roaring blaze of pure heat.

I sighed as his palms cupped my breasts. "I've wanted it to," I confessed. "I was just too afraid of getting hurt."

"I'd never fucking hurt you, Kenzie. I'd die to protect you without a second thought."

"I know," I told him, knowing it was the truth. "I'm not afraid anymore."

"Why?"

"Because you're worth taking a chance on," I said with a moan.

I squealed in surprise as he flipped my body over, and I landed flat on my back.

"Then I'm going to make sure I make it worth your risk," he growled, his big body looming over mine.

I looked at him, the moment stretching out like an eternity. His face was solemn, but the mischief in his eyes made my heart race. Dane *was* going to make it worth it.

I had no doubts about that.

CHAPTER 28

Kenzie

*A*ll I knew was that her name was Paige, and that she was at Harvard studying law. Other than those facts, I knew nothing about the woman I was about to meet.

Well, I did know *one* more thing: she needed a roommate.

Maybe this one will work out better. She's a student, so she's not likely to skip rent.

I'd already had several roommates who had left me stuck with the rent, and the last one had nearly left me homeless. I had to find a place to live, and I needed it quickly. I was already evicted from my former apartment because I couldn't pay both mine and my roommate's part of the rent.

I knocked on the door. The neighborhood was okay, better than my current place. The building was showing its age, but the exterior was well maintained.

All I wanted was a safe place to live, and a roommate who I could trust to keep making the rent on a regular basis.

"Hi! Are you Kenzie?" a pleasant female asked excitedly.

I nodded, afraid to hope that this woman would be the person I could finally trust. "I am."

She pulled me through the door, and I looked around the apartment. According to Paige, it was a two bedroom, but we'd have to share a bathroom. The space was neat, but the furniture was old, probably thrift store purchased. I had no problem with that since Goodwill was practically my go-to interior designer.

Maybe I'd found somebody like me.

"Sorry about the sad décor," she said. "Since I'm at Harvard, I can't afford nice stuff."

She showed me around the small apartment, and I was thrilled with what I saw. She even had a bed in her spare room, and I was hoping she wouldn't mind if I used it.

I had a bed, but it had seen better days, so I asked her if I'd have to get furniture.

"No. You can use mine, unless you want something better. If you do, I won't take offense."

"I don't," I said to her. "My stuff is even worse than yours."

"Great. Then maybe we can firm up the deal so I don't have to be here alone anymore."

I sighed. "To be honest, I'm pretty poor, but I always make my rent."

Paige smiled. "I guess we have a lot in common then."

Even though I knew she was probably super smart, I still liked her. Her openness put me at ease, and I got the sense that she and I could be friends.

What if she ditches me and her rent like my old roommates?

Yeah, I knew not everybody was like that, but I hadn't had the best of luck with any of my former roommates.

I'll make it. I just have to find the strength to keep trying.

At the moment, I had no other options, so I was going to have to hope things would work out.

I held out my hand. "You have a deal. I'll write you a check."

She beamed at me, and then took my hand to shake it.

CHAPTER 29

Kenzie

THE PRESENT...

I'd never wanted anything as much as I wanted Dane Walker, and even though it scared the hell out of me, the way I felt about him left no more room for caution.

If I was *ever* going to trust a man, it was going to be *him*. Nobody else had ever tempted me to leave my cocoon of self-preservation. But the man who was looking intently down on me at the moment had completely shattered any illusion of being safe.

I had to let him in, and to hell with the consequences.

I lifted my hand to stroke the stubble on his jaw. "I'm not very experienced," I warned him. "Only once in high school, and it wasn't very pleasant."

"I'll make it more than pleasant," he said gruffly. "I want you to come so hard you never want another man."

I wrapped my arms around his neck. "I haven't wanted anybody. Not really. I never knew what it was like to need someone this badly."

"It's more than mutual, baby," he replied, his dark eyes swirling with emotion as he lowered his head and kissed me.

His forceful embrace was overwhelming, and I had to hang on for the ride.

He plundered.

He explored.

And he definitely conquered me from the moment I opened completely beneath his powerful assault on my senses.

Desperate for more, I wrapped my legs around his flannel-clad hips, straining for the connection I *had* to have.

He released my mouth, and I tilted my head back as he attacked the sensitive skin on my neck.

"Dane," I moaned, unable to keep the pleasure from consuming me.

"Keep saying my name," he growled against my skin. "I want you to know exactly who's making you come."

Heat flooded between my thighs, drenching my panties.

I loved his dirty talk, and the intimacy that was flowing between us.

His bare chest moved against mine, turning my nipples into pebbles as they abraded against his red-hot skin.

My short nails dug into his neck, a silent plea for him to give me what I needed.

He moved down and put his scorching mouth on my nipples, one after the other, until I was half out of my mind.

I speared my hands into his hair and yanked. "Please, Dane," I whimpered.

He reared up between my legs, his hand seeking and finding the material of my panties. There was no time to pull them off delicately. He tore the material with a powerful tug.

"Mine," he rumbled as his fingers delved into the wetness and warmth of my pulsating core.

"Yes," I agreed, loving his fierce possessiveness.

His thumb started moving over my clit, a slick motion that zeroed in on where I needed him the most, and relieved some of my restlessness. But it wasn't enough.

I shoved to push him away, my blood pounding in my veins for me to get him naked.

"Kenzie?" he said in a covetous voice. "What do you want?"

I sat up and grabbed for the ties of his pajama bottoms. "This," I panted as I yanked on the strings. "I need you."

Dane was breathing heavy, his chest heaving with every intake of air. "Wait. You'll get it. Soon."

"I can't wait anymore, Dane."

He stumbled to his feet at the side of the bed, shucking off the flannel bottoms in record time.

He had nothing beneath them, and his cock sprang out of its confinement, heavy and beautiful when it was exposed.

My eyes ate him up, devouring the perfection that was Dane. He *was* the perfect male specimen in my eyes, and everything inside me that was female ached for the gorgeous, muscular body of the man I'd learned to care so much about.

His eyes appeared to be almost black, their chocolate color deepening as his greedy stare roamed over my form, making me feel taken before he even came back to the bed.

"This isn't going to go slow," he warned me in a feral tone. "I have no brakes when it comes to you."

My belly flip-flopped as I stared at him boldly, then reached out to touch the velvety head of his cock. "I never asked for slow," I said.

The feel of him was like an aphrodisiac to me. Not that I needed one. Watching Dane in all of his glory was plenty.

I fondled his cock, my desire rising to fever pitch as I glanced at the sculpted V beneath his abdomen that appeared to point right at the large erection I was stroking.

He felt so amazing that I couldn't stop myself from swiping the bead of moisture from the tip and tasting him.

"Christ, Kenzie!" he growled. "Are you trying to kill me?"

"Only with pleasure," I answered, my voice unrecognizably seductive.

"Stop, or I'll put you over my lap and turn that beautiful ass red."

My heart galloped as I imagined being at Dane's mercy. "I might like that," I bantered.

Dane pulled my hand away, and then came back onto the bed, his body pinning me to the mattress. "Be careful what you ask for," he answered, his breath warm on the side of my face.

"I'm not afraid," I said. "Any way you touch me would end up turning into pleasure."

He pulled back and stared down at me, his nostrils flaring as he appeared to be straining to keep himself in check. "Damn right I'd make it your pleasure," he rasped.

I wrapped my legs around his waist, and then strained up against him. "Now, Dane. I need you."

The ache inside me was getting painful, and more than I could handle.

"Easy, baby," he crooned. "Kiss me, Kenzie."

I wrapped my arms around his neck, and pulled his head down. It was all the encouragement he needed to kiss me like a man possessed.

His hard cock pressed against my core. I was so close to getting what I needed.

I strained up against him again, urging him to fill me as his intoxicating embrace went on and on.

When he finally surged into me with one powerful thrust of his hips, I moaned against his mouth.

Dane was built big, and my internal muscles struggled to accept him. Then the minor pain gave way to a greater sensation of being completely and totally filled.

"Yes," I moaned as he released my mouth. "Yes, please. Fuck me."

"You're so damn tight, sweetheart," he groaned, his body shuddering as he completely seated himself inside me. "And so fucking hot."

"That's all your fault," I whimpered.

"Jesus, Kenzie. I didn't realize it could be like this," he said in a raspy voice filled with molten heat.

I understood. It was perfect. Our bodies burned in tandem as Dane pulled almost out and then thrust in again.

"Oh, God, yes," I urged him on.

He grasped a huge piece of my hair and pulled my head back until he could ravage the skin on my neck with his teeth and mouth.

My focus narrowed in on his forceful thrusts, feeling nothing except him.

He surged inside me over and over, and all I could do was ride with him.

Deeper and deeper.

Harder and harder.

"More," I gasped, my short nails clawing at his back.

I was like tinder to his flame, and I was ready to explode into an out of control inferno, a blaze that couldn't be contained.

"Dane, I can't take it," I said in a desperate tone.

"You'll take it," he said in an animalistic voice beside my ear. "You'll take it and then beg for more."

I knew he was right. I couldn't get enough. My back arched as the tight coil in my belly began to unfurl and went straight to my core.

My legs tightened around his waist, and his thrusts became short and deep.

Our sweaty bodies slid together in a perfect rhythm that was erotic as hell, and caused each stroke of his cock to slide over my throbbing clit.

I imploded. And then, I began to sob as my climax took over my body until I felt like one big pulsating mess.

My pussy clamped down on his enormous cock, as though it didn't want to let him go.

I wanted to stretch out the moment, but my orgasm was too strong to be ignored.

"Dane," I screamed around my sobs.

"Fuck!" he said in a throaty voice. "I can't hold back."

"Don't," I pleaded as my core rippled around his cock, milking him to orgasm.

The climax hammered me, leaving me drifting in the aftermath.

Dane finally rolled off me, both of us completely spent.

My body was still trembling as he wrapped his arms around me and held me close.

"Don't cry, sweetheart. Why are you crying?"

They were tears of joy, a relief and happiness I just couldn't contain.

I clung to him as I answered, "It's not a bad cry. I'm happy."

I'd never felt that kind of belonging with somebody, that kind of joy. My emotions had poured across my usual, preset stopping point, and I hadn't been able to hold them back.

Everything had exploded in a sob fest that I'd never experienced in the past.

I love you, Dane. I love you so much it hurts!

My mind was screaming what my mouth couldn't utter. So I just clung to him silently as I recovered from the most extraordinary, mind-blowing experience of my entire life.

CHAPTER 30

Kenzie

THREE YEARS AGO...

"I got sacked," I told Paige as my eyes stayed glued to the *help wanted* ads in the paper.

I was on the couch with a bag of Cheetos Puffs, and chowing down on them while I was looking at the ads, my fingers starting to smudge the paper orange.

"What now?" Paige teased. "Oh, wait! Don't tell me. Mr. Patel is getting a new relative into the United States who needs your job?"

"His nephew," I answered flatly.

"You have to stop the night jobs at hotels," Paige observed. "They never last long."

I sighed as I looked up at her from my position on the couch. She'd just come in from class, and she looked as exhausted as I felt.

"I know. I'm looking for something else."

The night clerk at the hotel had been a second job for me. I already worked full-time during the day at another mindless job, but it didn't pay enough for me not to have a second employer.

Paige snatched the paper from me. "Stop looking. God, you just got fired."

I shrugged. "It's not like I'm not used to it."

I'd lost five evening jobs over the last few years, and none of the dismissals had been my fault.

A bankrupt business.

A business having layoffs.

A business cutting back on staff.

A business where a woman on maternity leave decided to finally revisit her job again.

And now...the Indian boss who wanted to employ his family coming into the U.S.

Hell, what chance did I have when I was weighed against a nephew?

"You don't need to find a job today," she griped.

Yeah, I actually needed something that would pay me before the end of the month, or I might not be able to squeak out my rent. But I didn't tell Paige that. She was working her ass off, too, and the last thing she needed was a deadbeat roommate.

Paige had turned out to be the best sort of roommate, the kind that made an excellent best friend. Over time, I'd shared a lot, and she'd told me things she'd never told another soul. We'd managed to get by together, neither one of us complaining when we had to throw in a little extra if one of us was short.

"I'll find something," I assured her.

She swiped my paper and strode over to hold it near the trash. "You have to quit. We never have an evening together. We can do a marathon movie or TV night."

Damn! That sounded good. We rarely got to spend more than an hour or two at home together, and it wasn't because either one of us had a hot guy. More often than not we were working or Paige was in class.

Sadly, I knew our roommate situation wouldn't last forever.

Paige could see an end to her poverty. She'd be a Harvard Law School grad, and I'd just keep on working dead end jobs.

There was no rainbow at the end of my tunnel.

I'll make it. I just have to find the strength to keep trying.

I let Paige have her way, and I stopped my job search for the night. I wouldn't have her for a roommate forever, and I wanted to enjoy one evening with my best friend.

Sooner or later, she'd be gone, and I was going to be all alone again. I wanted to just enjoy her company, and hope we kept in touch after she moved on to something better than our small apartment in Cambridge.

CHAPTER 31
Kenzie

I woke up in the morning surrounded by warmth in the form of a red-hot male body that was wrapped around me. Dane had spooned me tight, and never let go, even after he fell asleep.

I laid there for a few minutes, just enjoying the sensation of being cherished enough to have a place in Dane's arms.

We were both a little bit stinky since we'd fallen asleep soon after he'd fucked me to within an inch of my life, but I wasn't about to complain.

Eventually, I started to squirm slowly out of my place, needing desperately to empty my bladder.

"Oh no, you don't," Dane said in an adorable, sleepy male tone that sent shivers down my spine. "You're not leaving me."

He tightened his arm around my waist.

"Dane, I have to go. Literally. I haven't wet my bed in well over twenty years."

"Okay, then," he grumbled, but he still didn't let me go.

I actually giggled because he was so funny when he wasn't quite awake. "You have to let go."

"Don't want to," he complained.

Honestly, I had no desire to get up at the moment, but my bladder was screaming for relief. "I *have* to," I said with regret, and then wiggled until he loosened his hold.

"Come back to me," he growled.

I took a moment to lean over and kiss him on the forehead before I scampered to the attached bathroom. Judging by the fact that Dane hadn't even opened his eyes, he'd probably be back to sleep within moments.

I finished my business, and then turned on the shower. I was desperate to get my own stink off my body.

Come back to me.

I came so damn close to obeying his command because I wanted to, but the shower won because I really needed it to feel human again.

The powerful, jetted stream from the showerhead woke me up, clearing my muddled senses.

Now all I need is coffee!

But really, all I *wanted* was Dane again.

I guessed that was the problem in experiencing *that much* pleasure. I'd gotten greedy to experience it over and over again.

I washed my hair and ran the conditioner through it while I thought about what had happened the night before.

Dane was so damn dangerous to me. Not only was I crazy in love with him, but he could also be a damn good friend. My attraction to him was off the charts. And my soul felt a profound connection for the first time in my life.

Problem was, that combination could be disastrous, but I was at the point where I *had* to try. What good was there in life if all I ever did was survive? Maybe I was conditioned not to take chances, but Dane tempted me beyond anything I could possibly resist.

I wanted love.

I wanted connection.

I wanted...*him.*

My chest ached as I remembered how he'd made me come apart, my brain focused only on pleasure.

It was highly possible that the way I loved Dane might only come once in a lifetime. And I just couldn't throw it aside for safety. I wanted to experience everything I could before I missed the chance.

I closed my eyes and leaned back against the tile, my body primed and ready to orgasm.

Before I could think about it, I ran my hand down my belly, and it came to rest on my aching core.

"Dane," I whispered as I pictured him in my mind, that heavy-lidded, turned on expression I'd seen last night forming in my brain. "I need you."

I lifted my foot and propped it on the tub, my fingers still busy stimulating my throbbing clit.

My stomach clenched, and I bit back a moan as I visualized Dane surging into me. And Dane feasting on my pussy like he had the first time we'd been intimate.

I squeaked and my eyes popped open. A strong hand wrapped around my wrist, pulling my hand away from what I was doing.

Before I could quite process what was happening, Dane was on his knees and between my legs.

He looked up at me. "You're a very bad girl, Kenzie. Getting you off is *my* job," he rasped. "But I'll let it slide for now."

I shivered at the low timbre of his voice. I knew he was playing, but I didn't know quite how to join in. Or at least...I *thought* he was teasing. With Dane, it was hard to tell sometimes.

In seconds, I wasn't thinking about his words. All I could do was feel as he buried his face between my legs.

"Oh, God," I whispered, my legs trembling as he put his hands on my ass and pulled my pussy against his face.

I had to grab onto the bar in the shower, and I was grateful it was there. With my foot propped up, I was completely open to Dane, but my balance wasn't quite stable.

I let my head fall back against the tile as Dane's tongue flicked over the tender, pink flesh, then zeroed in on the tiny bundle of nerves that sent me through the roof.

I white-knuckled the metal bar, feeling my body reacting violently to every subtle touch of Dane's tongue.

With him, there would probably never be a time that I didn't go up in flames the moment he touched me.

"Make me come, Dane, please," I begged.

My core was already clenching, and I could feel my orgasm barreling full-strength toward me.

The pulsating stream of water was hitting my nipples, stimulating them almost in the same rhythm as Dane's tongue.

My back arched instinctively as my climax hit me like a tidal wave.

"Dane. Yes. Yes." I reached my free hand down to spear my fingers through his wet hair, my volatile release consuming me.

I wanted him close.

Closer.

Then closer still.

My body shuddered as I imploded, becoming a trembling mess as I gasped for breath and my sanity.

Dane's fingers replaced his mouth as he rose up, still gently stroking over me until I finally relaxed against him, my body completely wrecked.

"Good morning," he said in a low, sexy voice beside my ear. I was wide awake now, even without my morning coffee.

"Yes, it is," I panted.

His chuckle vibrated against my skin, and it was one of the best things I'd ever heard.

I wanted to make Dane happy.

I wanted to make him laugh.

There had been way too much solitude and sadness in his life.

"I thought I told you to come back to me," he scolded.

"I wanted to not stink first," I protested. "But I can make it worth the wait."

"You already have, sweetheart," he assured me.

My heart squeezed inside my chest. "I can make it even better," I offered, not waiting for him to answer before I slid down his body and knelt at his feet.

I'd wanted this last night, but things had been too volatile for me to fumble with my first blow job. Now, we had plenty of time.

"Kenzie, if you do that, I'm definitely going to come in record time," he warned.

I wrapped my hand around his rock-hard cock. "God, I hope so," I replied in a hopeful tone. "Well, not the record time thing, but the *coming* thing."

I savored the feel of his thick, hard shaft, hoping I could manage to give him the same pleasure he'd given me.

I looked up at him, and our eyes met with a powerful clash. "Help me," I said. "I don't exactly know how to do this."

His dark eyes lightened, and he grinned at me. "Trust your instincts. I guarantee I'll like whatever you do."

I moved my hands to his firm butt, my fingers tracing over the muscled, smooth flesh.

Like he said, I followed my instincts, putting my mouth to his wet abs, and tracing that seductive V with my tongue.

I let my mouth trail over his shaft, then opened to take him into my mouth.

Dane tasted like sin, and hard, stubborn, irresistible male, and I was intoxicated the moment I first sucked on his cock.

I fumbled, but Dane reached down and held my head, coaxing me into the rhythm he needed.

"Fuck, Kenzie! I told you I was never going to last. Watching my fucking wet dreams play out for real is too damn hard for me."

Had he dreamt about this, about me? God, I hoped so, because he'd been the star of my sensual dreams almost since the moment we'd met.

I picked up the pace, getting comfortable with his mammoth size. I tried to keep taking more and more of him, but I would probably never be able to handle all of Dane.

On instinct, I lowered my hand from his ass down to fondle his balls, and I was satisfied to get a guttural, sexy groan from his lips.

"Just like that, Kenzie," he groaned.

"Just!"

"Like!"

"That!"

I wrapped my hand around the root of his cock, finally getting to know his responses. I let my hand work with my mouth, and when I sensed his body tensing, I knew he was going to come.

"Back up, baby. I'm going to come."

I didn't want to back off. I wanted to taste him just like he'd tasted me. In fact, I craved it.

I got exactly what I wanted, and Dane's orgasm flowed powerfully down my throat, the warmth and his sensual groans fueling my own pleasure.

I did it! I didn't suck at giving head. Well, I guess I *sucked*, but only in a very good way.

Dane grasped me tightly under the arms and hauled me up and into *his* arms.

"Was that okay?" I asked hesitantly as I looked up at him.

"No, it wasn't," he said as he tried to catch his breath. "It was more than okay."

I smiled as he kept his eyes closed and his head tipped, his chest rising and falling rapidly.

"I'll improve eventually," I mused. "I just need practice."

He hauled me against him and he kissed me. I sighed into his tender kiss as I tasted the two of us mingled together.

When he finally released my lips, I rested my head on his strong shoulder, happy to just be with him.

"If you practice anymore, you'll probably kill me," he grumbled.

I smiled against his skin, knowing that he really wouldn't complain if I wanted to improve my skills.

We cleaned up lazily, taking our time before we finally left the warmth of the shower.

CHAPTER 32

Kenzie

ABOUT A YEAR AGO...

I was *not* going to cry.

"I'll miss you," Paige said in a forlorn voice.

"I'll miss you, too. But you're going to leave here soon yourself," I reminded her as we said our goodbyes at the bus station. My coach was just starting to load.

Maybe Paige's impending graduation was spurring me on to move and try out a different city. The New York gallery had kind of been an excuse. I'd applied intentionally for any positions in the art world, knowing my best friend would be moving on to bigger and better jobs. Since I had no experience, being a receptionist in a renowned gallery was going to have to be a place to start for now.

"Be careful. Don't walk alone after dark," Paige cautioned. "And don't forget to eat."

God, I was going to miss my honorary older sister. Paige was only a few years older than me, but she fussed like a mother hen sometimes. I was going to miss that so much. She'd always treated me like family, and it was something I'd never had.

"Come here," she said in a tearful voice. "I'm so worried about you."

I hugged her tightly, knowing that it was possible that I'd never have another friend who cared about me as much as she did.

"You be careful, too," I whispered. "It's not exactly small-town here."

I'd always been a lot more streetwise than my buddy. Paige had taken some hard knocks, but she hadn't spent as much time as I had roaming the streets.

"We'll stay in touch," she said, trying to be cheery while tears were leaking from her eyes.

I will *not* cry.

I nodded, knowing we'd probably lose touch eventually. Paige was destined for big things, and we wouldn't have much in common once she became a high-income attorney.

"I'll call you," I yelled over my shoulder as I raced for the entrance of my bus. It was getting ready to move.

I found my window seat, and saw Paige waving at the large vehicle as it prepared to pull away.

I'll make it. I just have to find the strength to keep trying.

I didn't start bawling until the bus had pulled away and I could no longer see my best friend on the sidewalk of the bus station. After that, my sorrow had free reign.

There would only be one Paige in my lifetime, and missing her was worth crying about.

CHAPTER 33

Dane

*M*ine!

I couldn't stop the tension forming in my body as I watched Kenzie eat the breakfast we'd ordered from room service.

Yeah, she *was* mine. She just didn't know it yet.

Christ! Just watching her suck a drop of syrup from her finger gave me a giant sized erection, and I wasn't even touching her.

Okay, I knew I was pathetic, but I just didn't give a damn. The only thing that mattered, my only objective, was to keep Kenzie by my side.

When she'd run away from me in the pottery room, I'd been terrified that I'd moved too fast, and done the wrong damn thing when I'd offered her money. I was pretty sure I'd blown it. Considering her history, I didn't blame her for not trusting anyone. Thinking about the hardship she'd gone through made my damn gut ache. And I couldn't help wishing that I'd been there for her earlier, but I was here *now*, and I wasn't going to let her be alone and frightened ever again.

I couldn't think about her being attacked without flying into a rage. Some low-life motherfuckers had nearly killed her, and left her for dead.

I'd been *that close* to losing her, and I'd never even met her.

It scared the shit out of me to think of Kenzie dying before I'd ever had a chance to have her in my life.

You know how sometimes you just *know* that something was meant to happen? Kenzie was that certainty for me. I knew we were supposed to meet. I don't know how I knew it, but it was true. I could feel it.

Problem was, Kenzie now had the power to completely destroy me, and that was fucking terrifying. But I wasn't going to let that fear stop me. She needed me just as much as I needed her. It just might take a little more time for her to see it my way.

There was no turning back for me. The minute I'd touched her, she was all mine. In fairness, I was all hers, too. All I needed to do now was convince her that she wanted a scarred up bastard like me.

"We're supposed to go snorkeling with the giant turtles today," she informed me between bites of her enormous stack of pancakes.

Hell, I loved the way she ate. There were no dainty salads for Kenzie. She enjoyed her food almost like it was some kind of religious experience.

"Are we going?" I asked as I picked up my fork and started to demolish the breakfast on my plate.

She looked at me with a frown. "You know I can't swim."

"I'll take care of you," I promised. "We could get you into a life jacket and let you watch the reef. Are you game?"

I should have started her swimming lessons on the island, but after I'd screwed up, we'd never had the chance.

"I'm not really afraid of water," she mused. "I just don't know how to swim. But I'd like to learn."

Yeah, I needed to get her swimming. I didn't like the thought of her getting in trouble in the pool or on the beach at the Cay without the basic skills to keep herself afloat.

She'd jumped into the shallow end of the pool so easily that I'd just assumed she knew how to swim until she'd told me otherwise.

"I'll teach you," I answered. "You like the water, so that's a good start. I'll have you diving with me eventually."

Her face lit up. "That would be incredible."

I was humbled by how easy it was to make her happy. Life had shit all over her, and she was excited by things I'd been doing my entire life. How fair was that? I couldn't think about it or it would make me insane.

"So you want to go?" she asked.

"Don't you?"

She nodded. "I do. I don't know if I'll ever get back to Hawaii again, so I'd love to see as much as I possibly can."

"We do have beautiful beaches on the island," I reminded her.

"I know. And I love it. But there's something magical about this place."

I agreed. The *something magical* was her presence here. I liked Maui. I'd been here many times to dive. But it had never been *this* good.

"I should get into my swimsuit," she said excitedly.

I held up my hand to stop her. "Finish your coffee. We have time."

She picked up her mug, and kept her seat, smiling at me as she put the coffee to her lips, and then drank. "About what happened last night," she started hesitantly once she'd slugged back some caffeine.

"And this morning?" I asked.

"Yeah, that, too. I was thinking that maybe it was just some kind of fling for us."

Shit. She was nervous, and I hated that. She didn't need to explain away what had happened. I'd been there with her. I was well aware of just how powerful it had been.

I put down my fork and looked at her stubbornly. "It was no fling for me," I told her with certainty.

I had to convince her that everything that had happened was real for both of us.

"But if it doesn't happen again, I'll understand."

I stood up, my gut aching at the thought of her throwing us away before we even got a chance to start. "I *want* it to happen again, Kenzie. Over and over. Every. Single. Fucking. Day."

Could I possibly make myself clearer? I didn't think so.

She stood up and walked up close to me. "I'm not on birth control," she blurted out. "It shouldn't have happened without protection, and I was stupid. I mean, it's not really the right time of the month to get pregnant, but it was still a dumb thing to do."

She looked so forlorn that I wanted to tell her that I didn't care if she got pregnant. I'd take care of her and any child I'd brought into the world, but I was afraid she wasn't quite ready for that. "We were both there, Kenzie. I was just as responsible as you, maybe more so."

At some point, I could have gotten some condoms. I'd never missed using a raincoat before, especially not with Britney. But I never even thought about it with Kenzie, probably because I already knew I'd never want anybody but her once I'd touched her.

She was it for me. Kenzie was the only woman I was ever going to love. She was my fucking everything. Now all I had to do was convince her what my gut and my heart had been saying all along.

"I know we were both participating," she answered. "I just didn't think about the consequences. I'm not sure why. I'm usually careful about *everything*."

"It's like that with us," I explained. "I think we both got caught up in the moment."

At least, I knew that I had. Hell, I couldn't even breathe when she was touching me, much less think.

"You've never done that before?" she questioned.

I took her hands and held them both tightly. "Never. And I should have thought about the fact that it would worry you. I'm sorry. But know that if it happens, you won't be alone."

Hell, if she was pregnant, I'd never be able to let her out of my sight. Not that I could now, but it would be a lot worse.

"But we could get protection," she suggested breathlessly.

"We *will* get it," I corrected. "I'm not letting you kick me out of your bed."

She flung herself into my arms, and I caught her around the waist.

"I'd never kick you out," she vowed. "*You'd* have to leave *me*."

"Then I guess we're stuck with each other," I teased, my heart a hell of a lot lighter knowing that she wasn't going to bolt.

I was as scared as she was, but I was going to stick it out and fight for what I wanted this time. I wasn't going into hiding, and I sure as hell was never going to let her go.

She wrapped her arms around my neck and pressed her warm curves into my harder body. And *Jesus*, she felt good.

"I don't feel stuck," she murmured. "I feel lucky."

"You feel lucky to be with an asshole?" I joked.

She sighed and relaxed against me, and my heart started to hammer against my chest wall. Kenzie was starting to trust me, and I felt like I had something really fragile and beautiful in my hands. All I had to do was handle it carefully.

"You're not an asshole, and believe me, I feel like I've met every one of them in existence during the last several years."

I hated the fact that she'd ever been at any guy's mercy. But there were some men who preyed on the innocent. It got their rocks off.

I stroked my hand over her silken hair, trying not to think of the tight situations that Kenzie had suffered through in the past.

If I considered it for very long, I'd end up homicidal.

"You're safe now. You know that, right?"

Please say yes.

"I feel safer than I ever have in my entire life," she replied. "But that isn't always comfortable for me, Dane. It's hard to let my guard down."

"Then take your time," I said. "We've got plenty of it."

I wasn't going to be fucking impatient.

Kenzie had a right to be careful, but I hoped that she'd eventually drop every single wall with me.

Sometimes, it was more comfortable being vulnerable with somebody who was just as terrified as I was.

CHAPTER 34

Kenzie

A FEW MONTHS AGO DURING THE HOLIDAYS...

"*Y*ou're fired, Mackenzie. Go collect your things from your desk."

I was sitting in the office of my boss, Keith Maxfield, getting ready to go over the morning schedule of prospective buyers coming in that day.

It wasn't something I'd expected him to say, especially not since I'd had to kick him in the balls yesterday for trying to assault me.

My blood ran cold at the thought of being without a job at the holidays. Especially my primary, full-time work. New York was so expensive that I'd be broke within a week, and nobody would be hiring this close to Christmas.

"Why?" I asked. "Is this about yesterday?"

I would have left if I could have. Keith was a prick, and I'd been fighting off his advances since I came to work here. In fact, it might be the reason I got the position in the first place.

Yesterday, he'd gone much too far by groping at me in places that never saw the light of day very often.

It had hurt, and I'd been fed up. Unable to stop him without a struggle, I'd resorted to the only way I know of to get him to let go.

"Of course not," he answered in a snotty voice. "I forgive you for losing control."

I wasn't stupid. It was his way of telling me that my story would never be believed. He was well-known in the art industry, and I was a nobody, a woman he could fondle and get away with it.

"Nobody is here, Keith. And we both know the truth. You're pissed that I put your balls in your throat because you couldn't keep your hands to yourself."

"Now, Mackenzie, we know that isn't true," he said in an annoyingly calm manner.

"Fuck off, Keith," I told him as my body trembled with anger.

I stood and dropped the schedule on his desk.

"No hard feelings, Mackenzie?" he queried.

When I got to the door I turned around and shot him a furious stare. "There are plenty of hard feelings, you jerk. I'm losing my job because you couldn't have your way. I get it."

I'd been through this routine plenty of times in my life, but to have it happen now was a nightmare.

"Mackenzie, you know you spent half of your day talking to your mother on the phone. I'm letting you go because you aren't a productive employee."

I pulled open the door as I said, "My mother is dead, you asshole."

I slammed the door behind me, and it echoed in the halls as my heels clicked on the tile while I made my way to my desk.

I *never* talked on the phone. The only one I spoke to on the phone was Paige, and we rarely talked these days since she was busy starting her career. But when my best friend and I talked, it was never on company time.

I drew a deep breath, and then let it out slowly as I searched my desk, looking for anything I wanted before I hightailed it out the door.

I'll make it. I just need to find the strength to keep trying.

I left the office only to hit the cold, New York air. It was snowing, so we were going to see a white Christmas. Not that it meant much to me.

I didn't care about the holidays. Never had. All I wanted was to live through the season without ending up homeless.

CHAPTER 35

Dane

"What in the hell do you mean that you aren't coming!" Sebastian bellowed into the phone.

I held the device away from my ear for a few seconds before I spoke. "It's a fairly simple concept," I explained patiently. "I'm not getting on my jet, therefore, you won't see me over the holidays."

I knew Sebastian had a fiancée, and the last thing I wanted to do was ruin his newfound happiness. I was going to stay on my island this year and miss the awkwardness of being with two happy couples.

I wasn't in a good place, and my art was suffering.

Maybe I had the holiday blues, but I knew without a doubt that I'd be the wet blanket to anybody's holiday cheer.

"You suck, Dane," Sebastian rumbled. "Paige really wants to meet you."

"You plan on being married to her for a while, right?"

"Forever, dammit!"

187

"Then I'll meet her when we get together again."

"Do you really want to be on that island all alone at the holidays?" he questioned.

No. No, I actually didn't, but I was getting used to being solo. It was preferable to feeling like I was ruining anybody's holiday. I didn't care about the holidays. I hadn't since the year I'd lost my dad. "Yes," I said through gritted teeth.

I hated saying no to either of my brothers, but this year, I had to.

I was fucking mopey and depressed. They'd thank me if they knew how much sadness seemed to hang around me like a thick fog.

"What can I do to make you fly home?" Sebastian queried.

"I *am* home. Denver has never been home to me."

"Are you going to be okay?" Sebastian asked in a rough voice.

"Yeah. I will." The last thing I wanted was for either of them to be worried about me.

I'm fine alone. I'll get used to it.

I made an excuse and hung up the phone with Sebastian, knowing my holidays were definitely not going to be merry at all.

CHAPTER 36

Kenzie

THE PRESENT...

"Today was amazing," I told Dane as he handed me a glass of white wine.

It seemed like the appropriate drink since we were sampling the hot tub that Dane had in the master bathroom of the suite. We probably could have hosted a Jacuzzi party since the tub was big enough for a large gathering. But I was glad to have him to myself, especially since we were both naked.

Letting the warm jets soothe my tension seemed so decadent. I was actually doing something to just relax and unwind.

It was something I wasn't used to, but my body seemed to appreciate it.

Dane slid back into the spa with something that was probably a little stronger than my wine. "You liked the turtles?" he asked.

We'd seen so many varieties of fish that I had them confused, but I'd never forget the wonder of one of those giant turtles flying by in front of my face.

"It shocked me," I admitted. "But in a good way. It's the most incredible thing I've ever done."

"You've been deprived," he pointed out.

I shrugged. "It made me very appreciative of the fun things I do here."

"Are you trying to say I'm jaded," he teased.

I looked up at him, astonished by his mischievous grin. "Not jaded," I observed. "But nothing is really new for you since you've done it all."

"Not anymore. I can see everything from your eyes."

"Oh, my God!" I said with surprise. "You actually have the most adorable dimple when you smile like that. I've never seen it before."

He reached up a hand and smoothed it over his face. "I hate it," he said.

I scooted closer to him and touched a hand to his face. "I love it," I told him earnestly. "It makes you more approachable."

"Okay. Then maybe I love it, too," he answered with a bigger smile.

"You *should* love it. It's so cute."

I was surprised that I'd never seen that adorable dent on his face, but Dane had never smiled quite so broadly before. I wanted to see that mark every day of my life from now on.

"I used to get teased in high school. My buddies said I was pretty."

I had a hard time imagining Dane as *pretty*, but his friends probably loved to torment him about the tiny dimple in his lower cheek. "I'm sure they were just jealous. It's rather breathtaking when you smile."

"That's not exactly how I want to take your breath away," he grumbled.

I put my wine down beside the tub and scooted closer to him. He snaked an arm around my waist and deposited me on his lap.

There was nothing I didn't love about being close to him. He'd been right beside me all day, especially in the water. Since I couldn't swim, he never left my side. I was a quick study since I loved the water, but even though I was wearing a life jacket, he always had a protective hand on me.

I turned and straddled him. Then I put my arms around him. "Thank you for all of this."

"For what?"

"For bringing me to Hawaii so I could see my best friend get married. For taking me wherever I wanted to go. For gifting me the beautiful dresses, and for the most beautiful jewelry I've ever owned." I knew he hated being out in public, but he seemed to get more and more comfortable with it every day.

He shrugged. "It's not like it's any big sacrifice."

"It's a big deal to me," I said softly. "Do you know I've never even been in a hot tub?"

He grinned. "What's the verdict?"

"It feels fantastic. Had I known how nice it was, I might have borrowed the one by the pool at home."

Home? Was the island becoming home to me?

"Sorry," I mumbled. "It's your home."

Dane put his drink next to mine and wrapped his arms around my waist. "It's your home. It's where you live. I want you to be at home there."

Tears flooded my eyes as I looked at his earnest expression. Dane meant every word he said, and the thoughtfulness of his words were devastating to my soul.

"I've never really *had* a home," I said tearfully. "I've never really belonged anywhere."

Every lonely moment of my past was overwhelming me. I'd never really thought about it until I actually said it, but I felt like I'd always been waiting to find out exactly where I'd finally feel like I was home. That had never happened...until now.

Home wasn't about the island or his house. It was about *Dane*. It felt like home because I felt like I belonged with him.

"What about when you lived with Paige?" he asked in a husky voice.

"It was good, but we hardly ever saw each other, and I knew it was going to end. I knew she'd be gone the moment she graduated. She had a future all planned out. And it didn't include a rundown apartment in Cambridge."

"You belong with me," Dane stated. "You always have. I think I was always just waiting for you, Kenzie."

He stroked his hands up and down the bare skin of my back, and I rested my head on his shoulder. "I feel that way, too," I confessed. "Is that crazy?"

"Possibly," he joked. "But I guess our neuroses complement each other."

I laughed, my heart so light it could probably float away. "I guess we'll just be a little bit nuts together."

"Always together," he vowed.

Thinking about a lifetime with Dane was something I couldn't completely contemplate, and I had to be realistic. It would *not* last forever, but I was going to enjoy every moment I got.

We hadn't really known each other that long. I'd fallen head-over-heels for him, but I couldn't guarantee he was ever going to return that emotional commitment. But it was a risk I was ready to take. I'd rather give him everything than to know I hadn't jumped into our relationship with all of my heart. My life was all about *trying*, and I was going to give this thing with Dane my best shot. If it didn't work out, I'd be devastated. But if I didn't let go of my insecurities, I'd never know what could have been.

"What happened between you and Britney?" I asked. Maybe it was none of my business, but since we were spilling secrets, I wanted to know.

"Paige told you," he guessed.

"She did. But she doesn't know the whole story. She doesn't know how it happened or what you wanted."

"It was a mistake," he told me. "I was missing human company, and she fulfilled a need."

"Sex?" I asked.

"Yeah."

"Did it help?"

"Not really. It just made me realize that not just anybody would be enough to help me shake off the emptiness. I just felt more alone."

I couldn't imagine what it had been like for him to isolate himself. "Social isolation isn't good for you. I've read articles that say it's dangerous."

"I know. I think I was on a slippery slope. When I didn't go home for the holidays, I knew I was in trouble. I just didn't know who to talk to, and I didn't want my brothers to worry that I was losing my mind."

"Did you think they didn't want you?"

"Some of it was just me. I know my brothers wanted me to celebrate the holidays with them, but I was just too far into my own shell. I didn't want to ruin anybody else's Christmas."

"Dane, that's not reality. They love you."

"I think I was losing track of what was real. I have Theo and Emilee, but I rarely see them. And I didn't even have Picasso to talk to. I think losing him was the beginning of the down-hill slide."

"Picasso?"

"My potcake dog. It's a mixed breed that inhabits some parts of the Caribbean. He got hit by a car when I was home for the holidays. He didn't make it."

"What was he like?"

"Sometimes he was a pain in the ass, but he was *my* pain in the ass. He was smart and would listen to me without interrupting," he said dryly. "I got him when I moved to my island, and he was around for several years until he got killed."

I knew that death had to have affected Dane pretty profoundly. The dog was really all he had. Maybe I'd never had a pet of my own, but losing something or someone he loved when he was so alone had to be a crushing blow.

"Have you ever thought of adopting another one?"

"No. He was unique."

"That doesn't mean you can't find another one just as unique. It would never replace him, but you can have another without trying to replace him."

"I wasn't really open to the idea before, but I might be ready to get another dog," he said thoughtfully.

"I think it would be nice to give another one a home."

"Then you can pick one out this time," he said with a little more enthusiasm.

"I've never had a pet," I shared. "I like dogs, but I could never get one. I couldn't afford it."

"Then we'll go look at some when we get back."

I was worried about Dane, so I asked, "Do you feel better being out in public again? I think you've spent enough time in solitary confinement."

"I can't say I'm completely comfortable with it," he admitted. "But yeah, I knew it needed to happen before I went bat-shit crazy on my own. I just wasn't sure how to do it on my own. Meeting you has changed me, Kenzie. I'm more comfortable in my own skin."

I hoped he was right. I didn't want to force him to rejoin society, but I *did* want to see him happy again. He had either been depressed, or at a high risk of depression. He'd gone from an active, normal high school graduate, to complete and total isolation. There had to be psychological effects, but he seemed to be adjusting well to being out in public again. It would take time, but I swore I'd eventually see him happy, and able to go anywhere he wanted.

I'd always been a loner, but I'd had social contact at work, and I'd had roommates and a small circle of casual friends to talk to.

Dane really hadn't had anybody except the occasional contact with Theo and Emilee.

"I think you need to spend more time with your brothers. They love you, and I know they've been worried about you."

"I'm here now," he rumbled.

"I know. I just want you to be happy."

"I *am* happy, Kenzie," he said huskily as he tightened his arms around my waist. "But I get it. Eventually, I think the isolation would have made me crazy."

"I'm glad we're here," I told him as I wrapped my legs around his waist.

Dane seemed to be coming out of his shell in public, and being in the company of people he trusted was the best thing for him right now.

"Me, too," he said, his hands moving to my rear.

I looked down into his gorgeous brown eyes, and I was lost. I saw so many shadows in there, and I wished I knew everything he'd gone through to make him so wary.

Heat flooded my body as I held his gaze. My body craved him, and it wasn't going to settle for anything less. "Fuck me, Dane," I said in a voice filled with longing.

"I plan on it," he answered. Then he put a hand in my hair and pulled my mouth down to his.

CHAPTER 37

Kenzie

I knew I was in trouble as soon as his mouth started to devour mine.

I was letting myself sink too deep into Dane.

But I was helpless to resist the allure.

With him, it was all or nothing. Emotions flowed too freely for it to be any other way.

For once in my life, I had to take a risk. I cared about Dane far too much to *not* take my chance to experience something wonderful.

I moaned against his mouth as he settled me more comfortably on his lap. Everything about him and the situation was erotic. Warm water licked my skin, and Dane was so raw and powerful that I shuddered as he finally released his hold on my mouth and stroked his powerful hand up and down my back.

Every touch was magnified, every emotion so strong that I was collapsing under the weight of feeling so many things at once.

His hard cock was pressing for entry against my core, and I couldn't wait. Dane must have sensed my impatience, or he felt the same urgency, because he hoisted himself and my body up until we were sitting on the tile beside the tub.

He stretched and snatched up a condom that I assumed he'd laid on the flat surface before he'd gotten in with me.

"Hold onto me," he demanded.

I wrapped my arms around his body while he expertly rolled on the rubber.

Then, without warning, he was suddenly adjusting my body to take him.

"God, yes," I moaned against his shoulder.

I needed this.

I needed him.

Being part of Dane was the perfect cure for every bit of loneliness I'd ever experienced, and I'd known that emotion profoundly for most of my life.

"Take what you want, Kenzie." His lower baritone hummed against my ear. "I'm yours."

God, I only wished that could be true, but I was going to savor the moment, wallow in the pleasure and safety that I felt when I was with him.

Dane helped me, his fingers biting into my ass as he guided my hips to ride him.

I leaned back so I could see his beautiful, chocolate-brown eyes. The moment our gazes met, everything was more intense. I put my hands on his shoulders as I admitted, "I just want...you."

"You have me," he grunted, his eyes flashing fire as our bodies moved together. "You'll always have me."

My head fell back, the pleasure of the moment way too intense.

"Don't," Dane growled. "Look at me, Kenzie."

I shook my head, but Dane reached for the back of my head and forced it up until I was looking down at him again.

"See me, Kenzie," he said in an animalistic, guttural voice.

My heart clenched as I got lost in his gaze. He looked tormented and vulnerable at that moment, and all I wanted to do was soothe him, make him understand that the last thing I wanted was to hurt him.

I kept my stare on him, knowing he could probably see everything in my eyes.

My joy.

My fear.

My insecurities.

And maybe, the intense love that I felt for him.

"I see you," I finally answered with a hungry moan, my hips rising and falling as I took him inside me over and over again. "Dane, I have to come," I whimpered. "It's too much."

The intense pressure in my belly was beginning to unfurl, and I was coming unglued.

His hand moved down to where our bodies were joined, and his thumb started punishing circles on my clit.

Strong.

Firm.

And so damn stimulating that I felt my orgasm rushing toward me like a perfect storm.

I tightened my legs around his waist, moving harder and faster against him, taking his cock in shorter, stronger, more furious movements.

"Kenzie," Dane groaned. He was rushing toward his own release.

I tumbled over the edge, but I couldn't stop looking at his face. He was beautiful to me, his pleasure totally unveiled.

His eyes turned darker, his facial muscles strained.

"Yes," I screamed. "Come with me."

"There was never any doubt of that," he rasped, his eyes still locked with mine.

My nails dug into his shoulders, but he seemed to relish it as my violent climax milked him into an orgasm.

Dane fell back, and I went with him, my body sprawled over him as we both tried to recover our breath.

Goose bumps were forming on my skin, and I was shivering, but I knew my reaction had nothing to do with being cold.

The bathroom was warm, and the hot water we'd exited made it even warmer.

"You're cold," Dane said, quickly sitting up, getting rid of the condom, and pulling us back into the warm water.

"I'm not cold," I protested. Not that I minded being back in the jetted tub.

"You're shivering," he argued.

"An appropriate reaction after what just happened," I teased, reaching for my wine at the side of the spa.

I settled beside him, nestled along the side of his body, my head on his shoulder. I took a sip of my wine, willing the drink to calm my body down.

Dane reached for his drink and downed it in one large gulp before placing it back on the tile.

I was grateful for the fact that he'd thought of protection. We'd stopped at a clinic after our outing earlier today, and I'd had an implant inserted in my arm. It would last for years, but since I was in the middle of my cycle, I had to use other protection. Once my period started, which would probably be very soon, I'd be safe.

"I'm glad this shit shakes you up as much as it does me," he finally answered.

I snorted. "You want me to be a messy puddle on your tile?"

"No. I want you to feel everything as much as I do," he confessed. "It would suck to be in this all alone."

"You're not alone," I told him.

"Neither are you, Kenzie. Never again," he stated forcefully.

Nothing good ever lasted for me, but I was comforted by his declaration. "Are we ever going to get out of this tub?" I asked jokingly. "Not that I don't love it, but I think I'm starting to prune."

Dane stood up, and I drooled over his powerful body as he said, "Then we're out of here. I'm ready to take you to bed."

He held out his hand, and I clasped it. My legs were still weak, and I was grateful that he pulled me out of the tub.

"I have my own bed," I told him as I waited patiently for him to dry my body. His touch was gentle, and I almost felt...cared for. It was a novel sensation since nobody had ever really taken a caretaker role in my life.

"You're sleeping with me," he stated.

I took a towel from the warming rack and started to pat him down once he was done with me.

The moment I was finished, Dane scooped me up and carried me toward his bedroom.

Not that I wanted to, but there would be no escaping Dane tonight.

Luckily, that was just fine with me.

CHAPTER 38

Kenzie

"*Y*ou look beautiful," I told Paige two days later at her wedding reception.

The entire day had been magical, from the breakfast this morning to the wedding that had taken place in the afternoon.

"So do you," Paige said sincerely.

Paige had purchased the dresses for me and her sister-in-law, Eva. We'd both stood up for her, right across from the Walker brothers.

I had to admit, she had amazing taste. I adored the black formal she'd picked out for Eva and me. The wedding had been small, but classy. She and Sebastian had said their vows on a spacious patio that had been transformed into what seemed like a gorgeous garden beside the sea. The weather had cooperated spectacularly, and there had been no reason to move inside for her backup plan.

The reception was being held outdoors in another fairy tale atmosphere beside the ocean. White tents had been set up for the drinks, food, and seating area. But most attendees were seated outside since it was a beautiful evening.

"I can't believe you're a married woman," I told her. "But that wedding dress confirms it. Not to mention the fact that I saw it happen just a few hours ago."

Paige was truly stunning in a long, traditional white dress. The only thing breaking tradition was that it had very little material in the back, and it was strapless. I remembered the moment when Sebastian had seen her walking down the aisle toward him. His face had lit up like a Christmas tree, and his gaze had never wavered from that moment until the end of the ceremony. He was in love with her. I was certain of that, and it made my heart sing.

"It feels good," she admitted as she sipped on her flute of champagne. "But it definitely still seems surreal. How did I get so lucky?"

"You deserve this," I said sternly. Paige's life hadn't been easy. She needed all the happiness she could get.

"Everybody deserves love," she replied. "But I think I really did luck out with Sebastian. He loves me as much as I love him. And he doesn't try to change who I am. Yeah, he's protective, but in a good way. He only gets impossible occasionally."

I watched her eyes scan the guests until they landed on her brand new husband, who was chatting with his brothers on the opposite side of the venue. It was evident the minute she found Sebastian. Her face softened, and her eyes glazed over with adoration.

"Only occasionally?" I teased.

"The Walker men are definitely used to getting what they want," she said with mock irritation. "Is Dane the same way?"

I stopped to think about her question for a moment before I answered, "Yeah. Sometimes. He's probably one of the nicest guys I've ever met, but he has his stubborn moments."

Paige rolled her eyes. "I think it's a prerequisite to being a Walker."

I laughed, nearly choking on champagne. "Maybe so," I said as I finally recovered.

"How are things going with Dane?" she asked curiously.

"Good," I told her. "Sometimes maybe too good. It's almost scary."

Paige lifted a brow. "What do you mean?"

"I mean that I think I'm falling in love with him," I confessed unhappily. "Or maybe I'm already there. Dane is too sweet. Too thoughtful. Too hot. He's just a little too much of everything. He understands me, which I find terrifying."

Paige reached out and put a comforting hand on my arm. "You're scared. Why?"

I gave her a dubious look. "You know why. Nothing good is going to last for me."

"Kenzie, there's nothing wrong with finding somebody to love. I think you and Dane both deserve it, and I know he cares about you. It's obvious," she said as she dropped her hand.

"I'm scared," I confessed with a sigh.

"I don't blame you," Paige answered in a soft, comforting voice. "Nothing good has ever happened to you, but that doesn't mean it won't or that it can't. Don't let your past determine your present. I did that with Sebastian, and it almost destroyed us. If Dane cares, let him love you."

"I'm not sure I have much of a choice right now. I love him," I said.

"But the trust is hard to give?" she asked.

"For me, yes. It's nothing he did. It's like you said...my past."

"I get it," Paige answered. "Maybe if you give it some time, he'll prove that he's trustworthy."

"He shouldn't *have* to prove himself to me, Paige," I said sadly. "He's been nothing but kind. Okay, he might be stubborn and bossy sometimes, but never in an abusive way. It's more because he's worried about me. I'm not used to that."

Paige smiled. "Believe me, it's easy to get used to it."

I grinned back at her. "I know. It's pretty damn addictive."

"You two are good for each other," Paige determined. "Just let things happen."

I nodded. "I already decided I was going to do that. I want to experience life instead of running away from it. Dane is worth trying my best to lose the demons in my past."

"I know it won't be easy, but I'd love to see you happy," Paige said quietly.

"I am happy," I said. "But for me, that's also scary."

"Because it's not something you're used to, and I hate that," Paige replied. "Life has been a nightmare for you, and none of it was your fault."

I shrugged. "Fate."

"Bad luck so far," Paige corrected. "You haven't found your fate yet. But I see a big guy over there watching you like he's about to change your destiny."

My eyes went from Paige to Dane, and I was startled by the intensity of his stare. He was watching me from across the patio. "God, I hate it when he does that," I said in a loud whisper.

"Why?"

"Because it makes me want to be with him. It's like a homing beacon for me."

Paige chuckled. "Let's go. I have to find my groom anyway."

I nodded as she started to find her way through the crowd with me following behind her.

She moved next to Sebastian, and Dane wrapped an arm around my waist and pulled me to his side possessively. "Missed you," he said in my ear.

"I was right across the patio," I teased.

"Doesn't matter," he said huskily, his eyes focused on my face. "I still missed you."

I flushed, feeling my skin heat as he continued to stare at me. "I missed you, too," I admitted.

I wasn't used to this kind of attention from any male, and getting it from a man like Dane made me flustered as hell.

When we were together alone, I was comfortable. But in company, I was feeling vulnerable. Public shows of affection were awkward because I had no idea how to act.

In an instant, his eyes caught mine, and our gazes held. It only took me moments to forget there was anybody else in close proximity to us.

"Kiss me," he demanded in a graveled voice. "I know the wedding and this reception make you nervous, but—"

He didn't get another word out of his mouth. I wrapped my arms around his neck and pulled that glorious mouth down to mine in a heartbeat.

I could see his own discomfort, and all I wanted to do was make him forget about the crowd. He enthusiastically took control, kissing me so thoroughly that I swore my toes curled.

When he finally raised his head, he grinned down at me. "That was unexpected," he rumbled.

"You wanted it," I reminded him.

"Oh, I didn't say I didn't want it. I did. Desperately. But I know the wealthy crowd makes you feel awkward."

I shook my head. "Not anymore," I corrected. "Not with you here."

Dane made me feel normal, and I reveled in that. I wasn't used to fancy parties, or trying to make casual conversation with strangers. But Dane made it feel right.

"Good," he said. "Did I tell you how beautiful you look?"

"Only a hundred times," I said with an even wider grin. "Probably as many times as I've told you how incredibly hot you look in a tuxedo."

I swore he actually blushed a little himself as I stood back and surveyed him. Dane *did* look smoking hot in his formal attire. His black tux was perfect, the jacket lovingly encasing his broad shoulders and ripped body. His hair was just as unruly as ever, but I'd clipped it before he'd dressed, and he'd been able to tame it some.

My heartrate accelerated as I took in the whole package of Dane, every detail ingrained in my mind. In everyday circumstances, he was already gorgeous. But in a tuxedo, he was breathtaking.

"I think you two need to get a room," Sebastian said jokingly.

"Have one," Dane grunted.

"Then maybe you need to find it," Sebastian answered. "You're making me look bad. I'm the one who's supposed to be salivating over my bride."

"You already are," Trace said as he put his arm around Eva. "I think maybe you and your bride need to find your room as soon as possible."

I bit back a smile. I'd never seen a groom as attentive and loving as Sebastian. He could put every other newlywed out there to shame.

"I can't," Sebastian complained goodheartedly. "We have a cake to cut."

"Then go do it," Trace suggested. "I've been eyeing that damn cake since we got here."

I'd seen the cake on the way in, and it was extraordinary. It had four tiers, and was painstakingly decorated with a multitude of different, delicate flowers which were all edible.

"I'm kind of craving it, too," Paige said. "Sebastian and I tried so much cake that I'm surprised we recognized what we wanted."

"They were all starting to taste the same," Sebastian said drily.

Paige nailed him playfully in the stomach. "They did *not* all taste the same, and ours is perfect."

"*Everything* today is perfect," Sebastian said in a quiet voice, but loud enough so I heard him. "You belong to me, now."

Paige pulled his head down for a brief kiss, then took him by the hand. "It's perfect for me, too. Let's go cut the cake."

I only sniffled a little bit as the bride and groom went to conquer their massive cake together, both of them so certain of a love that would last forever.

My best friend was going to be loved for the rest of her life. That was something worth crying about.

CHAPTER 39

Kenzie

I stared up at the beautiful full moon with my toes scrunched in the sand, and the peaceful sound of waves hitting the shoreline.

I sighed, a heartfelt sound that felt like it was released from my soul. "It's so beautiful here," I told Dane.

We'd snuck out of the reception for a few minutes to take a stroll along the beach. I'd slipped off my heels and left them near the stairs that led back to the reception area.

"Do you want to stay here for a while?" Dane asked.

"No. Not unless you do. I kind of miss the island, and we have a new dog to find."

I knew the last thing Dane probably wanted to do was hang out here after his family was all gone.

"Then we'll go home tomorrow," he answered, squeezing my hand. "We can celebrate our birthdays there."

Home!

The word had a nice ring to it.

"I'll make you a cake," I promised. "And something special for dinner."

"I wish I could promise you the same, but I think we'll have to share the cake. I've never tried to bake anything before."

"I'm okay with that," I said in a rush.

He chuckled. "Yeah, I figured you would be."

"It's been nice to see Hawaii, though. Thank you."

Dane wrapped his arms around my waist and pulled my body back against his chest. "We didn't really see much."

"I did. Remember? I've never been anywhere."

"We can travel more often," Dane suggested. "I can show you the world."

I leaned back against him, completely relaxed. "I'd like that when we have time."

"Make a list of where you want to go, and we'll work on it," he grumbled into my ear.

I laughed. "I'm not sure if all those places will fit into one list. I've always wanted to travel."

"We have time," he replied.

I didn't think about how long it would take to complete a list. I didn't have to. I was just enjoying the moment. But I loved him even more for agreeing to venture anywhere in the world for me. "We'll see," I answered noncommittally.

"Why the hesitation?"

"I know you hate to travel," I said honestly.

"I don't hate it anymore," he revealed. "Not when you're with me."

My heart clenched, and pesky tears formed in my eyes. Dane laid me bare when he said those things. "You aren't feeling self-conscious anymore?"

I felt him shrug. "No. Not really. I was even thinking of getting a second home, maybe in Denver."

My heart almost flew out of my chest. "Really? I think that would be fantastic."

"We could go back and forth between houses. Maybe spend the summer in Colorado and the winter at Walker's Cay."

God, how he'd changed. "Your brothers would be ecstatic."

His arms tightened around my waist. "And what about you?" he asked hesitantly. "Would you be happy? You'd get to be with Paige more often."

"I'm totally willing to travel back and forth with you."

Dane was finally ready to embrace civilization, and I couldn't have been more excited. "I'm glad you finally realized how gorgeous you are, and that you have nothing to feel awkward about."

"Because of you, Kenzie. That's why all of this is bearable."

"I don't think so," I denied. "I just think you're ready."

I was relieved, no matter how this change had come about. Dane needed to be part of the world. Maybe he'd tolerated isolation, and sometimes he seemed to like to be alone. But deep down inside, he wanted to be with other people, especially his family.

"I can't say I'm completely ready. It's going to take more time. But I don't want you to feel isolated. I know how hard that can be."

"I haven't been on the island long enough that it bothers me. And I'm not alone. I have you."

"I never want you to get to that point," he said roughly.

"Do you want to be somewhere else?"

"Yeah. I think I do. At least for part of the year. I hate feeling so disconnected, and even though Trace and Sebastian can be complete and total assholes, I miss them. They're all I really have left since Mom and Dad are gone."

A tear trickled down my cheek because I couldn't hold it back. Dane so deserved to have his family close to him again.

I slipped out of his arms, realizing how long we'd been gone from the reception. "I guess we should get back."

Our peaceful walk was ending, and the patio of the resort was in sight.

"I guess," Dane agreed. "If we don't, Sebastian will be gone. Probably Trace, too. After the cake, neither one looked interested in anything else except their wives."

I pushed my hair back behind my ear. My styling job was probably a disaster after the time we'd spent out on the beach, but it had been worth it.

"Sebastian and Paige are leaving tonight," I said as I walked along beside Dane. The beach wasn't lit, but the lights of the resort and the full moon had guided us just fine.

"I know. But we'll see them again soon. My main goal in life right now is to make you happy."

I stopped, making us both halt since I had a strong grip on Dane's hand. "I am happy," I told him emphatically. "I've never been happier than I am right now."

Dane made me ecstatic. I wish I had the words to tell him how much he meant to me, and how he'd changed my life. But I didn't.

"If you're happy now, wait until we get back to the suite," he said in a sexy, low, and very masculine tone.

I shivered at the thought of what he might have planned. But I didn't have to be screwing him to feel our connection. However, I'd probably never argue if he wanted to get me naked. I needed him as much as he needed me. Most likely, way more.

"Thank you for this," I said as we continued walking.

"For what?"

"Bringing me here. Showing me some of the island."

After our snorkeling outing, Paige and Sebastian had hosted two more days filled with sightseeing. And one evening at a traditional luau. Every moment had been sweet for me. Dane had attended every festivity, getting less and less reserved as we went along with the wedding events.

"You already thanked me," he reminded me.

"A while ago," I protested. "Now I'm thanking you for the last few days. It's been incredible."

"We'll come back eventually. I have a place in Kauai."

"What's it like?"

"Expensive," he said in a mischievous voice. "It's a resort."

"Another investment?" I joked.

"Yes. You'll love it."

"I'm sure I will," I said.

"We'll go there after we see more of the world."

That moment seemed so perfect, being able to dream about a future. Sure, I was scared, but I was determined to take Paige's advice and not let my past encroach on my future.

Dane was worth any risk I had to take to have a possible future with him.

Honestly, I needed him, and I hoped he continued to need me, too.

"I'll be right there," I told Dane as we reached the bottom of the stairs that led back up to the reception. I had to put my shoes back on, which meant I had to do a ton of tiny straps.

I waved him toward the stairs as I started securing all the straps.

He climbed the stairs, calling over his shoulder, "I'll be saying goodbye to my brothers."

"Go on. I'm on my way. Just give me a sec."

I sat down on the cement to keep my balance while I struggled with the pieces of leather.

In moments, I was rising again, and testing my heels on the cement.

"It will do," I said under my breath, preparing to go find Dane, his family, and Paige.

What happened after I was done occurred so quickly that I never had a chance to scream.

A warning chill coursed down my spine as I tried to speak against the hand that had slapped against my mouth.

Instantly, I knew exactly who was keeping me quiet and frozen to one spot.

He was familiar to me, and so was the terror I was feeling as he held me captive.

"Make one fucking stupid move and you're dead, bitch," the gravelly, hoarse voice said in my ear. He was holding me against his dirty, smelly body, the sharp point of a knife tearing into my skin.

Oh, Jesus! How could he possibly be here?

Nausea rose up in my throat, but I tried not to panic.

I knew his unpleasant voice, and I recognized his repulsive scent.

My time was up. I'd finally been caught.

There was no mistaking this man and his hatred for me.

I'd been living with it as long as I could remember.

I looked up to the patio as he dragged me away, my heart breaking as I realized I was never going to see Dane again.

CHAPTER 40

Dane

"I can't find Kenzie," I told my brothers when I came back to the patio. I'd gone looking for her twice, but she wasn't on the beach.

I cursed myself for leaving her at the bottom of the steps alone, but we were in a safe area, and I hadn't been far away.

The reception had slowly cleared out, and the only ones left on the patio were Sebastian, Paige, Trace, and Eva. I'd been searching for Kenzie for over an hour, hoping she'd just slipped away to the bathroom or another place where she could catch some privacy.

"Where in the hell did she go?" Trace asked gruffly.

I ran a hand through my hair in frustration. "I don't fucking know. We took a walk on the beach to get away for a few minutes. The last time I saw her she was putting her shoes on to come back up here."

"I haven't seen her since earlier tonight," Paige said, sounding alarmed. "I would have seen her if she'd come back to the reception. I assumed she'd gone back to your suite."

"She didn't," I confirmed. "I have the room key."

"We need to search for her," Eva said in a concerned voice.

"I've been up and down the beach, and I've been searching every public room in this venue," I growled, pissed off at myself because I hadn't waited for her.

"Then we'll have to spread out. And we should call the police," Eva said.

"Wait!" Paige exclaimed. "I think I might know what happened."

"What?" I asked in a graveled voice. "Tell me." I was fucking out of my mind with worry.

"Did Kenzie tell you about her past?" Paige asked, her face white with fear.

"Crappy parents, and an equally dismal life? Yeah, she told me."

"Did she tell you about her parents? Did she tell you that her father has been trying to kill her for years now?"

"What are you talking about, Paige?" I asked as I stared at her troubled expression.

She sighed nervously. "Then she *didn't* tell you. That makes sense, because she thought he'd finally given up several years ago. But maybe he didn't."

"Her father is in prison. She told me that," I answered.

"Her mother actually *died* in prison, but I know Kenzie tries not to think about that. Both of her parents were junkies, and her mother contracted HIV. She died of AIDS while she was incarcerated. Kenzie never had *parents*. Just enemies."

I scrubbed my face, trying to comprehend what Paige was saying. "She didn't tell me that her father was homicidal," I confessed. "But what does that have to do with her disappearance now?"

"Paige's father is still alive, and he's been trying to get to her, even from jail. She testified against him, Dane. She outed everything about her parents right before she graduated from high school. She put them away. Kenzie was a witness to a vehicular murder her father committed near their apartment. A drug deal gone wrong. Her account as a witness was what cemented the case against her parents."

Christ! I'd known that Kenzie's life had been rough, but I hadn't realized just how much courage she'd actually had as a teenager. It would have been so damn easy for her to just go the same route as her parents, but she'd struggled to do the right thing. "And her father wanted her dead for snitching?"

Paige frowned. "He was part of an organized crime ring, the U.S. part of a Mexican drug cartel. A powerful one that operates internationally. Her father transported drugs. He could have been a wealthy man, even though he was a horrible person, but her parents snorted and shot up the profits. Money went missing during the bad drug deal, over a quarter of a million dollars. Her father assumed that Kenzie had taken it. But she didn't. There's no way she did."

I shuddered at the thought of members of a drug cartel chasing Kenzie down. They'd apparently wanted to shake her down for the money they assumed she stole.

"I know she didn't do it," Paige said gently. "Not only did she tell me so, but she wouldn't have had to live hand-to-mouth if she'd stashed the money."

"You said he gave up?" I asked Paige.

"Kenzie did nothing but run away from her enemies that her father sent after her. If they were onto her, she ran. But after we became roommates, they either couldn't find her, or the guys on the outside lost interest and moved on to other things."

"And her father?" I questioned gruffly.

"He hates her. He always has. She put him in prison, and in his mind, she took his money."

"I'm going to see where he is right now," Sebastian said as he walked to the other side of the patio, already dialing his phone as he moved.

Paige called out the information Sebastian needed, but she didn't move away from me.

"I'll hit the computer," Trace said, and then left to jog toward the elevator inside.

Only Eva and Paige stayed in place.

"Why didn't she tell me everything," I asked angrily. "I would have protected her better. I can't watch out for her if I don't understand everything that happened. I had no idea that she'd had to keep running for her life, and that her father wanted her dead."

"I'm sure she wanted to, but she was always ashamed of where she came from, Dane. Who wants to tell *anybody* that your father wants you dead?"

"It's not her fault," I exploded.

"Of course it isn't, but Kenzie has spent most of her life on the run or looking over her shoulder. Her father was powerful in organized crime, and she blew the whistle on him. I can only imagine how hard that must have been for her. And then the incident that left her scarred destroyed her. Her chance for a new life was gone, and she had to move back to a place that was familiar to her. Granted, she didn't go back to Boston, but Cambridge is close enough."

I was livid. Yeah, I was pissed at Kenzie for not telling me, but the majority of my anger was toward her son-of-a-bitch father for the things he'd done to Kenzie. Nobody who is trying to do the right thing should have to live like a hunted animal. "You think it's him, don't you?" I asked Paige.

Her expression was terrified as she answered, "I hope not, but I can't come up with another plausible explanation, Dane. I don't want it to be him, because I'm afraid he's out for revenge. Once whoever is helping him is convinced that Kenzie doesn't have his money, he'll kill her. These people don't mess around. One more dead body is nothing to them."

I couldn't think of anything that made more sense, either. Kenzie's purse was still where she stashed it, so she almost surely hadn't left willingly. "Fuck!" I cursed, feeling like I was wasting time. "We have to find her, Paige."

"Did she tell you that she was in love with you?" she asked softly.

My head jerked toward her. "She's what?"

"She loves you, Dane. I think you should know that."

My chest ached so damn badly that I couldn't breathe. "She does?"

Paige nodded. "I'm hoping you feel the same way."

"Of course I do. Hell, I'd die for Kenzie without a second thought."

I was still trying to take in the fact that Kenzie loved me. But I was assuming that Paige knew the truth.

"I should have told her," I said with regret. "I was so damn afraid of getting hurt because Kenzie has that power. I was afraid I cared too much. But that doesn't mean a damn thing now that she's gone."

I hated myself for not spilling my guts to her. I should have. At least she would have known that I was going to hunt for her until I dropped dead, or we found her.

"She was scared, Dane. Please understand it had nothing to do with you. It took me years to get her to tell me the whole story."

"All I ever wanted was to fucking make her life better," I confessed to Paige.

"It was better," Eva spoke up. "I could tell."

Paige nodded. "For the first time in her life, she wasn't looking over her shoulder. You changed that for her."

"Shit! Maybe she was too complacent," I considered.

"It's been years since anybody hunted her down. She thought it was finally over, but she still kept alert for the possibility."

"Do you think those bastards in California were after her because of her father?" I rasped.

"No," Paige replied. "I think Kenzie initially suspected they were, but they were after drug money. It was an unfortunate crime, but they weren't connected to her father."

Sebastian came running back just as Trace flew out the door.

"He's out," Trace announced. "Her father was released from prison a few days ago. He ended up getting vehicular manslaughter, so he was up for parole. Since he'd behaved in prison, they granted him his freedom."

"I was just going to say the same thing," Sebastian said.

"Fuck!" I exploded, feeling like I was in agony.

The bastard had scooped her out right from under me. If I had only known that she was in any kind of danger, I would have watched her like a hawk. "He has her," I said.

Everybody nodded. Nobody believed this was a coincidence, especially me.

"We'll find her," Sebastian promised. "I have my security guys starting to search already. We need to track down where he would go with her."

"My people are on it, too," Trace confirmed. "We'll find her, Dane."

I'll be fine alone. I'll get used to it.

The words of my mantra floated through my head, but I wasn't accepting it at all. I wouldn't just lay down and be okay with being alone. Not after Kenzie. "I won't be fine alone, and I'm not fucking getting used to it anymore," I growled. "I want her back."

"What do you mean?" Trace asked.

"I used to tell myself that I'd be okay on my own. I thought I'd get used to it. Every time I started to feel lonely, I consoled myself with those stupid damn words. But they aren't fucking working anymore. Not since Kenzie plowed into my life like a tornado. I want people. I want my family. And God help me, I have to have her."

"You were never alone, Dane," Sebastian uttered in a low tone. "We were always here."

"I didn't see that back when I was really hurting. I didn't see shit. But I can understand it now."

Trace frowned. "You better understand it. We fucking love you, brother."

Now that I had clarity, I knew they'd always loved me, but I'd been too consumed with my own problems that I'd never seen myself as anything except a hindrance to them. I wanted them to live their own lives, something that didn't really include me. But I didn't feel that way anymore. "I love you guys, too," I grumbled. "I'll explain later. Right now I have to find Kenzie. I love her. And I'm not going to lose her. I can't."

My gut was twisting at the thought of her being with somebody who wanted her dead.

Honestly, I didn't understand how anybody could hate Kenzie, but her father was one fucked up asshole.

"Sebastian and I will work with our security," Trace told me as my two brothers retreated into the hotel.

For the first time in my life, I wished I had security. I couldn't stand to be idle.

"I'll go help them," I told Eva and Paige.

"The two of us will stay together and search for her. Maybe somebody saw something," Paige said.

"Be careful," I warned. "If anything happened to either one of you, your husbands would be completely destroyed."

Paige laid her hand on my arm. "Nothing will happen. I have to try to help. I'm the reason my best friend was here in the first place. And I knew about her father. I should have let Trace put more security in place, but I didn't know he was free. I'm willing to bet that Kenzie didn't know, either."

I grabbed Paige's hand roughly. "Don't!" I told her urgently. "Don't blame yourself."

"I'll stop when you do," she challenged, sending me a pointed stare. "Blame isn't going to help the situation right now."

I got that. And I probably knew I needed to drop my own emotions to search for Kenzie. But it wasn't going to be easy. "I understand," I mumbled as I let go of her hand.

"I just want Kenzie back," Paige said tearfully. "I've been so busy this week. We didn't really get to spend any time together."

"Hey," I cautioned. "No blame. She isn't going to die, Paige." I was willing to do anything to save her.

She nodded, but a big fat tear plopped onto her cheek right before she turned away, disappearing quickly with Eva to keep up the search around the premises.

I sprinted to the door, and then was nothing but irritated when I had to wait for the elevator to take me to Trace's top floor suite.

"Don't give up, Kenzie. We're right behind you," I said in a hoarse whisper as the elevator doors slammed closed. "Whatever it takes, I'll find you."

Somehow, I'd locate her. I'd always been like a heat-seeking missile when she was around. I just hoped that connection didn't fail me now.

CHAPTER 41

Kenzie

I'd had plenty of nightmares about my father finding me one day, but the reality was nothing like the scary dream. It was worse.

"I told you, I don't know what happened to the money," I told him nervously.

I looked into the cold, hard face of my father, Victor Jordan, still unable to believe that he'd been my sperm donor.

He was emotionally vacant, and I couldn't recognize a single hint of softness for his daughter.

He hated me.

He always had.

From my earliest memories, he'd been a monster, and it hadn't changed as I'd grown up. My parents had tried to use me to smuggle their drugs into school, but I'd refused. Yeah, I'd taken a beating that had left me unconscious for an undetermined amount of time, but none of my classmates were going to overdose and die because of me.

"You expect me to believe that, you little bitch. Tell me where it is."

So he could kill me immediately afterward? Oh, hell no. Even if I knew where his money was, I wouldn't tell him.

I knew this game. I grew up on the streets. All I had to do was give him a location, and I'd get a bullet in the head. I wasn't really hoping to convince him that I hadn't stolen the money out of the car the day he'd killed a drug buyer. I was pretty much just stalling for time.

My cheek exploded as my father backhanded me so hard I hit the dirty floor of his hotel room. I saw stars for a moment before I opened my eyes.

We weren't far from the resort, but at the moment, it felt like a million miles away.

Dane had to be looking for me. I wished I had told him all of my history instead of leaving out the part about having a homicidal father.

I thought it was over. I never stopped being afraid that one of my father's mobsters would find me, but I thought they lost interest.

Had I known that my father had been paroled, I would have been more careful. I wouldn't have left anything to chance.

I should have told Dane that I love him.

Because I did.

With all of my heart.

"You can hit me all you want," I said stoically. "It won't change the fact that I can't lead you to the money."

My suspicions were that it had been spent a long time ago. There had been other junkies and dealers on the street that day, people who wouldn't have hesitated to swipe satchels full of money.

"Then I'll find another way to get what I deserve," he said maliciously.

I propped my upper body up, using the bedframe to support me. "How?" I asked, dreading his new idea.

"You were with Dane Walker, one of the billionaire Walkers. Does he want you back?"

I panicked, afraid to draw Dane anywhere near this crazy bastard. "No. I'm only an employee. He can find another assistant."

My father hadn't aged well in prison, and his expression was crazed. He looked the same, but older. Much older. And he still scared the shit out of me.

"I'm thinking you're lying, girl," he said as he held up the 9mm pistol, leveling it near my temple. "Look at you in your fancy dress, and where else would you get jewelry. Are those stones real?"

I cringed at the way he was eyeing my birthday present from Dane. "I'm not lying, and I bought this cheap costume jewelry at a thrift store," I argued, knowing I'd die before I told him what Dane really meant to me.

He'd twist it and use it.

If he knew that Dane would be worried, he'd use me to get anything he could get.

The only thing I could think about at the moment was my need to protect Dane. My life had brought me here to finally confront the man I'd run from for so long. My father didn't have to tell me he wanted to see me dead. I already knew. I wasn't leaving this filthy room alive unless I could manage an escape, and my chances weren't looking very promising.

"If he thinks I know where you are, I could snatch him. His brothers would pay for his safe return," Victor mused.

"You wouldn't return him. You'd kill him," I said angrily.

No innocent victim who knew anything ever walked away from my father. He preferred not to leave witnesses. Luckily, I'd stayed alive, but I'd always feared this moment, the day that I'd have to face the father I'd betrayed.

Victor Jordan was ruthless, and I already knew this wasn't going to end well.

"You know me well, daughter," he said with an evil smirk.

Unfortunately, I knew *way too much* about him.

"I do," I answered simply. "And you can't kidnap a Walker. They're too high profile. You'd have police on your tail before you ever forced him into a car."

Victor hated the police, and I was hoping he'd back down. No such luck.

"Fuck the police," he ground out. "I'm smarter than they are, except for when my own family member rats me out."

"You killed somebody," I reminded him. "Do you think you deserved to go free?"

"Yes. I'm your father, but you never did have any respect for me."

I could have respected him if he hadn't loved hurting people so much, or if he'd wanted to get out of a criminal life. Maybe even if he'd had the capability to care about his daughter.

But this man didn't know how to love.

My father was pure evil.

"You tried to kill me. Several times," I said.

"You deserve to die," he said maniacally. "And you will. Nobody betrays me and lives to tell about it."

I swallowed the large lump in my throat. I knew I was going to die, but I wasn't going to beg him for anything, even my life. He'd never spare it, and I didn't want to bow down to him during the last moments I had on Earth.

"Do it," I instructed. "Just kill me."

"Not yet," he said. "I'll do it when I feel like it."

I knew I'd be taking a risk by challenging him, but I *did* know him well, and if I wanted something, he'd do the opposite of what I wanted. He was just twisted that way.

He leaned down and hauled me up by one arm, his hold so brutal I felt like my limb was going to snap.

"What are you doing?" I asked, trying to keep the fear out of my voice. He'd get too much pleasure out of that.

"Taking your freedom, just like you took mine."

He body slammed me to make me move, and I stumbled toward the bathroom.

I shielded my head as he forced me into the bathroom, knowing I was going to fall.

My protective measure didn't help much. I could hear my head slamming against the bathtub.

I wasn't fast enough to get to my feet. I laid there for a few moments, trying to get my brain to work.

I listened as he locked the door from the outside. Had he bought the lock and put it in place before I'd arrived? I had no idea, but it would be pretty strange to have an outside locking bathroom door.

A tremulous breath escaped my lungs as I heard a slam of the main door, signaling that my father had left the room.

Looking around frantically, I realized I was trapped.

The tiny window over the tub was miniscule. Probably small enough to fit my hand or part of my leg.

I got up from the floor and yanked on the doorknob, but the door was locked tight.

"Dammit!" I cursed in frustration and fear. "I have to get out of here."

I was fairly certain that Victor had gone after Dane. He was desperate enough to go after anybody right now.

"Watch your back, Dane," I whispered to myself as I continued to try to pull the door open.

But it wasn't budging.

"Please, Dane, please. Don't go anywhere with him," I uttered as tears filled my eyes.

I was desperate and frantic, trying and failing at fighting off my fear of my father hurting Dane.

I had to focus.

I had to figure out an escape route fast.

My life and Dane's depended on it.

CHAPTER 42

Kenzie

*T*he next evening, I was still stuck in the tiny, dirty bathroom. I'd worked on getting the door open until my fingernails were bleeding, and then I'd finally collapsed in the bathtub, unable to stay up any longer without any sleep.

I'd heard my father return in the morning, then leave again this evening. I was assuming he'd slept. He certainly hadn't let me out of the bathroom, even when I'd screamed at the top of my lungs to get the hell out.

I wasn't sure how long I'd slept, but I'd just been awoken by a noise coming from the bathroom door.

It was still dark, so I probably hadn't been asleep for long.

Jumping out of the tub half awake, I stood near the door, hoping I could escape if my father needed to use the restroom, or if he was coming to kill me.

There was no way I was going to let him shoot me dead while I slept in a bathtub.

I held my breath as he fumbled with the lock, hoping I could slip by him before he turned on the light.

Jesus, I really wasn't ready to die. Not now. Not yet. Not when I'd discovered the most amazing man on the planet, and he cared about me.

After thinking about my situation and Dane's, I knew there was no way my father was going to be able to actually capture Dane. The only reason Victor had been able to conquer me was because I was unaware.

By now, the Walkers probably knew everything about me, and Dane would be on high alert. More than likely, security and police would be everywhere around the Walkers, or at least I hoped they would be.

I was ready to push my way through the door when it opened, but rather than moving forward, I was pushed backward by a very solid form before the door swung shut again.

I stumbled from the weight of the body that crashed into me, trying to keep myself from flying back against the bathtub—again.

Victor hadn't even turned on the light, so I squealed in the darkness as the unknown form stepped in behind me, keeping me from taking another tumble into the porcelain tub.

"Kenzie?" A familiar voice said into the darkness.

"Dane?" I couldn't believe he was actually here with me.

I flipped on the light as soon as I regained my balance.

It *was* Dane, and he looked much worse for wear. "What in the hell did Victor do?"

I was furious. Dane looked like he'd been beaten up, his face sporting some fresh bruises and a few lacerations that were still bleeding. His arms were bound in front of him with some kind of cheap twine, and I debated about whether I could get it undone.

"It's nothing," he grumbled. "But it looks like that bastard hit you."

Dane was angry, an emotion I didn't see from him that often.

I shrugged. "I'm used to him hitting me. What did he do to you?"

We were stuck in a small space together with very little room to move. Since the room was so small, I hopped back into the tub. "Sit down," I demanded. "You don't look very steady."

He sat, resting his back against the wall next to the tub as he asked, "Can you get into the pocket of my jacket? I have a knife to cut this rope."

"Why in the hell did he hurt you?" I said angrily.

"I called him several names he didn't like," Dane said, sounding more satisfied than regretful. "I would have killed the bastard if I'd had the chance. But I didn't. I needed to get to you."

Dane was sporting a light leather bomber jacket, an article of clothing he hardly needed in a tropical climate. I didn't have to reach far to get inside the garment. "How did he get to you? I was hoping you'd be protected. I didn't want him to take you."

I found the jackknife in his pocket and started cutting the twine from his bound hands.

"I wanted him to take me," he answered matter-of-factly.

I looked at him in shock. "For God's sake...why? Do you have a death wish? Victor doesn't let any witnesses live. He'll kill you, Dane. He'll kill both of us."

Finally, Dane's hands were free, and he tossed the rope underneath the sink before he dug into his jacket pocket again. "Nobody is dying."

"You don't know Victor—"

"He'll be leaving soon. And then we can get the hell out of here."

I watched as he pulled out a small object that looked like a remote and switched it on. "Is that a tracking device?" I asked, still flabbergasted that Dane was here with me.

"Yes," he answered simply.

He put the small tracker back in his pocket.

"I don't understand." Maybe I still wasn't quite right from the blow to my head because I didn't get why Dane had let Victor take him.

Dane moved onto his knees and put his hands on my shoulders. His tone was a husky whisper as he said, "My brothers will lure Victor out of here with a promise of money. Then somebody will come in and let us the hell out of here."

"You set all this up?" I frowned at him, not happy that he was risking his life.

We kept our voices low. Victor wasn't far from the bathroom door, and if he knew Dane had tricked him, he'd shoot first and never ask questions at all.

"Did you think I'd ever leave you here alone?" he asked, his mouth close to my ear.

"You should have," I answered honestly.

"Not happening. I just found you. I'm not losing you now."

Tears leaked from my eyes as I answered, "I don't want you to get hurt. What if something happens to you?"

He pulled back and our eyes met and locked. His gaze was turbulent. "How in the hell do you think I felt? You were there one moment, and gone the next. I almost went fucking crazy. When my brothers and I found out about your father, we knew there was a chance that Victor would come after me or at least call to try to get something from us so we could get you back if he couldn't get money any other way since you and I were connected. I made sure I was prepared just in case, and I made myself available. Luckily, he showed up."

My tears were pouring down my face without stopping. "You're crazy," I accused, my heart clenching hard in my chest.

Even after I hadn't told him the truth, he'd still made himself a sitting duck to rescue me.

His stare was intense as he whispered, "I'm insane when it comes to you. I'd rather fucking die trying to save you than to live without you, Kenzie."

His mouth enveloped mine before I could blink, his embrace rough and urgent.

Winding my arms around his neck, I sighed into his mouth, trembling with fear for him, and the emotions coursing through my body.

I needed him.

But I wanted him safe.

The last thing I'd wanted was to have him anywhere near my crazy father.

When he finally lifted his head, I stumbled to my feet. "You're bleeding," I said.

"It doesn't matter."

I reached over him and swiped a thin washrag and got it wet in the sink. I crouched back down and started to wipe the blood from his face tenderly. "It matters to me."

Once the blood was removed, I could see the lacerations on his face, and the swelling near his eye. "Why did you let this happen?"

"I couldn't fight very hard," he replied. "I wanted him to take me to wherever you were."

"You shouldn't be here at all." I was suddenly confronted with the fact that Dane knew everything. "He's my father. My problem."

The outside door slammed shut, and I realized that Victor had finally left.

He took the rag from my hand and tossed it under the sink. "He's not your *father*, Kenzie. He's a goddamn monster. And he *used* to be your problem. He's not anymore. He's our problem."

Even if we escaped, Victor would never stop looking for me. When he had a vendetta, he never gave up. He was crazy that way. "He won't go away, Dane. He'll never go away."

"He's going to meet up with my brothers for ransom. The cops will be there. He's going back to jail, Kenzie."

"It doesn't matter. He'll get to me somehow," I answered. Victor had always found me if he wanted to, whether he was incarcerated or not. He had too many outside contacts, too many affiliates in organized crime. Maybe they'd all lost track of me for a period of time, but if my father got sent back to prison, he was going to do anything to get his organization back on track to kill me.

Victor was going to be pissed when he got caught so soon after he'd gotten out of prison. He'd reach out to somebody from the inside who could kill me. Maybe he'd gone on to other things when he hadn't been able to find me before, but now, he'd never stop looking for me.

I'd be running.

Always running.

My life would go back to the way it was before I'd moved in with Paige.

I flinched as Dane put a finger on my face, tracing the mark where my father had belted me.

"Does it hurt?" he growled, the muscle in his jaw flexing, his expression angry.

"No. Not anymore," I answered honestly.

"I could kill the bastard myself. Believe me, I wanted to, but I wanted to find you more."

"You're crazy," I told him again. Who did that? What man would let himself be kidnapped just to find somebody else?

He shrugged. "I'm not crazy. I love you."

My breath seized in my lungs as I looked at the sincere expression on his face.

He *did* love me. I could see it in his eyes.

I thought of all of the things I regretted not telling him as I answered, "I love you, too. Which is why I don't want you here putting yourself in danger."

"There's nothing I wouldn't do for you, baby," he said. "Nothing."

I felt like my heart was being torn from my chest. After all of the years I'd spent running alone, his words and actions nailed me. "I feel the same. Dane, you have to get out of here."

I was terrified that Victor would come back, that he'd hurt the man I loved more than anything or anyone else in the world.

"*We* have to get out of here," he corrected. "And I expect our rescue any minute now. You promised me a birthday cake and dinner, and I'm going to collect."

"Today is your birthday," I said remorsefully, having thought about it being Dane's date of birth several times before I finally collapsed in the tub.

"Actually, it's after midnight. It's actually *your* birthday."

I squeaked as he wrapped his arms around me and bodily hauled me out of the tub, dropping me on his lap.

My arms went around his shoulders, holding on as he settled me comfortably.

My beautiful dress was pretty much ruined, the fabric bunched around my thighs.

"How did you know he'd come for you?" I asked, my fingers pushing his hair back from his face gently.

"I didn't. But if he did, I was going to be ready. I figured he was desperate for money, and I have a lot of it. When we didn't get a ransom demand, I assumed he'd found another plan. I just hoped he didn't kill you before we found you." His muscular body shuddered.

"I told him you wouldn't care about me. That I was just an employee. Even if you paid him, he would have killed me. He wants me dead."

"Jesus! He's your goddamn father."

"Doesn't matter," I replied. "He's so twisted that he doesn't even recognize the connection. I was never anything except an inconvenience to him and my mother. I'm so sorry I didn't tell you. I wanted to, but I was afraid."

"Yeah, some day I'm going to make you tell me why you didn't think I'd understand," he warned. "But right now, I'm just fucking relieved that you're okay."

There were a million reasons why I didn't want to share all of my past.

My shame.

My embarrassment.

My fear.

My hang-ups.

But none of them seemed to matter now. "I do love you, Dane. Maybe I have for quite some time, but I didn't want to admit it."

"Why?"

"Because nobody has ever really loved me except for Paige. I don't do relationships. I don't know how."

"We're going to learn, baby. I don't know how to deal with loving a woman like this either, but I'm not letting you go. Ever. I just went through two days of hell. I'm going to make sure I protect you from now on."

I wasn't quite sure how to handle that. Nobody had ever cared enough to protect me, even when I'd been an innocent kid.

So I kissed him, trying to relay to him everything I was feeling.

Dane took control, his hands on both sides of my head to hold me in place.

It was the last bit of intimacy we had before the troops arrived to let us out of our makeshift prison.

When we finally got outside, my knees collapsed as I realized that Dane and I were safe. Neither one of us was going to die.

Dane lifted me up and put me into the police car as I sobbed against his shoulder all the way back to the resort.

CHAPTER 43

Kenzie

"Victor is dead."

I looked up at Paige as she sat beside me in Dane's suite at the resort the next day. Her expression was gentle, and it took a moment for the news to set in.

"How?" I asked.

"He tried to escape the police at the location set up to collect the ransom. He drew on them, and the police were forced to shoot him."

Paige reached out and took my hand as reality set in.

"I'm free," I whispered in shock.

She squeezed my hand. "You are. Thank God."

"Is it bad that I'm glad he's dead?" I asked her.

"Of course not," she denied. "I'm glad he's dead, too. We all are. I think it's the only way you'll ever heal. You've spent your whole life terrified of him, and looking over your shoulder. He doesn't deserve any remorse. He was *never* your father."

"All he wanted to be was my executioner."

"He failed," Paige said angrily.

"Thank you," I said quietly. "Thank you for everything."

She rose and moved to the couch to sit beside me before she swept me up in a giant hug. "All I've wanted was for you not to be afraid anymore. I wanted you to be able to stop running and looking over your shoulder in fear."

I hugged her back. "I'm not sure I know how, but now that I'm free, I'd like to learn."

"Dane will take care of you. He loves you."

"I love him, too," I confessed as we let go of each other.

"Take what you want, Kenzie. Don't let the demons of your past win."

I swiped a tear from my face. "I plan on shooting those bastards down," I said jokingly.

Paige laughed. "Good. It took me a while to destroy mine. But we have to brush them off before we can really move on."

I knew my best friend had exorcised her own demons. "I'll do my best. Have fun on your honeymoon."

I hated to see Paige go, but Dane and I were leaving ourselves within the next hour.

She winked. "I plan on it. How could I not? I'll have Sebastian all to myself."

Paige and her new husband were going to do some international travel before they went back to Denver. I was almost envious about their travel itinerary. "Try to see some things while you're gone," I teased.

"Seeing Sebastian naked is on the top of my list."

I chortled. "You see that all the time."

"And it never gets old," Paige said with a sigh.

"I'm sorry that you had to deal with my disappearance right after your reception."

I was remorseful that I'd forced her to postpone her honeymoon.

"I'm your friend, Kenzie. Do you think I care about that? Tell me you wouldn't have done the same thing for me."

I couldn't tell her that because I certainly would have done anything I could for Paige. "It still sucks," I told her.

"That's what friends are for," she said. "I actually see you as family. Thank God we can pick our friends even though we can't choose our family."

"You've always been my only friend."

"Same here," she confided. "There aren't many people I wanted to share my secrets with, but you understood when most people wouldn't have."

I nodded. I did understand. Both of us had guarded our secrets until we found someone who would understand. "If I hadn't told you everything, Dane would probably never have found me."

"I hope you forgive me for telling, but I knew you were in trouble."

"I'm glad you did."

Paige smiled. "Me, too. Try to be happy with Dane."

"How could I not?" I said, amused. "I'll have him all to myself once we get to Walker's Cay."

"Maybe you'll see him naked," Paige shot back at me.

"God, I hope so."

We laughed together, both of us amused at the fact that we were so hung-up on our Walker men.

Paige finally stood up and smoothed down her sundress. "I have to run. Sebastian will be waiting."

I rose from the couch. "Be safe," I said. "Be happy."

There was nothing more satisfying than seeing my friend so upbeat and carefree. Paige had always had a serious demeanor, probably because of her own past.

She hugged me again briefly. "You, too. I wish you lived closer to Denver. I miss you."

"I miss you, too," I said as I briefly hugged her back. "Why don't you guys come to the island to visit?"

"Dane never asked Trace or Sebastian to visit. I think they felt like they were intruding," Paige mused. "They thought Dane needed his space."

"He doesn't," I told her. "He needs his brothers. Dane was going half-crazy on the island alone, but he was afraid to be out in public. I suspect he didn't ask his brothers to visit because he felt...different. He couldn't move on with his life, and he never quite healed."

Paige nodded. "I think Sebastian realizes that now. He loves Dane. You have no idea how much. He just didn't know what to do. He wanted to give Dane his space, but it was killing both him and Trace not to intrude."

"They should intrude," I shared. "As much as they like. Dane might grumble about it, but it would make him happy."

Paige sighed. "Now that Sebastian knows that, he'll be there. So will Trace. I know I wouldn't complain about spending time there. It must be heavenly."

"It is," I assured her. "It's quiet, but it's beautiful."

Paige picked up her purse. "We'll be there often. I know Trace and Eva will as well. It might take Dane a while to completely let his brothers in, but they'll keep trying until he does."

"I think he's ready," I replied.

"Get him to come see us if you can," she suggested.

"I will. I promise."

There was one last hug before Paige left the suite, and I shut the door behind her.

My heart was light now that Victor was permanently gone from my life.

Nobody would ever come after me.

Nobody would hunt me down.

I wasn't quite sure how to believe I'd never have to run again, but I'd definitely get used to it.

I'll make it. I just have to find the strength to keep trying.

I smiled as I went to my bedroom to pack. I wasn't going to need my old mantra anymore.

Dane hadn't said anything about the future, but I didn't even have to find the strength to keep trying.

Dane gave me strength.

He gave me love.

And I *was* going to make it.

Being free had opened up my whole life. If I didn't have to run or be afraid, I'd find a way to be the person I'd always wanted to be.

No more shadows.

No more fear.

And best of all, no more secrets.

I packed my clothes with a confidence I'd never had, knowing I was more than ready to go home.

CHAPTER 44

Kenzie

"*I*'ve never seen Mr. Dane this happy," Theo remarked as I poured him a cup of black coffee and handed it to him.

Dane and I had been back on the island for a week, and he'd taken some time away from his painting.

We'd been to Miami and Nassau, spending every single day together, whether it was off the island or at home.

Dane and I had celebrated our birthdays belatedly. I'd made him the promised dinner and a cake.

I smiled as I thought about the creative things Dane had discovered to do with the sweet icing. We'd both ended up a sticky mess, but it had been worth it.

"I'm happy, too," I confessed to Theo.

"It shows," he answered with a grin. "You two were made to be together. Just like my Emilee and me. I knew it from the way he looked at you on that first day."

I put my own coffee down and crossed my arms. "How could you know that? He was horrible to me."

"Because I ignored his anger. I only saw the way he looked at you."

"How did he look?"

Theo took a sip of his coffee before he said, "Like he'd just found something priceless, but he was afraid to take it. Glad he finally came to his senses."

Dane wasn't the only one who'd needed to get some clarity. I hadn't completely banished my demons, but I was working on it.

"Thanks for bringing the puppy," I told Theo. "I hope Dane is ready for it."

I'd arranged for Theo to bring another potcake dog, a female this time. I was hoping Dane would love her. Since she was as different as she could be from his deceased Picasso, I was pretty sure he could form a bond with her.

Theo grinned. "I'd say he's about ready for anything you give him."

"He loved Picasso," I mused.

Theo bowed his head. "He did. I've always felt horrible that he got away from us, and he died because of that."

"It was an accident. It wasn't your fault."

"Maybe. But it nearly killed Mr. Dane."

"I think he's ready for another dog," I answered. "I thought if we had a female, he might be open to the idea. You said the puppy looks nothing like Picasso."

He nodded. "Her coloring is different."

"Good." I wanted Dane to have another dog. The female Theo had delivered would never replace the animal he'd loved, but I was hoping he'd still be able to care for another canine.

Theo drained his mug and took it to the sink. "I'm off. I'm sure Mr. Dane will be fine. I don't think there's anything that can ruin his mood right now."

I knew Theo had a schedule of things to check on around the island. "Tell Emilee I said hello, and don't forget that tomorrow is your anniversary."

Theo's wife had shared that her wedding anniversary was approaching, and she was hoping for a vacation.

I'd passed on the information to Theo, and he'd promptly started planning. I knew that he'd booked a getaway for himself and his wife.

He grinned at me. "There's no forgetting an anniversary. I'll never forget the date that I married the prettiest, smartest woman I've ever met."

I smiled until Theo was gone. He and Emilee were still in love, and they'd been married for a very long time. It was amazing to see the two of them together.

I picked up my coffee mug, cradling the precious pottery cup as I polished off my caffeine fix. I'd made the mug myself a couple of days ago, and Dane had painted it. It was nothing like his usual painting. The abstract figures were much lighter than his usual, appearing more as an expression of hope than one of despair. He'd left a space in the middle to paint "I love you more than you'll ever know" into the space.

I'd been surprised when he'd brought it to me yesterday, and I'd certainly had no plans to use it, but Dane had cajoled until I'd promised that I'd treat it just like any other mug. He'd insisted that he could paint more if it got broken.

I'm slugging coffee from a container that's probably priceless because it's a very unique Dane Walker piece.

It felt strange to be drinking from a mug painted by one of the most revered artists in the world, but I didn't think of it as a priceless piece. I saw it as an act of love.

I put the mug back on the counter carefully. I'd start making breakfast soon, but I couldn't resist looking into the box at my feet. The potcake puppy Theo had chosen was adorable, and her dark brown eyes were beckoning as she whined softly for attention.

I knelt down and scooped her out of the box, holding her against my chest. I giggled as she promptly started licking my face.

"Do you need to go out?" I asked the cute canine. "Can I put you down, or will you pee on the floor, girl?"

I had no idea how to raise a dog, but somebody else in the house certainly did.

"She'll pee, but we can clean it," Dane said from above my head.

I looked up at him. He'd just gotten out of the shower. He was dressed in a pair of jeans, his upper body bare. His hair was still wet, and he looked delicious enough to eat.

"She was a surprise," I told him nervously. I hadn't meant to spring the dog on him this way, but he didn't look upset.

"Let her run. She'll have a lot of energy to burn off."

I set her down, and she immediately started sniffing Dane's feet before she shot off to dance around the kitchen.

I straightened up. "I don't know how to potty train her. I hope you're not mad. I know you wanted a dog, and I wanted one, too."

We watched the puppy run around the area curiously before Dane scooped her up. His eyes were wary for a few moments, but once the female started licking his face enthusiastically, I knew he was hooked.

"She's friendly," he said huskily.

"She likes you."

Dane cradled the pup with one strong arm. "They're smart. She'll potty train fast."

"You'll have to help me. I've never had a dog."

"I'll always help you. You don't even need to ask."

My heart was almost exploding through my chest wall. I loved this man so much that it almost hurt. "What will you name her?"

"You decide," he suggested.

"But I bought her for you."

"She'll love both of us."

I stared at the dog for a moment before I said, "Right now I'd call her Lucky since she's cuddled up to you."

"Jealous?" He cocked a brow as he looked at me.

"Maybe," I teased.

He gently put the dog down on the floor. "You'll always be the most important female in my life,' he said huskily.

My heart tripped, just like it always did when Dane said something like that to me. I should be getting used to it. He didn't skimp on affection with me, and I ate it up.

He wrapped me into his arms, and I put a hand behind his head and pulled it down to kiss him.

"Lucky it is," I murmured once he'd lifted his head.

Would I ever get used to feeling so out-of-control with him? God, I hoped not.

CHAPTER 45

Dane

*D*amn! I was nervous.

I strode downstairs a few mornings after Kenzie had gotten our new puppy, wondering if I was ever going to get up the nerve to propose to Kenzie.

The ring had been burning a hole in my pocket since we'd arrived back from Sebastian's wedding.

I wanted to ask Kenzie.

But the last thing I wanted was to rush her.

What if she said no? Or that she wasn't ready. I didn't think I could handle that. Yeah. Okay. Chances were that she'd agree. But what if she didn't?

I wasn't the kind of guy to really jump headfirst into anything. But with Kenzie, everything was different. I needed her tied to me in every way I could possibly make happen.

I fucking loved her.

I needed her.

And I couldn't imagine life without her anymore.

Some fucked up, primitive, possessive part of me needed her to be mine in every way. Problem was, I doubted even marriage would be able to calm down my protective instinct.

She'd been hunted like an animal before she'd ever really been an adult.

Maybe I should let her have her freedom.

Or...maybe not.

"Fuck! I'm pathetic," I whispered irritably to myself as I went to search out my woman.

Kenzie was usually awake before me, and she was almost always in the kitchen.

"I'm doing it today, dammit!" I said fiercely under my breath. I wasn't going to be able to wait anymore.

I met with Theo in the kitchen. "Where's Kenzie?" I asked.

He motioned toward the French doors. "She took Lucky for a walk. Coffee is made. I'm taking mine to go. Got work to do."

Theo grabbed his travel mug that I assumed was full, made his way to the front door, and exited.

I filled a mug and went to the French doors to look for Kenzie. I wasn't used to the house being so damn silent.

Kenzie had changed my home, and my life.

Usually, it was alive with her energy, and I never wanted it to be quiet again.

I'd spent too much of my life alone, and I'd never *really* gotten used to it. Maybe I'd told myself that I was content, but I wasn't.

I think I'd always just been waiting for *her.*

"She's going to marry me," I grumbled as I made my way out to the beach. If she wasn't ready, I'd wait. Hell, there was no time limit on how long it took to convince her. I just knew that I'd never survive without her anymore.

I stopped on the sugar sand, covering my eyes as I scanned the beach along the coast of the island.

No Kenzie.

Logically, I knew she hadn't gone far. We were on a goddamn island. Where *could* she go?

Still, my heartrate accelerated, and my adrenaline kicked in as I searched for her.

Because of her past, and the way I felt about her, I was always going to worry when I couldn't find her. Losing her was my fucking nightmare.

I heard the distant sound of a dog barking over the sound of the small waves hitting the shore. It was calm, and there wasn't really an angry surf this morning.

I sprinted down the sand, stopping abruptly as I finally saw Kenzie, and my body tensed as I spied her out in the water.

"She can't swim that well yet. What in the fuck is she doing?"

We'd been slowly working on her ability to keep herself afloat, but she still wasn't a strong swimmer. It was going to take more time.

Lucky had her paws in the water, but even she didn't attempt to follow Kenzie into deeper water. The canine was barking up a storm, trying to convince Kenzie to come back.

"Smart dog," I rumbled.

I quickly shucked off my jeans, then tossed them on top of Kenzie's clothing. I hadn't bothered with any other clothes, so I was naked when I waded into the water.

"What in the fuck are you doing?" I grabbed her arm as I approached.

She visibly startled before she turned to face me.

Jesus! I hated it when I saw fear in her expression, but I was pissed because she'd ventured into the water without me. There were strong currents along the island at times, and given her novice swimmer status, it scared the hell out of me to see her alone.

"I'm fine," she bristled. "The water is calm, and it's not deep enough to have to swim."

"There's a drop-off just a few more feet ahead." I was pissed, but my anger was caused by my fear.

Her face fell. "I didn't know. It seemed safe enough."

She probably would have been safe. Even if she'd stepped off the sand bar, she could have easily swum back to where it was shallow, but there was no reasoning with my anger.

"Get out of the water," I demanded, letting go of her arm so she could trudge back to shore.

"You're here now," she reasoned.

"Get. Out."

For an instant, she looked like she wasn't going to move, but then she turned toward shore and made her way back to the sand.

I followed closely behind her, my temper barely contained.

She picked up her T-shirt and plopped down on the dry top. "I'm fine. You can go now," she huffed.

Oh, hell no. I wasn't leaving until she understood that she couldn't do anything that could risk her life. I spread out my jeans and sat beside her. "I'm not leaving until you do."

Lucky pranced around for a few moments before she finally scampered into the shade to take a puppy nap.

"I don't need a keeper," she answered in a snippy tone.

"Too bad. You have one anyway. I can't leave you alone for a minute without you trying to get yourself killed."

"Is that why you're angry?" she asked softly. "You thought I was going to die? Dane, that's not reasonable. I was perfectly safe."

"Bullshit! You can't swim well yet. One bad current, one wrong step and you could easily get swept away. Dammit! Don't you understand that if anything happened to you, I'd never survive it, Kenzie? You're my whole damn life now. There won't be a 'me' without 'you.'"

Maybe I was pathetic, but it was the truth.

Kenzie's eyes filled with tears as she looked at me for a minute before swinging her body over mine, straddling me.

I told myself not to be swayed by her beautiful naked body over mine, but I was starting to fail miserably.

All I had to do was feel her soft skin touching mine, or catch a whiff of her seductive scent, and I was toast.

"Thank you for worrying about me," she said against my ear. "But you can't boss me around like a drill sergeant. I don't like it."

Had I been that bad? "I was scared," I admitted.

She stroked my wet hair back from my face. "I get that. But the risk was minimal, and it's hot this morning. All I wanted to do was get wet."

"I can get you wet," I rasped, my mind snapping the moment she mentioned getting *wet*.

She laughed, a musical, happy sound that made my heart swell up in my chest.

Kenzie hadn't had many reasons to laugh in her life, and I loved it when she did. It was happening more and more, and the shadows in her eyes were slowly fading.

"There's no doubt you can get me very wet," she said seductively.

I looked up into her eyes, my heart hammering as I saw the love that I needed right there in her expression.

Holy fuck! I knew instantly that I was a goner.

CHAPTER 46

Kenzie

I'd been hurt when Dane had yelled at me, bossing me around like he owned me. But all of that faded as I saw the fear in his gaze.

He isn't angry. He's scared. And he's afraid for me.

I'd get him to lose the anger, and talk to me about what was bothering him. While I wasn't the kind of woman to put up with somebody bossing me around, I could handle Dane's fear. It nearly brought me to tears that he cared that much.

"You're not mad," I told him. "But your concern is coming out as anger. And it hurts me."

"Fuck! You're right," he said. "But I can't fucking stand the thought of anything or anybody hurting you ever again. I'm sorry," he said remorsefully. "I don't want to control you, Kenzie. I just want to keep you safe. I feel so damn possessive I can't stand myself."

I put my hands on his shoulders as I looked down at him. "I think I can handle it. Maybe I even like the way you want to protect me."

"Do you?" he asked.

I nodded. "It's kind of sexy."

"I'm glad you think so, because I can't seem to control it. I'm one of those jealous, obsessive guys I used to laugh at, like my brothers. I never got how they could get so damn crazy over a female."

I smiled. "But now you do?"

"Karma is a bitch."

"I love you, Dane. I don't want to go anywhere, and I don't want anybody else."

"Yeah. I find that hard to believe sometimes."

"Believe it."

"You could do better, but I'm not planning on giving you that chance."

I chuckled. "Really? I could do better than the most handsome guy on Earth who has a ridiculous amount of talent? A billionaire who also happens to be kind and wonderful. Excuse me if I don't believe that. There *is* no better man. And I happen to be insanely in love with you."

Dane had never realized his worth, and it had nothing to do with money or his painting. He saw me. He always had. He was kind and generous. He was loving and protective. All those reasons made me love him.

He tightened his arms around my waist. "Then I sure as hell am not going to try to talk you out of it."

"Good." I leaned down and kissed him, trying to show him just how much I needed him.

Dane had become part of my soul, part of the fiber of my being. I had no idea how I'd found him, but I needed him so desperately that my heart ached.

Our mouths never came apart as he rolled me onto my back, taking possession of my body as it trembled beneath him.

I gasped as he released my lips and found the sensitive skin on my neck. "Yes," I encouraged. "Please."

"Baby, you don't have to beg," he said against my skin.

"Does it turn you on?" I asked in a shaky voice.

"Hell, yes," he growled.

"Then I don't care if I beg. Not with you."

"There can't be anybody else, Kenzie. Ever."

As his mouth moved down to my breast, I said in a raspy tone, "Never."

There would never be another Dane. I could never feel this way again, so I cherished what we had.

All thoughts of conversation fled as his teeth latched onto a hard nipple, jolting sensation through my body. When his fingers teased the other one, I nearly came unglued.

It was like that with Dane. All it took was one touch to make me crazy. My core flooded with heat as his fingers trailed down my belly, finally finding what they sought.

Our bodies were almost dry, so the sand had begun to fall off my body until it felt warm beneath me instead of sticking to my skin.

"Oh, God. Dane," I moaned, needing more.

His fingers found my clit, and he was teasing rather than satisfying.

"Fuck me, Dane. I don't want to wait this time," I pleaded.

It had never taken him long to make me fly into a frenzy. But I couldn't stand it. Not today. Both of us needed each other so desperately that I just wanted him to send me into orgasm. And I wanted him inside when he did.

What we felt was primitive and raw, and that was what I craved.

"What do you want, baby?" he said hoarsely.

"You!" I cried out. "I just want you."

"You've always had me," he growled as he covered my body with his.

I could feel every hard inch of him pressing against my belly.

"I want everything," I whimpered.

"You've got it," he said gruffly as the tip of his cock pressed against my core.

There was no hesitation. Dane entered me in one powerful thrust.

I wrapped my legs around his hips, silently asking him to fuck me as hard as he could.

"Christ! You feel so damn good." He pulled out and entered again. "But I need more."

He pulled out, making me whimper with the pain of losing his cock inside my body. But I was panting as he prompted me onto my hands and knees.

He brushed the clinging sand from my ass sensually before he grasped my hips.

"You okay?" he asked.

"Yes. Just do it," I demanded, eager to feel him take me.

Being with him this way incited some kind of madness I couldn't explain. All I knew was that nothing was more important than having him fuck me.

We'd never assumed this position, yet it matched the insane way I had to have him.

I let out a squeak as he buried himself to his balls again, his hard grip on my hips almost painful. He was so deep that it satisfied the ferocious need that was overtaking my entire body.

"I love you," I panted. "I love you so much."

He pulled out and entered me with an even greater force. "I love you, too, baby. Probably way too much."

I wanted to tell him that he could never love me too much. I craved his fierceness, and I adored his protectiveness. Maybe he went a little over-the-top sometimes, but I understood it. I felt the same way.

My head dropped as he plowed into me.

Over and over.

Harder and harder as I encouraged him.

When he grasped my hair and pulled my head up, I screamed his name as my body started to come undone.

Heat fired in my belly, and it went straight to my pussy.

I didn't even flinch when his thumb slid roughly over my ass, probing my anus. "This will be mine someday, too," he insisted in a husky voice filled with greed.

I'd never done anal, but I could see myself giving anything and everything to Dane. He'd make it pleasurable. He always did. "Yes," I consented with a tortured moan.

When his finger probed that untried area, my climax didn't just begin, it rushed toward me with a speed I couldn't control.

"You're mine, baby. I'll never let you go," he said with a groan.

Like I'd want him to? All I wanted was Dane.

"Don't," I cried. "Don't ever leave me."

"I'm not going anywhere."

When that wandering hand moved to my belly and down to my clit, I imploded. He was rocking my body with sensation, and I couldn't hold back.

The muscles inside my channel spasmed almost painfully, milking Dane to a heated release.

I collapsed, and Dane came down beside me, his hand searching and finding mine.

We stayed just like that our hands clasped, and our labored breath slowly recovering.

"What in the hell did I ever do in my life to deserve you?" he asked huskily.

I sighed. "I wondered the same thing."

Dane let go of my hand and sat up, then grasped my hands to pull me up beside him.

"I wasn't planning on doing this right now, but I can't wait." He let go of my hands to fumble in the pocket of his jeans.

My heartrate, that was almost back to normal, increased again as I saw the small jewelry box in his hand.

He flipped the lid, and sat directly in front of me. "Marry me, Kenzie. I can't spend another minute without officially making you mine."

I covered my mouth with my hand as a sob escaped from my body. "Dane, are you sure?"

It was obvious that he was deadly serious, the expression on his face hopeful.

"Surer than I've ever been in my life. I know I'm no Prince Charming, Kenzie. But I need you so damn much."

The enormous diamond sparkled in the sun, and it was the most beautiful thing I'd ever seen.

I shook my head. "That's not true. You're *my* Prince Charming," I said between sobs.

My heart was galloping as I took in the moment.

The man I loved more than anything in the world wanted to marry me?

"Being yours is all that matters," he explained. "Put me out of my misery. Marry me. I'll never be perfect, but I can promise that I'll always love you."

I could promise him the same thing. "Yes. Yes. Yes."

"Thank fuck," he answered in a relieved tone as he took my hand.

The diamond fit perfectly.

"How did you know my ring size?" I asked as tears flowed down my cheeks.

"Paige might have helped me a little," he replied.

I threw my arms around his neck and sent him tumbling onto his back. "I love you so much."

He wrapped his arms tightly around me. "I love you, too, Kenzie. I always will. There's nobody else for me but you."

We stayed there for a while, absorbing the sense of peace that washed over us now that we were committed to making each other happy for the rest of our lives.

Honestly, I didn't know how a woman like me had captured a guy like Dane, but I wasn't going to question my fate. I was too damn happy about it to keep wondering about my destiny.

The sun was getting warmer by the time Dane lifted me from the sand and carried me back inside.

Lucky followed us, barking playfully as she scampered behind, apparently approving of the way we'd just sealed our love.

In the blissful weeks that followed, we did very little except celebrate our engagement.

By the time we married in Vegas, our bond was so strong that nothing and nobody was ever going to pull us apart.

I was grateful for every day I spent with the man I loved. And knowing we had a lifetime together was the greatest gift I'd ever received.

The two of us were stronger together, and the fear that I'd always carried with me eventually dissolved.

It was funny what the powerful and absolutely undefeatable power of love could do to repair emotional damage that had been piling up for a lifetime.

EPILOGUE

Kenzie

"*W*hat are we doing here?" I asked Dane curiously, not certain that I wanted to exit the warm vehicle we'd traveled in.

He shrugged as he opened the car door. "It's Christmas. I have a present for you."

Like I hadn't already gotten enough stuff? Between Dane, Paige, Eva, Trace and Sebastian, I'd gotten more presents this Christmas than I'd ever seen in my entire life.

I loved Denver, and it was beautiful at Christmas. The only downside was the cold. Dane and I were used to our tropical island, so I was pretty sure my blood had thinned, but it was nice to see a real winter again.

We'd been here for three weeks, spending time with his family. It had been so wonderful to actually have family nearby that I never wanted to leave.

Paige and Eva had pulled me into their circle long before we'd arrived in Denver. Dane's brothers and their wives were frequent visitors to Walker's Cay, so we'd all gotten to know each other fairly well.

When the holidays were rolling around, my husband hadn't hesitated to take his jet to Denver.

I was pretty certain most of his hang-ups about his appearance were gone. We'd traveled together across the world after we were married, seeing places I'd only ever dreamed of visiting.

"The last thing I need is another gift," I told him jokingly as I exited the car.

Dane met me on the passenger side, grasping my hand firmly as I shut the door.

"You need this one," he said mysteriously.

I tromped through the snow with him, and was surprised as he opened the door of the enormous high-rise with a code. He waved at the beaming doorman, and the older gentleman waved back at him.

After we got into the elevator, I asked, "Seriously. Where are we going?"

He put two fingers over my lips. "No questions until you see it."

Okay. Fine. Maybe I could figure it out for myself.

It was a luxury building, so he obviously had a rich friend who owned a residence in the high-rise.

But what in the world was he storing here?

Before I could wrack my brain any harder, the elevator came to a stop. My eyes flicked to the panel, noticing we were on the penthouse floor.

Tugging me from the elevator, Dane searched in his pocket as we walked.

"Here." He handed me a key as we stopped in front of a door.

I took it. "What is this?"

"The key to our new home."

I was shocked into silence.

We had a new home in Denver?

I quickly opened the door and we stepped inside, but I didn't get very far before I noticed that the place had been professionally decorated in a beautiful contemporary style.

"This is beautiful," I said in a breathless voice. "Is it really ours?"

"All ours," he confirmed. "I probably should have consulted you, but I wanted you to be surprised. If you don't like it, we'll sell it and move."

"What about Walker's Cay?"

"We'll keep it. I'll always love spending time there, but I don't need the island anymore, Kenzie. I know you want to go to college, and this place has a studio with amazing light. I can work here and so can you."

I walked into the penthouse in a daze, still clutching Dane's hand.

I don't need the island anymore.

Those words were his way of telling me that he no longer wanted to hide, that he finally believed in himself.

His actions spoke volumes, and this place was more than just another home. It was a location where he could be closer to his family, and I could be closer to Paige and Eva.

I was quiet as we toured the enormous top floor mansion with amazing views. I hadn't counted the bedrooms, but I thought I'd seen six or seven. The chef's kitchen was amazing, and the home included an indoor pool and spa, a workout room, a huge studio where Dane and I could work, a theater room, and master to die for.

"Do you like it?" Dane questioned as we returned to the kitchen.

"I love it," I told him honestly. "It's very private, yet we're in the heart of the city."

"We'll only be a few minutes from both of my brothers' places.

I nodded. "I know. It would be really nice to have family close by."

I thought of all the things I'd like to do, like going to college, and all of those things were now possible. Dane had just laid the whole world at my feet.

Looking up at him, I asked, "Is this really what you want?"

"I do," he answered.

"You won't miss the island?" I didn't want him to regret leaving there to live back in the city.

"I won't miss it. We'll still spend time there. But I think it's time we both joined civilization again. I grew up in Dallas. You grew up in Boston. Denver is a compromise."

We had both grown up in the city, so it wasn't like we didn't know how to survive here. "Then I'd love to live here," I told him earnestly.

I had occasionally missed the amenities of the city: shopping, restaurants, other dogs for Lucky, the movies, and all of the other things that couldn't be done without more people around.

Most of all, I'd missed being close to friends.

I would have gladly given them up forever if Dane couldn't tolerate the city, but I was ecstatic that I didn't have to.

"I don't think it's possible not to be happy as long as I have you," Dane said huskily.

When I flung myself into his arms, he was ready. He caught my bundled up body, winter clothes and all, and pulled me into him.

"I love you so much. I just don't want you to give up something you love for me," I said in a tearful voice.

"I love you more than anything. And the island was something I used to need, but I don't anymore. At times, it was a prison. Now I can just enjoy it occasionally."

Maybe I had to remember that at one time, Dane had felt trapped there and incredibly alone. "You're not alone anymore."

He nodded. "I know. That's why it doesn't matter where I live. And it would be nice to be close to Trace and Sebastian. I've missed a lot of their lives."

"Do they know?"

"They know. They're both happy to have all of us in one city."

I was pretty sure that Dane's brothers were glad to pull their little brother back into the fold.

And me? I was happy to have any family. It wasn't something I'd ever had, but I'd craved it.

"Thank you," I said simply.

"For what?"

"For giving me two homes and a family, and for being the best husband a woman could ask for."

Dane was still possessive and more than a little jealous at times, but it wasn't anything I couldn't handle. Other than that, he was the most thoughtful, loving spouse in the world.

He grinned down at me. "Technically, we have a lot more homes. I just never go visit them."

"All of those are basically investment houses. But this and the island will always be homes."

"I'll keep trying to make you happier," he warned.

"I can't get any happier than I am right now."

"We'll see," he said. "Should we break the new place in?"

I could tell by the mischief in his eyes exactly what he meant.

Playfully, I punched him in the shoulder. "We have to be at Trace's house for Christmas dinner very shortly."

"I'll call him and let him know we're running a little late," he teased.

"You can't do that," I said firmly. "I'd be mortified because everyone would know exactly why we were late."

"I think they all know that I can't keep my hands off my wife."

"Which is exactly why we can't be late."

I was saying no, but my body desperately wanted to be late for dinner.

"I'll lie," he offered. "I'll tell them we got a flat tire."

He pulled the knit cap off my head and buried his hands in my hair.

"We can't," I moaned as Dane unbuttoned my warm coat.

"We can," he countered.

I unzipped his coat just so I could feel his rock-hard body beneath my fingertips. He felt good. Absolutely amazing.

"Maybe a quickie," I conceded.

His mouth came down on mine, and I wrapped my arms around his neck so he could plunder as much as he wanted. My hand speared into his hair, and I knew I wasn't leaving until my body found satisfaction.

Dane lifted his mouth and looked down at me. "Not too quick."

When his tongue started tracing my sensitive earlobe, I suddenly didn't care if we arrived at Trace and Eva's a little late. "I'm hungry," I informed Dane.

His expression changed to one of concern as he answered, "Then we should go. You shouldn't be skipping meals."

"I need you more than I need food right now," I said seductively, not allowing him to push me away.

I should have kept my mouth shut. I, more than anyone, knew that Dane was going to take care of my basic needs if he thought I needed something.

"Okay. But it *will* be a quickie. I want to feed you."

He swept me off my feet and plopped my ass on the kitchen table.

"We'll get to food later," I told him. "Right now, I just want you."

It wasn't even a contest.

Dane fucking me or food.

I'd take the first choice every single time.

"I love you, Kenzie," Dane said in a husky voice.

"I love you more," I replied.

If I had one last wall, it had already tumbled. Dane had bought this home for me because he knew I still had things I wanted to accomplish. Perhaps he was ready to leave the island, but I knew damn well that he hadn't been thinking about himself when he'd decided to relocate.

"We're going to be happy here, Kenzie," he said hoarsely, his voice full of emotion.

"I know we are."

I'd be happy being anywhere with Dane, but I knew we were going to build great memories in this home.

I knew that Eva and Paige both wanted to have children, and Dane would like to have a family, too. Our children and his brothers' kids would grow up together here in Denver. Maybe it wouldn't happen soon, but eventually we'd all be ready to have kids, and our kids would have cousins to play with.

We started to tear at each other's clothing, desperate to be skin-to-skin. "I need you," I told him feverishly.

"I need you more," he rasped.

I sighed. "I forgot where the nearest bedroom was."

"Don't need it," he grumbled. "I was thinking of just bending you over this table and—"

"You're right," I interrupted. "No bedroom required."

I liked his idea so much better than searching for a bed.

In the end, we were more than a little late for dinner, but what had happened before that had been too good for me and Dane to have any regrets.

Sometimes, I still wondered how a poor, scarred, damaged, imperfect female had ended up married to a guy like Dane.

I had family.

I had a husband who loved me.

And I was no longer looking over my shoulder, prepared to run.

My scars would never go away completely, but it didn't matter. The damage to my psyche was healing, and I needed *that* more than I wanted to have a perfect face.

All I'd needed to do was keep trying. I *did* make it, and all of my years of running had a purpose. I was trying to get to Dane.

My husband considered himself damaged, too. But I'd never, ever see him that way, just like he didn't see me as scarred. We'd recognized each other with our hearts instead of our eyes.

When we looked at each other, all we could see and feel was love.

~ *The End* ~

BIOGRAPHY

J.S. "Jan" Scott is a New York Times, Wall Street Journal and USA Today bestselling author of steamy romance. She's an avid reader of all types of books and literature. Writing what she loves to read, J.S. Scott writes both contemporary steamy romance stories and paranormal romance. They almost always feature an Alpha Male and have a happily ever after because she just can't seem to write them any other way! She lives in the beautiful Rocky Mountains with her husband and two very spoiled German Shepherds.

Please visit me at:

http://www.authorjsscott.com
http://www.facebook.com/authorjsscott
https://www.instagram.com/authorj.s.scott

You can write to me at
jsscott_author@hotmail.com

You can also tweet
@AuthorJSScott

Please sign up for my Newsletter for updates,
new releases and exclusive excerpts.

Books by J. S. Scott:

The Billionaire's Obsession Series:

The Billionaire's Obsession
Heart of The Billionaire
The Billionaire's Salvation
The Billionaire's Game
Billionaire Undone
Billionaire Unmasked
Billionaire Untamed
Billionaire Unbound
Billionaire Undaunted
Billionaire Unknown
Billionaire Unveiled
Billionaire Unloved

The Sinclairs:

The Billionaire's Christmas
No Ordinary Billionaire
The Forbidden Billionaire
The Billionaire's Touch
The Billionaire's Voice
The Billionaire Takes All
The Billionaire's Secrets

The Walker Brothers:

Release!
Player!
Damaged!

A Dark Horse Novel:

Bound
Hacked

The Vampire Coalition Series:

The Vampire Coalition: The Complete Collection
Ethan's Mate
Rory's Mate
Nathan's Mate
Liam's Mate
Daric's Mate

The Sentinel Demons:

The Sentinel Demons: The Complete Collection
A Dangerous Bargain
A Dangerous Hunger

A Dangerous Fury
A Dangerous Demon King

The Curve Collection: Big Girls And Bad Boys
The Changeling Encounters Collection